EDMONDE

The erotic angel of the S.S.

Edmonde is everything that went wrong with the Third Reich. Beautiful, educated, sensual. In another time she might have grown serenely to fulfilled womanhood. But left alone by her mother's desertion and her father's death, she is engulfed in the dementia of history. From her first sexual explorations with a girl friend to her recruitment by the Gestapo—where she performs perverse favors for Hitler's high command and dooms her most cherished lovers to save her own life—Edmonde emerges as a diabolical symbol of the times: daring, sensitive, full of bravado and humor, but unable to escape her fate as Shakespeare mixes with sadism, Wagner with whippings, Mozart with mass murder...

Decadent, lyrical, controversial,
THE QUEEN OF THE NIGHT
is a novel that will be talked
about...in whispers.

The Queen of the Night

Marc Behm

AVON
PUBLISHERS OF BARD, CAMELOT AND DISCUS BOOKS

AVON BOOKS
a division of
The Hearst Corporation
959 Eighth Avenue
New York, New York 10019

First Avon Printing, September, 1978

AVON TRADEMARK REG. U.S. PAT. OFF. AND IN
OTHER COUNTRIES, MARCA REGISTRADA,
HECHO EN U.S.A.

Printed in Canada

"Ein mächtiger, böser
Dämon hat sie ihr
entrissen."

Die Zauberflöte

"This 'star-flaming Queen' is certainly not a personification of darkness, any more than the glittering coloratura of her arias can by any stretch of interpretation be said to represent darkness. What her arias may legitimately call to mind, as the high soprano notes fly from her spectacularly and separately, like sparks, is light suddenly manifested in darkness."

BRIGID BROPHY,
Mozart the Dramatist

I HATE FURNITURE and clowns.

My father took me to the circus only once, in May 1922, and we left almost immediately. It was appalling, all of it. But the clowns were absolutely grisly.

And after my mother vanished, in March 1925, we gradually threw away all her chairs and armoires and tables and footstools and chiffoniers, until the rooms of our house were almost bare.

I started to smoke when I was eleven years old. An American brand called Wings. Herr Dorpmüller gave us each a pack, Lisa and me, every time we let him take us into the back room of his shop on the Ludwigstrasse. We would unbutton our blouses and show him our breasts, and he would stand before us with his hands moving in his pockets, grunting and snorting.

We did this every Monday and Friday.

Then Lisa moved to Dresden and I was afraid to face him alone. So I stopped smoking.

Lisa hanged herself in Berlin, in 1945.

I was born in Bad Tölz on the thirteenth of January, 1915. I am a Catholic, legitimate, of the feminine sex, and at birth weighed three kilos.

My mother worshiped Wagner and wanted to give me an operatic name. She hesitated between Brunhilde,

Sieglinde, Isolde, Ortrud, and Elsa. But Papa, who translated *Hamlet, King Lear,* and *Richard III* into German, insisted on calling me Edmonde, in honor of his favorite villain, Edmund, in *Lear,* the bastard son of Gloucester. So I was christened Edmonde Seiglinde Kerrl.

I am a Capricorn, willful and remote, cold and lonely, and sufficient unto myself. But I hate astrology. It's so Germanic and tribal.

I love Shakespeare. In *The Winter's Tale,* Leontes explains his jealousy by saying, "I have drunk, and seen the spider!"

And when Prospero is told that he is no longer an exile and free to return to Milan, he says, "Every thought shall be my grave."

My God! A genius wrote those lines!

I love *Die Zauberflöte* too. I saw it six times. I saw *Don Giovanni* four times and *Le Nozze di Figaro* twice.

Lisa and I used to hide in Papa's garage and smoke our Wings. She was blonde and silvery, with long legs and shining gray-pewter eyes. She was my Pamina. I would often hug her tightly, squeezing the breath out of her, and sing:

> Zum Leiden bin ich auserkoren;
> denn meine Tochter fehlet mir.
> Durch sie ging all mein Glück verloren,
> ein Bösewicht entfloh mit ihr.

We first made love on a summer afternoon in 1929, when I was fourteen and she was sixteen. We were in our house, in my late mother's boudoir. It was a small green room with two white doors and a gray rug. I painted it myself and bought the rug with my allowance. It cost one hundred reichsmarks. And it contained not one single piece of furniture! The walls were absolutely blank except for a photograph of the divine American actress Louise Brooks.

Lisa and I suddenly decided to commit a mortal sin together, so we took off all our clothes and kissed each other's lips. I bit her shoulders and neck and she caressed my hips.

I went mad with joy and so did she. We wept and licked each other's tears and did a thousand things too incredible to be believed.

She knew a bit more about the business than I did, for she pushed me down on my knees and guided my face between her legs. But *I* was the one who discovered we could do it simultaneously.

After that, on other afternoons, we would spend hours and hours with our mouths buried in our bodies, like mice in a beehive, ransacking our honey until we were stupefied with exhaustion.

Once we fell sound asleep on the floor and the maid almost caught us.

Lisa's father was a director of the Kaiser Wilhelm Gesellschaft. He got entangled in some terrible homosexual scandal with a Communist boy. That's why the family had to move to Dresden.

And during the battle of Berlin she killed herself in the basement of the Harnack House.

My father was the internationally known Bavarian tragedian Erich Kerrl. No, that is not true. I should not be sardonic. He was never as world-renowned or prodigious as he pretended to be, poor man, but he was fairly popular and certainly talented.

He played all of Shakespeare's young men. Hamlet, Troilus, Romeo, Pericles, Malcolm, and, naturally, my namesake, Edmund in *King Lear,* which he translated and directed himself.

We both loved Edmund. He is a much more charming and gayer monster than Iago or Claudius or Richard, and far more evil.

Referring to Regan and Goneril, he quips:

> To both these sisters have I sworn my love; . . .
> . . . Which of them shall I take?
> Both? one? or neither? . . .
> Hah! hah! hah!

Papa always laughed merrily here, and the audience would applaud, like happy confidants.

During the war he was Oberleutnant Kerrl of Jasta 12/JG 2. He flew a Fokker D VII with a fork of lightning painted on its fuselage. He wasn't an ace; he shot down only two enemy planes. Or so he said. But did he, really? "Both? one? or neither?" Who can say!

Anyway, he knew most of the heroes, Voss (forty-eight victories), Udet (sixty-two), von Richthofen (eighty), Dörr (thirty-five), and the others. And Hermann Göring (eleven victories), when he was commander of Jasta 27, once spent two weeks at our house in Bad Tölz. I was only three or four at the time and don't remember the occasion at all, but the neighbors were always talking about it.

My mother worked in a bank in Augsburg. Papa married her in 1914.

I hate banks. They represent debits and foreclosure and devaluation.

After the war he played in hundreds of films. Silent

films. There is no recording of his voice anywhere, except in my memory.

He was murdered in a riot, in Munich, in 1930.

I've already mentioned my mother's disappearance. She ran off to London with a British doctor in 1925. We never saw her again.

It was about then that Papa and I began to take our long, long walks together. Up and down the river and in the woods and through all the streets and lanes and byways of Bad Tölz and along the boulevards of Munich.

We knew every centimeter of Munich. Every park and square and alleyway. Ah, we must have walked a thousand kilometers, side by side, talking about this and that.

On the afternoon he was killed, I was going to meet him in a tearoom on the Kaiser-Ludwig-Platz, and that evening we were going to see Louise Brooks in *The Canary Murder Case*.

Instead I went to the hospital morgue to identify his body.

I made all the funeral arrangements myself. I told the mortician I was expecting a fabulous inheritance, so he gave me all the credit I asked for. I never paid him.

I was enrolled in Mademoiselle de Marigny's École des Jeunes Filles on the Kaulbachstrasse, near the Englischer Garten.

I could no longer afford the tuition, but trimesters would come and go and Mademoiselle de Marigny just never brought up the question of paying, so I remained there.

Then her assistant, Fräulein Liebel, offered me a job

in the office, typing letters after classes, from five to
seven. And I suppose that paid for my so-called education.

I was also put in charge of the bookkeeping, which
enabled me to help myself to a thousand marks every
now and then.

Thanks to Papa, my English was almost perfect. In
any event I was the only girl in the school, and probably in all of Munich, who knew five Shakespearean
plays by heart. Now my French too became more and
more fluent, and I read *Les Oeuvres Complètes de
Molière*, Balzac, *Le Comte de Monte Cristo*, *Fantômas*,
Flaubert, and Racine.

Speaking three languages, and with the school's funds
at my disposal, I had no fears about finding a place
for myself in the world.

I love French. I've never forgotten a little song Mademoiselle de Marigny taught us in the *sixième classe*.
I was only nine or ten, but I still remember all the
verses.

> Promenons nous dans les bois,
> Pendant que le loup n'y est pas,
> Si le loup y était,
> Il nous mangerait,
> Mais comme il n'y est pas,
> Il nous mangera pas.

I love German and English, but French is exquisite.
It's a perfect third language to keep tucked away in
one's purse for an emergency.

Fräulein Anna Liebel was twenty-eight years old, an
incredibly beautiful woman who would have been an
ideal Portia.

She was my second feminine experience.

One Sunday afternoon we were in the library, reading Krafft-Ebing's *Psychopathia Sexualis* together. Mademoiselle de Marigny and the other girls had gone downtown to a Furtwängler concert and we were all alone. L'École was as silent as a mausoleum.

Krafft-Ebing was too much for Anna. She was petrified with shock. She admitted that she herself had had a violent infatuation for her athletics instructress when she was a student, but apparently their escapade had gone no further than writing sonnets to each other. She had no idea at all that two girls could actually indulge in mutual physical intimacy.

When I casually mentioned my "affair" with Lisa, she was dumbfounded. She wanted to know what we *did* specifically.

In the back of the library was a small dusty room filled with ledgers and boxes of files. We went in there and locked the door.

We sat on a bench and kissed and held hands. I was seized with such a strangling throatful of lust that I thought I would go stark raving mad! But I feigned innocent serenity and just sat there as demure as a doll, with my head on her shoulder, letting her fondle my wrists.

Mon Dieu! I was boiling with excitement! It was marvelous!

But then, unable to bear it any longer, I jumped up and pulled off my skirt and sweater. Beneath them I was wearing my bathing suit, for I had intended to go swimming that afternoon. I removed that too.

She was more difficult to undress, covered with buttons and buckles and hooks and knots. But eventually she was as naked as I.

And what a surprise!

Her body was superb. Not at all like my own, or like Lisa's. It was astonishing! Lisa and I were long and narrow and angular. But Anna was *immense!* The distances were unending! Her hips were far, far, far away from her shoulders, and there were no angles, only curves, curves everywhere, circuits that went down, down, down, and around and around her waist and her spine and under her arms to her derriere and the backs of her thighs and then down and around again to her knees and . . .

She was a landscape!

I imagined I was in Papa's Fokker with the lightning fork on its fuselage. I flew over her mountain peaks and along her valleys and savannas. I soared into her forest over and over again and swept across her coves and coasts until my jaws ached.

She bit her arm to keep from screaming. She thrashed beneath me like an earthquake and almost pulled my hair from my skull, but I hardly noticed.

I just could not taste her or savor her or scent her enough, or follow her pathways and jungle trails to their extremities, or moisten all her meadows and hollows completely. There was always another isthmus to explore, another inlet to swoop upon, one more dry acre of countryside I had to irrigate, even though my tongue was numb and my lips raw.

When it was finally over she lay sprawled on the floor like a map of the Versailles Treaty, her frontiers awry, her villages in ruins, and her railroads and highways demolished.

It was four-thirty. I went to the swimming pool.

Despite all this, I was a virgin. The only boy I knew was Hans Breker. His mother was Rosl Breker, the actress who played in all those dreary mountain-climbing films. She had been one of Papa's girlfriends.

Hans was a lifeguard and we were more or less lovers.

When I arrived at the pool he was—as my *Dictionary of American Slang* would say—"fit to be tied." The pool was closed on Sundays and we had planned to use the privacy to eliminate my maidenhead. But he was in such a state of gibbering nervousness that he wanted to postpone the act.

But I wouldn't hear of it. I insisted we go through with it and we went into the shower room. For the second time that afternoon I undressed.

I had glimpsed his penis before and had even held it in my hand on several occasions. But that was the first time I'd ever seen it in its entirety in the natural décor of his nudity.

After Anna's naked festival, the revelation was somewhat uninspiring. The thing looked like one of those crooked, spotted, minced-beef sausages hanging from the rafters of an inn.

I too must have been singularly unexalting, for he could only gape at me, twitching with revulsion, as if I had just been run over by a streetcar.

We tried everything, in vain. I knelt before him and put it in my mouth. But my poor maxilla was useless, I suppose, because he just dangled there.

We abandoned the project and went to see Greta Garbo in a sound film called *Anna Christie.*

I'd never heard her speak before. That voice! She had an accent, of course—*my* English was a thousand times better—but the grave rhapsody of those tones! Ah, the melodiousness! Mon Dieu! It was extraordinary. I longed to lie upon her, prone, and stroke her vocal chords with the tips of my fingers.

But Hans, the idiot, was totally unaware of her performance. It was the story of an immigrant girl who went to the United States and became a whore after being raped by a family of peasants. So, naturally, according to him, the whole film was merely a commentary on American degeneracy.

We went to a tavern to drink some beer. We met Röhm there.

Let me tell you about *Romeo and Juliet,* a play Papa did not particularly like. There is an absolutely astounding scene in the first act. Romeo and Mercutio (Papa played both roles in different productions) and several of their friends are walking through the streets of Verona on their way to a party.

Mercutio, who is an insufferable bore, begins telling them about a dream he had had the previous night.

This, to be sure, is the famous Queen Mab speech and actors and directors and scholars—and even audiences—are convinced that Shakespeare wrote the scene simply to give the actor who plays Mercutio a chance to show off, just as Mozart and Beethoven gave pianists a cadenza to play with in their concertos.

It's an incredibly insipid monologue, tedious and crudely written, and it goes on and on forever!

If, as everyone believes, Shakespeare really intended this to be a passage of genuine poetry, he would have done a much better job of it, believe me.

But the truth of the matter is, he didn't care in the least about Queen Mab. He was interested only in creating a theatrical hiatus that would point like a blazing arrow to surely one of the most sublime moments in the history of the drama.

After Mercutio has been babbling on for hours, one of the boys, Benvolio, I think, finally tells him to shut up. If they don't go to the party now, he reminds them, they will be too late for supper.

And Romeo replies—and here is the scene's dramatic bombshell—"I fear, too early."

They all stare at him, puzzled by this cryptic remark. And he looks up at the sky and speaks four majestic lines of verse that nobody in the world but Shakespeare could have written:

> . . . for my mind misgives
> Some consequence, yet hanging in the stars,
> Shall bitterly begin his fearful date
> With this night's revels . . .

When Hans and I met Röhm in that tavern, I kept *my* fearful date.

2

HANS WAS A MEMBER of an organization called the Sturmabteilung. This was the bodyguard of Herr Hitler's anti-Semitic, anti-Communist, anti-everything National Socialist German Worker's Party (the NSDAP).

They wore shabby, dun-colored uniforms, and everybody called them Brown Shirts, or Brownies, or Tanners—a pun on the German verb *bräunen,* because they were armed with cruel leather truncheons that they used, as they themselves admitted proudly, for tanning hides.

They were always running amuck in the streets, committing all sorts of mayhem, smashing shop windows and burning down synagogues. It was in one of their brawls with the Reds that Papa was killed.

Ernst Röhm was the Sturmabteilung's chief of staff. He was sitting with four or five other Brownies in the tavern when we came in. When he saw us he jumped up and swaggered over to our table. Hans jumped up too, and they both heaved their arms into the air, as if they were picking cherries. This was NSDAP salute. The Munich nightclub comic Willi Olbricht called it "waving to Jerusalem." They pounded each other on the shoulders, braying with laughter.

Röhm was a beefy man with a square, oxlike face, a little mustache, and a coy, ogling, corners-of-the-eyes stare à la Clara Bow. He had hairy fingers and fetid alcoholic breath.

He sat down with us, still mauling Hans, and asked me what I thought of, first, the Young Plan, then, the American crash, and finally, the Naval Reduction Treaty.

Being only a female, I was supposed to know nothing about any of these subjects. But, in fact, I was an expert on current events and we talked for three hours. Hans consumed lakes of beer and kept going off to urinate.

During one of his absences, Ernst put his hand on my knee and asked me if I were prepared to make a great sacrifice for Germany. I thought he was going to invite me to go home with him. That would have been a sacrifice I wasn't ready to submit to! He was repellent! But no, all he wanted was a thousand marks to pay for the drinks. I gave it to him. He scribbled my name in a pad and presented me with a card.

I had become NSDAP member number 5365.

From Monday to Friday I lived the life of l'École, but on weekends I always went back to Bad Tölz.

The house was terribly lonely. Papa's study was like a crypt. His bottles of whiskey were there, with his books and his piles of scripts and his photographs on the wall. But where was he?

I would turn off the lights and wander through the bare rooms looking for him, hoping to see his ghost. But he was probably afraid of frightening me and always kept hidden, not making a sound. I would beg him to come out of the shadows, just for an instant, so that I could see him again. But he wouldn't answer me.

I knew he was there, though. And once I heard him,

upstairs, tiptoeing like an elephant around the boudoir. When I ran into the room he was gone.

So I would talk to him, all night sometimes, chatting about this and that, as we used to do on our long walks together.

That Sunday night I finally decided to make a clean breast of it. I confessed everything, blurting out the whole business—Lisa, Anna, Hans, the money stolen from l'École . . .

I think he laughed. No, that was probably just the wind in the yard.

Anyway, he heard me. And he forgave me, of course.

A papa is so wondrously soothing! Much more so than God in a drafty cathedral, or the moon or the stars. In the whole wide world there is nothing more appeasing than a father.

He pierced my despair like a boil!

My insides exploded with an agony so comforting that I prayed the rapture would never end. Blood poured out of me, splashing down my knees and flooding the floor, liters and liters of it, thick with clots of sludge, smoky dark muddy blood, emptying me like a cask of swill.

I bled and I bled. And then the madness passed, and I found myself lying in a quagmire in the middle of the salon.

I tore off my sweater and stuffed it between my legs. I sat there until dawn, afraid to move.

Then, at six o'clock, I started to crawl to the telephone to call Dr. Grüber. But I changed my mind.

I took a bath and wrapped myself up in two towels like a package. Then I drank a glass of schnapps and ate four apples.

By noon I found I could walk and even put on my

shoes. I threw my sweater in the garbage and cleaned up the mess in the salon.

On the train back to Munich I read Chapter Ten of *The Annals of Imperial Rome* by Tacitus.

I was "ill" for three days. Mademoiselle de Marigny and Anna put me in the guest room, and an expensive doctor came to l'École to stick a needle in my derriere.

It was heaven, the whole experience.

At night, Anna would slip into the room and hold my hand and nibble my fingers. She was convinced she was responsible for my condition. Poor girl!

A priest visited me, le Père de Haraucourt, a friend of Mademoiselle de Marigny's, a handsome old gentleman from Verdun with a Victor Hugo beard.

Anna was terrified. She was afraid I would confide in him and—as my *Dictionary of American Slang* puts it—"spill the beans."

But all we did was talk about Molière, he correcting my mispronunciations and I correcting his misinformed interpretations of the characters of George Dandin, Don Juan, and Tartuffe.

He gave me a bag of mint bonbons. I love the French!

Before he left, he said something extremely odd. As he was going out the door he turned and looked at me keenly. And he whispered, *"L'Allemagne. Quel mystère."*

Papa visited me too. Very late the second night. He stood beside the bed and touched the pillow. I was wide awake. He thought I was asleep, but I wasn't. I saw him quite distinctly, standing there in the moonlight. I cried, of course, like an imbecile, and that drove him away.

I hope he didn't think I was afraid!

I had another hemorrhage, but just a tiny one.

The following weekend I didn't go to Bad Tölz. Hans took me to an NSDAP meeting in a gym on the Rosenheimerstrasse across the river.

There were over a hundred people there, most of them gangster-looking Brown Shirts, a few civilians—schoolteacher types, and only four or five girls—including me.

Ernst, wearing his grubby chocolate-colored uniform, met us at the door and kissed us both. He was slobbering drunk. Absolutely sozzled!

Then he stood on a platform before a gigantic swastika flag and made a completely incomprehensible speech about, I think, inflation and unemployment. It was hilarious! But everybody applauded as if he were Marc Antony delivering Caesar's funeral oration.

And then, all of a sudden, a huge plump man in a natty tunic appeared on the platform beside him. Ernst embraced him, driveling and swaying, and introduced him to the crowd as Comrade Göring.

There was another tempest of shrieking and applauding.

I was anesthetized with surprise. Göring! The ace! Papa's famous house guest, the commander of Jasta 27!

Hans told me he was one of the most important men in the party.

He made a speech too, a witty anti-Semitic harangue, outrageously vulgar but, compared to Ernst's gibberish, a masterpiece of rhetoric. We all giggled like fools. Mon Dieu! He even told Papa's old joke about Meyer and Dreyfus in the whorehouse! Only, in his version,

Meyer was a stockbroker, not a tailor, and Dreyfus, instead of being a junkman, was a banker.

And he concluded, no longer grinning but becoming unexpectedly ominous, that the Fatherland had not only been betrayed by the Western Allies and the Weimar Republicans, but, thanks to something called Pan-European Zionism, it had been turned into an Israelite pigsty, and that Meyer and Dreyfus were, at that very moment, in the Reichstag in Berlin, writing a new German constitution that was to be called the Talmud.

There was an instant of hushed stupefaction, then everyone in the gym sprang to their feet and sang "Deutschland, Deutschland über Alles."

Just to be arbitrary, I sang "The Star-Spangled Banner."

After the meeting I went up to the platform and introduced myself to ex-Oberleutnant Göring. He didn't recognize me, but he pretended he did. And, naturally, he remembered Papa. When he discovered that I was a party member, I thought he would weep with happiness. He took his own swastika button from his tunic and pinned it on my lapel, rubbing all ten chubby fingers against my breasts as he did so.

Hans glowed with pride.

He had to catch a train to Stuttgart at midnight and invited us all—Ernst, Hans, and I—to dinner at the Bahnhof restaurant.

During the meal he and Ernst argued loudly about who was going to pay for renting the gym. They ranted and snarled at each other like two shrews in a market. Hans just sat there, petrified with hero worship. I ate a big steak and drank a half-bottle of Tokay.

Another man wearing a party badge joined us, a shapeless, round-faced, bespectacled fellow in a black overcoat and a Borsalino. His name was Himmler. He ended up paying not only for the gym but for the meal too.

Göring then became nostalgic and talked about Papa and the war, about Baron von Richthofen and Guynemer and "Bloody April" and the great dogfights over the Marne.

I had heard all this before, often, every time Papa had had a few drinks. Ernst too was obviously familiar with the aria. He yawned continuously, bombarding us with his vile beer-keg breath.

Herr Himmler, when he learned who I was, asked me confidentially if the rumor was true that Conrad Veidt was a Jew.

Herr Veidt was an old dear friend of mine and I knew for a fact that he was *very* Jewish. We had often argued vehemently about Shylock and *The Merchant of Venice*. But I thought it would be best not to mention that in the present company. I told Herr Himmler that he was a Buddhist. He actually believed me.

At eleven o'clock a bizarre change came over the three of them. They began fidgeting and glancing at their watches and drumming their fingers on the table, mumbling and coughing and licking their lips. It was rather weird! As if they all had an abrupt and simultaneous urge to visit the men's room.

Then, at precisely eleven-ten, they crowded into a booth and telephoned somebody in Berlin.

Hans explained this queer comportment. They were reporting to the "Chef"—Herr Hitler himself.

Göring and Himmler caught their train to Stuttgart.

Ernst took Hans and me to a party near the Rundfunk-Platz.

It was in the penthouse of a new apartment building on the edge of a vacant lot. We took a teak and stained-glass lift up to the top floor and rang the bell of a tall white leather door.

It was opened by a ravishing girl in an evening gown covered with pearls.

Ernst presented her offhandedly. "Her" name was Erwin! She, *he* was a male!

Papa had told me tales about this sort of thing, but I had never before encountered a boy in a dress. He wasn't the only one there. The flat was swarming with dozens of the creatures, all clad in chic frocks and ensembles that must have cost baskets of reichsmarks, all wearing silk stockings and gorgeous glorious jewelry, all made up like lovely simpering Pierrettes.

The other guests were Brownies, garbed in their hobolike *caca* uniforms. But tonight they were peculiarly nonbelligerent. In fact, they were as docile as lambs, and even more outlandish than the "girls." They squealed and yodeled like a choir of *castrati*, filling the room with soprano and contralto bleatings. They pranced and waved hankies. They smoked cigarettes in long ivory holders and ate cookies and shook their derrieres. They pointed at me and screeched.

I was the sole and unique girl present, and I began to have serious doubts about my own gender.

But the food was sensational! Ham and turkey and foie gras and nuts and oranges and peaches and whipped cream. And cheeses! Camembert and Gruyère and Roquefort and *fromage de chèvre*. And ice cream!

Like a pig, I sampled everything, gaining at least five kilos. I love ice cream and cheese!

By two o'clock in the morning everybody was irre-

vocably sozzled. I lost Hans somewhere and went into
the bathroom to look for him. I found two pretty
young ladies there. One of them was sodomizing the
other.

I fled into a bedroom. And there he was! He was
lying in a stupor on a chaise longue, wearing only a
black brassiere. Ernst was kneeling over him, holding
his penis in his mouth, making spigot noises as he
feasted on it. He turned and waved at me.

I was too thunderstruck to react. I just stood there,
Alice in Wonderland.

And Hans! He was *colossal!* Ernst had only the
dome of the thing between his lips. The rest was a
steeple! an obelisk! a promontory!

If he had been that erect in the shower room on
Sunday, my virginity would have been pulverized!

A young man with a monocle in his eye was sitting
on the floor, smoking a cigar and watching them. I sat
down beside him and we introduced ourselves. His
name was Otto Kasper.

He thought I was one of the transvestites and danced
his fingers up my thigh under my skirt, searching for
my nonexistent object. When he couldn't find it he was
dismayed. He drew away from me quickly and apologized. So did I.

Then Hans began to neigh. He arched his body,
almost flinging Ernst off the chaise longue. Ernst gob-
bled and gulped. Hans flapped his arms like wings.

Otto and I laughed. It was really comic.

Hans shriveled up, rolled over and smiled at us
stupidly. Ernst pushed him aside, flopped down on his
back, and lowered his trousers, exposing his own stump.
It was a thick snail emerging from a nest of twigs.
He took Hans by the ears and forced him down upon

it. Hans blinked at it, touched it with his nose, whispered to it, lapped at it. Ernst crowed with joy.

Otto offered to drive me home.

He had a new American Packard, a splendid machine that hummed as if it were conducted by Furtwängler. We floated through the empty streets, turning south for a cruise along the river before returning to the Kalbachstrasse.

It was three-thirty when we reached l'École, and by then I knew the entire story of his life.

He was born in Bremen in 1909. He left school when he was thirteen to work in his father's butcher shop. Like all butchers, old Herr Kaspar had made a fortune during the war years and by then owned slaughterhouses in Hamburg, Vienna, Berlin, and Munich. Otto was in charge of imports and exports in a meat-packing concern and had spent almost all of the 1920s traveling in South America. He joined the party two years ago and had become the Brown Shirts' auditor and head of the fund-raising committee.

I asked him if he knew the "Chef."

His response to this question was just as curious as Göring's and the others' behavior in the Bahnhof restaurant when they made their long-distance telephone call.

There was something about this Herr Hitler that charged even a casual reference to him with kinetic tension!

Otto threw back his shoulders, like a soldier snapping to attention, and informed me solemnly that he knew him well. He frequently reported to him on questions of finance and the previous summer had actually sat beside him at a banquet in Cologne. I made believe I was impressed. He nodded and his eyes lit up insanely.

The "Chef" was the greatest statesman since Bismarck! The "Chef" was Germany's Joan of Arc! He was the Savior and the Redeemer! He was Siegfried, the slayer of dragons, and Parsifal in quest of the Holy Reichstag. He was . . .

I thanked him for the lift and promised him we would have lunch together soon. As I stepped out of the car he lifted his arm in the party salute. But I was too tired for that nonsense.

I hate zealots!

Anna was waiting up for me. When she saw my swastika pin she was outraged. One of Mademoiselle de Marigny's students a Nazi? It was unheard of! How could I possibly be part of that rabble of guttersnipes and murderers?

I was still sleeping in the guest room, so she could rant at me to her heart's desire.

She castigated me mercilessly. What was I thinking of? National Socialism was an abomination! The Brown Shirts were all ex-convicts and hooligans! Adolf Hitler wasn't even a German! He was an Austrian pimp! And furthermore, what did I mean, coming home at this hour? It was almost four o'clock!

She was—as my *Dictionary of American Slang* put it—"madder than a wet hen."

It probably would have gone on longer, but she was wearing a silk kimono, and as she lurched about the room I could see her naked shoulders and legs.

The drunken vision of Hans and Ernst dining on each other's organs came back to me. Puffs of warmth gushed up and down my spine and made my armpits drip. Little evil spiders' claws walked in my stomach, scratching and tickling my insides.

I pulled off my dress quickly. Anna gasped. I moved

to her, opening the kimono. I saluted her à la NSDAP. Heil! I stood against her, placing her lips under my upraised arm. She swallowed the wet fragrance eagerly.

And we both went berserk.

We crushed our abdomens together and ground our knees into our bonfires. We ripped our throats with our fangs like vampires. We gashed our breasts with our nails. We tore out our tongues by the roots.

Haunted by the image of the "girls" in the bathroom, I spun her around and stood behind her, squashing her into the wall, my hips flogging her. She bent into me, whining, yielding to me, her hands flying up and down our four legs.

Then we were on the bed, our heads deep in our thighs, our palates gourmandizing our crescendo.

Besides the bookkeeping and the typing, I was responsible for the laundry, the servants' payroll, and all the kitchen purchases. Mademoiselle de Marigny gave me a full booklet of signed blank checks for the payments. Not only that, but since I was by then practically a member of the staff, she let me keep the guest room.

Anna and I slept together every night, from eleven-thirty or thereabouts to six o'clock. Just after lights-out she would slip into my bed and we would make love. Then we would sleep. Then we would wake and do it again. And at dawn she would hurry back to her own room.

I would spend the night in her bed every now and again, but not often, because it was too dangerous. We were just next door to Mademoiselle de Marigny's apartment and once we woke her up, or rather Anna did, pealing in climax like a carillon. Mademoiselle came charging in and I had to hide in the closet à la

Feydeau while Anna, green with terror, pretended she
was having appendicitis or something.

I hardly ever returned to Bad Tölz on weekends because she would have insisted on going with me, and
I didn't want Papa witnessing our wrestling matches.

Every month I managed to pilfer a horde of cash
from my various accounts, but I didn't know where to
hide it. I was too young to have a bank account. Besides, all the banks were closing and money was value-
less anyway.

The comedian Willi Olbricht told a joke about buying a loaf of bread for a million reichsmarks and trad-
ing it for a Mercedes-Benz, then selling the Mercedes-
Benz for two million reichsmarks to buy a Lüger to
hold up a bank, only the bank was now a bakery shop
selling loaves of bread for three million reichsmarks,
providing you brought your own flour.

So I just spent the money on clothes. I bought a
new pair of Italian leather boots, an Irish wool sweater,
an American corduroy skirt, a stunning suede Oslo
jacket, and scores of men's shirts, which were much
cheaper than blouses. I became positively chic!

Anna finally met Hans and Ernst and we all per-
suaded her to join the party—they using ideologic
arguments, I beseeching her tearfully, as if it were a
matter of life or death to me. It wasn't, of course. I was
simply being circumspect. Every time we had a fight,
which was tediously often, she threatened to expose my
Nazism to de Marigny.

So we became accomplices in guilt and she was
forced to shut up.

At first the Brown Shirts horrified her. She was
convinced they planned to carry her off to some basement and rape her en masse. But I assured her that
there was absolutely no danger of that.

I soon surmised what was what among the Brownies. Hans, Ernst, Otto Kasper, that crowd at the orgy—yes, indeed! The entire Sturmabteilung was a festival of rampant homosexuals!

Hans actually began wearing lipstick.

Anna, once the scales were lifted from her lovely eyes, was delighted. She turned into a militant fanatic and became the mother hen of all of them. They called her Aunt Annie, and she was allowed to sit on the platform beside Ernst at the rallies.

I wasn't too sure of the extent of Otto's abnormality. We had lunch together every week, then twice a week, and finally every day. He gave me all sorts of gifts— a watch, a diamond swastika, a jade cigarette case, a Gaucho whip—and he kissed me often and was evidently smitten by me.

But I remained a virgin.

Then, one Saturday, we went to Frankfurt in his Packard, and on the way back to Munich we spent the night in a hotel in Ulm.

I waited for him in our room while he was having a drink down in the bar.

Mon Dieu!

I remembered Papa at the theater every night, cowering in the wings, quaking with stage fright just before he made his entrance. That's exactly how I felt. But I was overjoyed too. I was going to be *entered* at last!

But it turned out to be a typical Brown Shirt session. He wanted my mouth immediately and I consented, thinking that it would be only a preliminary. I didn't quite know how to go about it, so I simply ate it like an ice cream cone. He clamored like a horn and geysered in my face.

Then, later, he crawled on my back and tried to penetrate me there. I don't know whether he did or not. He howled in my ear, like a seashell, and I experienced nothing whatsoever.

The merest touch of Lisa's or Anna's fingers or lips could make me fester and burst. But with Otto I was only saddened.

He slept and I smoked cigarettes and read *Der Stürmer*. And the next day we drove on to Munich.

A month later Otto resigned from the Sturmabteilung to become one of Herr Himmler's aides-de-camp.

Himmler and Göring were in and out of Munich continuously and we became a *cohue*—they, Anna, Ernst, myself, Hans, Otto while he was still there, and a half-dozen others.

Himmler was a mystery. The bespectacled, balding top of his head stuck out of the water, the rest of him was an iceberg deep in the Arctic Sea. All that I knew about him was that his name was Heinrich and that he raised chickens.

Göring, on the other hand, was a jolly dancing bear. It was impossible not to like him, despite my aversion to clowns.

They say that the character of Falstaff was really Hamlet, in exile in London. Göring was Don Giovanni, disguised as Leporello.

One evening we went to the theater to see *Egmont*. In the middle of the second act Göring popped out of his seat and went stumbling off down the aisle to the exit. I found him out in the parking lot, in his shirt-sleeves, trembling and wheezing. He was sticking a syringe into his arm.

That is how I discovered he was an addict. No one else in Munich—or, for that matter, in Germany— ever knew that.

We spent the rest of the night in bed together, in the transvestites' penthouse on the Rundfunk-Platz.

I had one injection. He had three more.

His body was a Venusberg of blubber and his penis no longer than a toe. I fondled it while he told me about the twenty-two planes he shot down. It was an andante, sorrowful and meek, played by three fingers on a minuscule fife.

Poor Hermann.

In 1932 Anna was appointed head stenographer of the Bavarian Sturmabteilung. I was nominated chief of the Foreign Press Department. That is to say, I translated the headlines of the American, British, and French newspapers for Ernst.

By then I was familiar with most of the NSDAP's preposterous cast of characters.

There were Ernst, Göring, and the stealthy third murderer, Himmler.

There were also the deputy leader, a man named Hess, and his secretary, Bormann, two sly high priests in charge of party ideology. They showed up at the Brown House periodically to listen to Ernst's drunken situation reports, staring at him and at all of us like two owls, then going off into a corner to mutter together and jot down notes on the backs of envelopes. I called them Guildenstern and Rosencrantz. Mon Dieu! What a pair of blockheads!

In comparison to the so-called party intellectuals, though, they were Hyperions!

A schoolteacher from Nuremberg named Julius Streicher was the editor of the illiterate *Der Stürmer.* He was a racist bigot so rabid that he referred to all non-Aryans—even the French!—as Mongols. And another wild crank was one Rosenberg, author of the

NSDAP bible, *The Myth of the Twentieth Century.* I
never met anyone who read it because it was unread-
able—a monstrous slab of rancid Teutonic gingerbread!
These two oafs were supposed to prove to the masses
that National Socialism was not merely a political
movement, but a philosophy!

And up in Berlin, forever blaring like a trumpet, was
an unsuccessful scenario-writer-turned-rabble-rouser
named Goebbels. He was a fervent admirer of American election campaigns and was in charge of making
loud party noises. Hanging swastika banners from one
end of Germany to the other was his doing. So were
all those ostentatious slogans—"One Fatherland! One
Reich!"—blazoned on walls wherever one looked.

He was also an old foe of Papa's. They once almost
fought a duel over some actress. In '28, criticizing a
UFA epic in a Berlin paper, he wrote: ". . . and then
there was Erich Kerrl, looking, as always, as if he was
cheating at cards."

But he was at least dynamic. The others were soggy
and vapid. Ernst was sozzled all the time, and I was
never sure whether Hess was awake or asleep. Bormann, Streicher, and Rosenberg were insipid display-
window dummies. Himmler . . . who, *what* was Himmler? *Nosferatu!* And Göring was Göring.

And high above them all, reigning in cloud cuckooland, was the "Chef ex machina," the only begotten,
alias Herr Hitler.

Although he was omnipresent, I could never seem to
meet him. When he was in Munich, I was in Stuttgart.
When I was in Berlin, he was in Hanover. When we
were both in Nuremberg, he was displayed on a dais
surrounded by a hundred thousand spearholders, while
I was sitting far away in a grandstand.

The closest I ever came to him was in his autobiog-

raphy, *Mein Kampf.* I got as far as page thirty, then
threw the book away.

I worked, dined, partied, danced, nightclubed, traveled
about, and whatnot with all these gentlemen. Except
Hitler and Goebbels. Only Bormann and Streicher made
any serious attempt to seduce me. They both failed.
Streicher was just too asinine to take seriously. And
Bormann, on top of all his other faults, was perpetually
unwashed and malodorous.

My virginity, like a successful stage farce, ran on for
season after season.

Oddly enough, none of them ever found out about
Anna and me. We were "the two French teachers," or
"Trooper Liebel and Trooper Kerrl," or "Aunt Annie
and Eddy." But our true relationship was never even
suspected.

Then I met Eva, and she knew immediately.

She came down from Berlin to help us during the
elections. She held some vague position of importance
in the party, and everybody in Munich treated her like
a countess—even Ernst. He was disgustingly servile
when she was around.

She had loads of reichsmarks and moved into an expensive studio in the middle of the Neuhauserstrasse.
I helped her furnish the place.

It was a ghastly experience!

She had no taste at all and filled it to the brim with
hideous bogus antiques and a piano and crystal chan-
deliers and ottomans and porcelain lions and pink
lampshades. I tried desperately to stop her, but she
wouldn't listen to me. Finally the rooms were so
crammed with junk that it was impossible even to open
a window.

I swore I would never visit her. But when she invited me to tea one afternoon I went.

There was no tea. There was gin, and we both got sozzled.

Eva was a cinema fan and knew more actors and actresses than I did, especially all the newcomers. To impress her I had to go all the way to Hollywood and invent hair-raising anecdotes involving Papa and Gary Cooper, Jeanette MacDonald, Maurice Chevalier, Richard Barthelmess, and God knows who else. She hung on every word. Or did she?

We *seemed* to be discussing motion pictures. But, actually, we were doing something else. I could not fathom *what* exactly. Then I began to understand.

She kept staring at my knees and at the buttons on my shirt and at my ankles. Once she touched my arm. She bit her lips frequently and her eyes glowed eerily.

These were sexual telegrams, I was certain.

I prompted her a bit and we opened another bottle of gin. And, in a while, I solved the mystery without too much difficulty.

I was not wrong. It was all sexual.

She was the mistress of somebody near the summit in Berlin. She wouldn't tell me who he was because it was supposed to be a secret. Mon Dieu! Party dalliance up there was conducted with far more discretion than it was in Munich. Eva's affair, in fact, was so discreet that she had to sleep alone! She had remained untouched for over a year!

Now she was footloose in wicked Bavaria. But she wouldn't dare accost a man, because it might become known. Heavens! That would be a disaster! If her Abélard in the Reichstag ever found out, it would have been the end of everything! But extempore infidelity with another woman was hardly a risk. Nobody bothered about such bagatelles.

And that, she concluded flatly, was why *I* was there.

I couldn't believe it. She was soliciting me. *Me!* As if I were a plumber, summoned to unplug her bathtub. Her coldbloodedness stunned me. I threw the gin into her face and got up to leave.

Tears squirted out of her. She dropped to her knees and hugged my legs. She blubbered and sobbed and begged me to be kind.

I looked down at her, astonished by this effusion. I always knew, categorically, when even the cleverest actress was performing and when she was not. Eva was neither clever nor an actress. This wasn't a performance, it was real.

I was touched.

She wasn't coldblooded at all, the poor thing. She was—as my *Dictionary of American Slang* put it— "caught between the devil and the deep blue sea."

I took her in my arms and helped her to her feet. We kissed chastely.

I undressed us both and we sat down on the carpet.

She refused to take the initiative. Oh, no, that would have been perversion. I was to be the aggressor and she the prey.

But I simply refused to play the role of the venal hireling. Never! I sat back and made her begin, ordering her to kiss first my elbows, then my shoulders, then the back of my neck, then my feet. She obeyed, dry-mouthed and shy.

But then the sorcery of our flesh took command, the magic odors and the nectar tastes.

The panther caged so long within her pounced out at last and almost tore me to shreds.

She needed no further urging. She found her way to

me all by herself. I stretched out on my back and let the firestorm overwhelm me.

When she reached my core she stopped dead. She had never beheld such a sight before! She hovered there, agog, like Edmond Dantès peering into the cavern of Monte Cristo. A vision of unicorns and griffins frolicking in the Tiergarten could not have surprised or beguiled her more than this revelation.

I eased myself up to her and, at the same time, pulled her legs to my face. I was indeed sorry the gentleman in Berlin wasn't there to see what happened next.

It would have served him right!

Having two women on my hands was no problem. Anna and I were together fifteen hours a day, but we hardly ever saw each other. We never got back to l'École before midnight and were too weary then to make love. We didn't even sleep together anymore, because that would have meant getting up too early to scurry for cover. And at the Brown House we each had a thousand separate things to do.

Occasionally, when no one was about, she would kneel before me—or vice versa—in a closet, or under the stairway, or down in the cellar—and we would relieve each other quickly, like pickpockets.

Then she began spending more and more of her free time in a grim Lesbian bar on the St. Anna-Platz. I refused to enter the place. I would go and see Eva instead.

Poor Eva!

She insisted that our little trifle was over and done with, but she kept postponing the ending. There was always one more last time, over and over again, all during April, May, and June.

She had raging climax spots concealed all over her in the most unlikely places. In her ears, on her eyelashes, in her nostrils, around her calves, in the fuzz on her arms. Once I touched a mole on her back with the nipple of my breast and a cataclysm ensued. It was remarkable! Salvos of spasms obliterated her and she fainted dead away, her tongue hanging out. I thought she was having an epileptic fit!

When I chided her wantonness she would only smile and nod. Our bodies were her sustenance, and she was famished. She accepted that as matter-of-factly as she accepted everything else.

We spent two weeks in Bad Tölz, but I never touched her inside the house. We made love in the woods and in haystacks. She accepted that too.

She cleaned the place from top to bottom, scrubbing and mopping and brushing everything like a hausfrau, washing the kitchen walls and polishing the silverware and shaking blankets out the windows. She was sweet.

Papa watched us from the shadows, guffawing.

We slept in separate rooms, and once she woke up in the middle of the night yelping with fright. She swore somebody had tickled her feet.

I told her about the ghost. She even accepted that.

And when I felt like walking she came along with me. And we walked and we walked, hiking distances Papa and I had never dreamed of. From Bad Tölz to Pensberg and back. From Munich to Pasing to Dachau and back. Then we went to Stuttgart to hang up Goebbels's posters and roamed all over Feuerbach and Ludwigsburg and Esslingen and Göppingen.

On one of these excursions we explored a deep, deep cave in a quarry. We got lost in the labyrinth and couldn't find our way out.

She decided, as matter-of-factly as always, that we

would die there. Just like that! And she kissed me
good-bye and thanked me for all the kindness I'd
shown her.

I thought she was joking. But no, she was dreadfully
serious. She sat down on the ground and waited for
the end. It chilled me.

It took me an hour to find the exit, and when we
wobbled out into the daylight she turned and looked
back into the pit almost regretfully.

I made up my mind right then and there that I
adored her and made love to her on top of a boulder.

And then catastrophe struck.

Mademoiselle de Marigny brought some bank audi-
tors to the school to have a look at the account books.
They discovered a debit of 875,000 reichsmarks.

Within twenty-four hours I was arrested and locked
in a cell.

The party—to quote once again from my *Dictionary
of American Slang*—"dropped me like a hot potato."
They wouldn't even hire a lawyer for me. I suddenly
found I was persona non grata, like a contagious leper.

Ernst was the only one who visited me. It was the
first and only time I'd ever seen him in civilian clothes.
He wore an awful green double-breasted suit and a
white cap. He looked like a hoodlum in a Fritz Lang
movie. And he was, to be sure, sozzled.

He explained the predicament. The election was
forthcoming and NSDAP's reputation was already un-
savory enough. If they were to associate themselves
now with an embezzlement trial, the resulting publicity
would be devastating. So orders had come from Berlin
to dump me quietly by the wayside.

He told me to keep my mouth shut and have faith. And he gave me a carton of American Marvels.

I was sentenced to ten years for fraud.

I was only seventeen years old, otherwise I would have been sent to Stadelheim Prison. As it was, I was immured in a children's institution in Landshut.

It wasn't as ghastly as it sounds. The chief matron was a Nazi, and she forged a medical certificate that permitted me to sleep in the dispensary ward, which was usually empty. L'École sent me my books and I reread all four volumes of *Le Comte de Monte Cristo,* thinking of Eva on every page: "*. . . vous ne vous laisserez point aller ainsi à vos mauvaises pensées. Ne pouvant m'avoir pour femme, vous contenterez de m'avoir pour amie et pour soeur . . .*"

At night I would play with myself under the covers until I went to sleep; then I would dream of Lisa.

Lisa. We would be standing together showing our breasts to Herr Dorpmüller for two packs of Wings, then she would turn and flee and I would chase her through the corridors of my brain.

How I adored her!

Keats said, "A thing of beauty is a joy forever."

It's not true!

Beauty is cruel and means only loss. And loss is too appalling to be borne.

Everything that's beautiful is taken away from us and we're miserable when it's gone, miserable forever.

Lisa lost, Papa lost, Eva lost, even Anna—all lost everlastingly.

One moment they were there and the next they evaporated and we were all alone, driveling for them in the dark.

Where's the joy in that?

It would be far better to be born in a grotto or a bog and raised with toads and lizards and scorpions and be surrounded always by fiends and ghouls and crippled freaks with gangrenous faces and never even glimpse beauty.

Then if we lost everything we would lose nothing.

Shit!

I kept waiting for Papa to find some way of coming to see me.

He was the only one who understood my vast misery. He would never leave me alone like this.

But where was he?

He arrived one night during a thunderstorm. That was typical of him! Flashing lightning and the wind howling mournfully. I was alone in the ward and the door opened. It was locked. I was positive of that. It was always locked. Yet it opened. Then it closed. Then it opened again and banged and rattled and shuddered and thumped. And the thunder roared and the rain pounded on the windows. Oh, he had a fine time!

Finally one of the surly guards came and shut it.

I slept in peace and had my period.

The July elections were an enormous success. The Social Democrats gained 133 seats in the Reichstag, the Catholic Center, 75, the Communists, 89, and all the other barnyard parties about 80. And the NSDAP 230!

Unbelievable!

I could not for the life of me understand *why* anybody would vote for the Nazis. And yet they did, massively.

Incredible.

The matron smuggled in a bottle of schnapps to celebrate and I got sozzled.

Then one afternoon in September I was summoned to the director's office. Bormann was there, looking very dapper and smug and carrying a briefcase. He gave me innumerable papers to sign and told me that if all went well I would be out of jail by 1941. He presented me with a box of chocolates and left.

I cursed him furiously and went back to the ward and cried.

I decided to kill myself.

Not immediately, of course. First I would eat the chocolates. Then I would finish the last volume of *Monte Cristo*. Then, next Friday or Saturday, I would smash a windowpane and slash my wrists with the broken glass.

When I told Papa my plans he kept me awake all night, rapping on the walls and creaking floorboards. But I wouldn't listen to him. My mind was made up.

Soon there would be *two* ghosts in Bavaria.

The next day I was released.

The door closed behind me, and I found myself standing out in the road, *free*.

I was numb with shock.

Bormann, of course, had known all along that this would happen. The sadistic beast! Nineteen forty-one indeed! That was his idea of a joke. He should have warned me. Suppose I had killed myself last night?

But I was too overjoyed to think about him.

It was still summer; the air was thick with bees. I tried to tease one of them into stinging me, but he was too friendly.

A big cat was asleep on a windowsill. I caressed his ears and he purred and rolled over on his back.

My insides were smoldering delightfully; next month it would be smoky October, and after that, Christmas.

A chauffeur was standing beside a limousine parked at the curb. He opened the door and a stooped, tired-looking man with uncombed hair stepped out of the rear seat.

"Fräulein Edmonde Kerrl?' he asked timidly. I nodded. Up swung his arm in a tired salute. Mine too.

"Eva couldn't come," he explained. "She's in Berlin. She asked me to pick you up and drive you to Munich." I thanked him and we got into the car.

"My name," he said, "is Adolf Hitler."

3

I SAT IN THE CORNER of an auditorium on the Friedrichs-Platz in Mannheim and watched Ernst—as my *Dictionary of American Slang* would say—"cut off his nose to spite his face."

"Of course I'm a homosexual," he bellowed. "What of it?" He glared like a baboon. "But don't be deceived, comrades. Homosexuality is just an excuse."

He was addressing a packed audience of silent Brown Shirts. And he was sober. It would have been better if he had been drunk and incoherent. But he was loud and explicit, alas.

"They're not trying to get rid of me because of a so-called abnormality," he hooted. "That's only a pretense. Now that they all wear neckties and striped pants they want everybody to think that old Comrade Röhm's private sex life is an offense to the nation. Balls! That's not it at all! What really offends them is that I'm not playing along with their lies and their betrayal!"

I had pleaded with him all afternoon not to make this absurd speech. But he wouldn't listen to me. He wouldn't listen to anyone anymore. He was beyond recall.

"There have been successes." He leaned against the rostrum and scratched his belly. "I'm the first to admit that, sure. Bravo! But winning a few elections and occupying a ministry or two isn't my idea of achieving

the goals we've been aiming at all these years. No, sir!
Maybe they've forgotten what those goals are! But we
haven't! We've been on the march since the twenties,
comrades. And, I might add, marching in the vanguard . . ."

Cheers and applause.

". . . the vanguard, yes! But, may I ask, marching
where? To a cocktail party at the chancellery? To tea
in Göring's palace?"

Boos and jeers.

"Don't worry," he chuckled. "Big Hermann wouldn't
let us in. He doesn't want to be seen in public with
goons like us."

Laughter.

"No, soldiers, our objectives haven't changed. The
goal is still the same. We're marching now"—he shook
his fist—"as we've always marched, shoulder to shoulder, toward total victory! And total victory means total
revolution!"

There it was. Revolution. The poor nitwit. I got up
and left the auditorium as a squall of hurrahs acclaimed
this nonsense.

What Ernst did not—could not—understand was that
the marching to victory was over and done with. Hitler
was chancellor, and all his faithful toadies were com-
fortably installed in large offices with platoons of pretty
secretaries servicing their every need.

They weren't interested in revolutions. In fact, they
were no longer interested in the Sturmabteilung, either.

But the army was. The officers of the general staff,
watching these antics in the background like gray
wolves on the steppes, didn't relish the idea of having
several million armed and angry Brownies stampeding
hysterically throughout Germany proclaiming anarchy.

That's why that speech was pure madness.

It forced Hitler to make a choice: Ernst or the army.

I went around the corner to a café on Elizabethstrasse and telephoned Goebbels in Berlin.

When I was released from prison, Hitler invited me to move into Eva's studio on the Neuhauserstrasse. The rent was paid for six months in advance.

I lived there until March 1933. The first thing I did was to put all the furniture into storage, every bit of it. I bought a cot to sleep on and, except for that, the place was as bare as a tennis court.

When Eva came down from Berlin to visit me she made me buy her a mattress, and that became our "flinty and steel couch of war" on the floor.

Anna dropped by only once. We didn't *do* anything. She was completely in the clutches of some Austrian girl, a violinist in the Munich Philharmonic.

Anna saddened me terribly. She had gone altogether —according to my *Dictionary of American Slang*—"off the deep end." She had a cadet haircut and wore a man's suit and tie. It was awful. She looked like an evil lounge-lizard. She was still lovely though, under all that camouflage, and I felt like kissing her. I didn't.

I met her Austrian. Her name was Birgit. She came to see me late one night, brandishing a razor and threatening to slit my throat if I tried to take "Annie" away from her.

She was terrifying! But appealing. Blonde and vulnerable and unhappy. I could understand her despair— oh, yes. I was capable of murder too for Lisa or Eva. I think. Anyway, we passed the night on the mattress, lying in each other's arms, like sisters.

I never saw her again.

I went back to work for Ernst, but funds were low and he couldn't pay me anything. So I got a job as a receptionist in a dentist's office on the Beethoven-Platz.

His name was Dr. Frankovitch. He was fifty-eight years old, a widower, and Jewish.

That was in November. In January he asked me to marry him.

I had been expecting something like that ever since the day he hired me. Oh, not marriage, of course, no. But the inevitable wooing and clumsy horseplay men feel they must indulge in with their secretaries.

The formal proposal, though, took me aback. I decided to accept, temporarily at least, while I thought it over. I could always change my mind later.

He was elated. He invited me to dinner. Then we went to a cinema and saw an American film, *Kongo*, with a remarkable actor named Walter Huston. He was marvelous. I was so enthralled by his performance that I forgot all about Frankovitch sitting there beside me and wasn't aware of his presence until the picture ended and we were leaving.

He wanted me to go home with him. I refused. He didn't insist. He kissed my hand, and I left him standing there on the corner of the Marien-Platz.

I hurried away from him, almost running, as if pursued by the Eumenides. But I had no idea what I was really fleeing from. Marriage? Why not marry him? What else did I have to do with my time and myself and my future? Maybe I would have a child. A little girl. We could go on long walks together and . . . What shit!

I could never have a daughter with Dr. Frankovitch! Suppose she looked like him? What a revolting possibility!

It began to snow.

But a husband *was* useful—to make decisions and pay the bills and fix things and supply my body with hormones.

I was wandering through the streets à la Lady Macbeth. *Our* streets. Papa's and mine. Our park, our Hofgartenstrasse, our Joseph-Platz, our shops and bookstores and sidewalks and trees. And there was his theater, just across the square, like a black vault!

I wondered if he was there tonight, sitting in his dressing room, or standing on the stage before all those empty seats, rehearsing some phantom play.

Perhaps if I waited for him he would come out of the alleyway eventually. He would see me, and wave to me . . .

But of course he wouldn't! He wasn't there. Why should he be?

The dead stayed in their cemeteries. It was the living who were the ghosts, haunting the cold night.

I was sobbing now, I couldn't help it. I didn't want a husband, I wanted my father!

I sat down on a bench and let the snow cover me.

My behavior was becoming more and more psychopathic!

So I was a fiancée. But not for long.

A week or so later one of Dr. Frankovitch's patients waddled into the reception room with a toothache. A stout, rosy gentleman in a camel's-hair overcoat. He was, according to his dental file, Herr Müller. But when he saw me his many chins quivered with glee and we embraced rowdily.

It was Göring!

Dr. Frankovitch came out of the office to see what all the fuss was about. He stood watching us in amazement as we hugged each other. We paid no attention to him.

Fabulous things had happened to Hermann since I'd seen him last. He had become minister of the interior of Prussia, in absolute control of two-thirds of Germany. But it had not changed him in the least. He was still a hilarious, lopsided grizzly bear with a buffoon's grin.

He made me swear melodramatically that I wouldn't reveal "Herr Müller's" identity to anyone. It was a necessary precaution, he explained, because he was in flagrante delicto. He had been Frankovitch's patient for years, and still was, despite the new anti-Jewish regulations. If it were to become known that a Nazi minister was patronizing a Hebrew doctor, the party would court-martial him.

He laughed uproariously at the joke. So did I. Frankovitch just looked bleak.

Then it happened.

As soon as Hermann left the office, Frankovitch bolted the door behind him and walked up to my desk.

"You are a Nazi," he whispered.

And he slapped me. His hand sailed toward me and I felt a searing pain on my cheek. I jumped to my feet. I couldn't believe it. *He slapped me!*

He took me by the collar and pulled me around the desk, shaking me like a wet raincoat.

"You Munich bitch," he rasped.

I was dense with humiliation. My father never touched me, not once in his entire life, never! But this pigfucker ... This dentist actually *slapped* me!

I picked up my typewriter from the desk and threw it at him as hard as I could. It struck him in the face and he stumbled away from me, holding his nose. I followed him, lifted a lamp from the waiting room table, and hit him with it, smashing it down on the top of his skull with all my might. He dropped to his knees, sputtering. I kicked him between the legs. He rolled over, screaming. I kicked him in the ear. Then in the neck. Then I brought the heel of my boot down on his balls again.

His arms opened and flopped to the floor.

He was *blue*. I knew at once that he was dead.

I telephoned Ernst. He arrived a half-hour later with a truckload of Brown Shirts. They handcuffed Frankovitch's dead wrists together and dragged him downstairs. They put him in the truck and drove away.

Ernst and I stayed in the office. He tore the place apart, searching for loot. Then we went up to Frankovitch's apartment on the fifth floor. I'd never been there before. It was a glorious, six-room Palais de Versailles filled with Louis XV and Louis XVI furniture. A dozen Renoirs and Van Goghs hung on the walls.

In a closet in a shuttered bedroom I discovered the late Frau Frankovitch's wardrobe. It was incredible! Three mink coats, a hundred leather handbags, thousands of scarfs, dresses, jackets, sweaters, bathrobes.

I undressed and tried on several garments. They fit me beautifully!

Ernst found her jewelry in the drawer of a dressing table. Brooches and necklaces, bracelets, rings, pins, tiaras—a fortune! He "requisitioned" everything and told me I could have the clothing.

We remained in the apartment all day, packing things in valises and sacks. Ernst called an antiquary, who came and bought the furniture and paintings, the tapestries and rugs, and all the bric-a-brac. Two other men showed up and carried off the dental equipment, the refrigerator, the gas stove, a washing machine, the radio, two vacuum cleaners, and an ironing board.

Ernst attacked the liquor supply and got sozzled. I took a bath.

When Hermann found out about the business there was a nasty scene. It wasn't the loss of his dentist that peeved him. He wanted the Renoirs and Van Goghs.

Ernst informed him blandly that the matter was already out of his hands. Hermann was furious and promptly had the antiquary arrested on some trumped-up charge and reconfiscated everything.

The next time Eva came to Munich she took me back to Berlin with her.

Her sex life was still a shambles. Hitler just would not sleep with her. She was sure he wasn't homosexual, so he was either impotent or simply indifferent. In any case, she wanted me to move in with her permanently.

She was living in a suite in a small hotel in Grunewald, just beside the Hundekehlesee. I took a room on the same floor, and that's where we slept, because, naturally, she'd turned her place into a hovel.

Berlin was booming with operas. I saw *Die Entführung aus dem Serail* and *Cosi Fan Tutte* for the first time, and *Die Zauberflöte* for the seventh, eighth, ninth, and tenth times, four nights in a row.

I could see it every night for the rest of my life and probably still wouldn't understand it. Is the Queen of the Night a villainess or isn't she? Is she a she-demon and a witch, or is she *"die Sternflammende Königin"*? The work is so fantastically confusing and contradictory that it's impossible to unravel.

I wonder if Mozart himself knew.

I also saw four new American films: *The Mask of Fu Manchu, The Bitter Tea of General Yen, Frankenstein,* and *Gold Diggers of 1933.*

And I saw Lisa too.

It was at the opera, the second night I saw *Die Zauberflöte.*

Monostatos and the others were singing:

> Das klinget so herrlich, das klinget so schön!
> La-ra-la, la la la-ra-la!
> Nie hab ich so etwas gehört und gesehn!
> La-ra-la, la la la-ra-la!

I looked up and there she was. She was sitting in a box, wearing a silver evening gown, and she looked like a resplendent, frozen, dozing effigy.

But no, of course it wasn't Lisa. I borrowed the binoculars from the man sitting next to me and aimed them across the audience, bringing her into closer focus.

It was she! Mon Dieu! It was!

During the intermission I flew out into the foyer, looking for her. She was in the bar, sitting at a table and drinking champagne. She was with a general staff officer, a colonel. Three or four captains and lieutenants were standing around them, besieging them.

She was absolutely magnificent! Her hair was piled on the top of her head, held in place by—I looked closer—by a golden clasp. How old was she? Twenty-one? Twenty-two? And that gown! Silver and glimmering, *argent!* Like a blade! Radiant and frosty, icy, glinting!

Was the colonel her husband? Or was she just his girl—a general staff lay?

I tried to hear what she was saying. She put a

cigarette between her lips. They all thrust lighters at her, igniting her face in a forest fire of flames. She wasn't saying *anything!* She just sat there, narrow-eyed and bronzed, shining, golden, ablaze. The warriors did all the talking. She wasn't even listening to them. She was gazing at the wall, touching her lips with her tongue, whispering smoke into the air.

I thought I would suffocate. My throat tightened. I couldn't breathe.

During the second act I tiptoed to the door of her box, then fled, then tiptoed back, then fled again. A sullen old usher with a jellyfish face asked me for my ticket. I told him to go fuck himself.

When the curtain went down I followed them to the cloakroom. The colonel draped a dark hooded cape over her shoulders and they went out to the street. I ran after them. They walked to a small restaurant on the Lützow-Platz. I waited outside and watched them through the front window. She ate a cake and drank two cups of coffee.

The colonel was about forty, tall, lean, slit-mouthed, lipless, unsmiling. A cobra! He drank a large cognac.

There was no intimacy between them. They sat apart, remote and lowering, like monarchs at a coronation.

They were married, I was certain!

When they came out I hid behind a tree. The colonel marched across the pavement and waved to a passing taxi.

Lisa turned and stared at me.

Could she see me? I hoped not! I was wearing one of Frau Frankovitch's 1925 evening gowns and must have looked like a bumpkin. If she recognized me and called my name, I would pretend I was someone else—

Hilda Schultz from Wilhelmshaven! Or a foreigner—Jane Jackson from Boston!

But she didn't. They got into the taxi and drove away.

Eva and I were out shopping one morning when we met Magna Goebbels in a department store on the Brandenburgischestrasse. She was a friendly, unpretentious, straightforward woman who knew all about Eva and the chancellor. We had lunch together; then she invited us home to a cocktail party.

"Home" was the Ministry of Propaganda, a mountainous granite edifice on the Wilhelms-Platz. She and her husband were living there while their house was being renovated.

Everybody was there—Hermann, Bormann, Hess, Streicher, Rosenberg, Himmler, and dozens of others I knew. We all greeted one another with stiff solemnity, not like the former back-alley conspirators we were, but as party dignitaries in the public eye, each of us ceremonious and reserved. What a dismal charade!

Even Hermann was punctilious. He took me in hand and ushered me like a maître d'hôtel across the ballroom-sized reception hall to meet our host.

Joseph Goebbels, one-time scenario writer and film critic, the man who dared compare Papa's acting to "cheating at cards," was a bent, swarthy gnome with tiny muskrat teeth. His eyes scrambled over me like cockroaches—breasts, face, breasts, hips, legs, breasts. Ho! ho, I said to myself, the little fellow is a satyr!

Hermann ran through my party biography, making it sound Homeric. Goebbels was impressed. He snapped his fingers at a lackey, summoning drinks. Then he took me off into a corner and asked me sarcastically what Ernst was up to these days. I thought he was referring to the Frankovitch incident. But no, it was intraparty business.

"What does he want exactly?" he demanded. "Why is he being so difficult?" Difficult? Ernst? I knew he was disappointed about not being a minister, but aside from that I always thought he was perfectly satisfied. "What does he want to be minister of?" Goebbels snapped. "Fellatio?" We both laughed.

Himmler joined us, carrying—of all things!—a copy of the *New York Times*. He wanted me to translate an article on the inauguration of the new American President, Roosevelt.

"He's an invalid," Goebbels declared. "He wears a harness and walks on crutches. He'll never last four years."

"A wounded animal," Himmler murmured, "is dangerous."

"Rubbish!" Goebbels huffed, gulping down his drink. "He's a fossil."

I translated the article and Himmler thanked me and stalked off.

"Heinrich," Goebbels drawled, "was born in the wrong time. He should have been Vad the Impaler's butler. You can imagine what kind of impression he makes on foreign ambassadors." He pointed to Hess and Bormann, whispering together nearby. "And those two! Laurel and Hardy!" He turned to me, his eyes flashing to my bosom again. "Kerrl. Where have I heard that name before?"

Then his wife came over and led him away.

I looked around for Eva. She was sulking by a window, eating cookies, trying to make herself invisible. No one would talk to her. They were far too discreet to dare strike up a conversation with the chancellor's concubine.

We left the party.

The next day Goebbels telephoned and offered me a job.

I wore a smart pale gray uniform with black boots and sat at a desk in a vast office with twenty other girls translating party propaganda into French, English, Italian, Spanish, Hungarian, Arabic, and every other imaginable language—including Hindustani.

I was part of a team of four responsible for the English versions. Gritting my teeth, I turned out page after page of official garbage entitled "National Socialism and Education," "The Four-Year Plan," "Hitler Youth," "Nazism and Motherhood," "The Aryan Principle," "The Jewish Problem," "Adolf Hitler and the New Order," and so on.

It was insufferable. But my salary made the torture bearable.

Goebbels picked me up every evening, and we would go out on the town together until midnight. He was a master of lecherous stratagems, but all his tricks fell flat. Going to bed with him was out of the question. After what he had said about Papa, I could never let him inside me.

One night he came creeping into my hotel room like a burglar and found Eva and me in bed.

But there was nothing he could do about that. He wouldn't dream of running to the chancellor with such a disclosure. Oh, no. The ancient Pharaohs sacrificed messengers bringing bad news. Hitler's reactions to misdeeds were even more terrifying because they were unpredictable.

So little Joseph had to hold his tongue.

Hitler left Berlin for Obersalzberg, taking Eva with him. All the party courtiers followed them, including Joseph.

Just before he left, he called me into his office and fired me.

"Don't be here when I come back," he grinned, all his tiny rat teeth exposed. "I don't want my ministry associated with your girlish peccadilloes."

So that was that. I was once again unemployed.

In the archives room, just next to the translators' office, was a shelf piled high with general staff dossiers. I read through them all. The one I was looking for was marked "HEYE, Richard (Colonel, Infantry)." His wife was "Elisabeth Heye, née Stieff." There it was! They had been married in 1932. Their home address was 144 Warthe-Platz.

It was a small house in a copse of trees, not far from Tempelhof Airport.

I went out there the next afternoon, planning just to ring the bell and say, "Hello, Lisa!" when she opened the door.

But naturally I didn't. I sat down on a bench across the street and waited for a glimpse of her.

By two o'clock I knew all the windows by heart. There were nine of them: four downstairs, five upstairs. Then I memorized the bushes and trees in the garden and counted the bars of the fence and the number of shingles on the roof.

At three o'clock two officers in a staff car arrived, went inside, remained a half-hour or so, then came out and drove away.

At four o'clock I walked down the Warthestrasse as far as the stadium, then up the Oderstrasse to the Saint Jakobi Cemetery, then along the Siegfriedstrasse to the Hermannstrasse, then back up the Warthestrasse from the opposite end.

She was sitting on the bench, waiting for me.

*　　*　　*

We spent the rest of the afternoon drinking whiskey (I had five scotches!) in the airport bar.

She *had* seen me that night outside the restaurant! And ever since then she'd been waiting for me to reappear. When she told me this, I put my face in my hands and sobbed.

I was dazed with happiness. I'd forgotten how *green* her eyes were!

She wanted me to come back to the house and meet her husband, but I didn't feel up to that. Besides, I was getting sozzled.

I'd forgotten so many things about her. Her shades and hues, the twist of her lips, the arches of her eyebrows, the hollow of her throat. Mon Dieu! She was awesome!

After they moved to Dresden her father was sent to Russia to build a factory. That's where she met her husband. He was the military attaché at the embassy in Moscow. They went to Venice on their honeymoon. Next month they were going to Lisbon.

Then it was six-thirty and she had to leave. She insisted on paying for the drinks. I insisted on buying her a gift. In a souvenir shop in the lounge I found a small swastika pennant with "Welcome to Berlin!" emblazoned across it. I presented it to her. She bought me a novel in the bookstall, an enormously thick American best seller called *Anthony Adverse*. She wrote our names and the date on the inside of the cover. I sobbed again.

Two mornings later she came to my hotel.

While I was waiting for her I took two showers and began *Anthony Adverse*. It was an absolutely *immense* volume, almost too heavy to lift, over a thousand pages long, divided into nine books, sixty-seven chapters,

and an epilogue! Attempting to read the whole ele-
phantine thing from beginning to end would be a saga!

Then she arrived.

I was just coming out of the shower for the second
time; that helped. If we had both been dressed, it might
have been awkward to begin. But there I was, nude
and dripping. She took the towel and dried my back.
And when her hands touched my breasts, everything
was all right.

She put her cheek against my shoulder.

Then she took off some of her clothes. Her coat,
her scarf, her shoes, her blouse, her skirt, her slip. Mon
Dieu! I took off the rest. My knees turned to water,
and the floor swooped like a flying carpet.

Then I was in bed, under the covers. I don't for the
life of me know how I got there! And she was beside
me, whispering my name, putting her nipples between
my lips. I tried to swallow her whole, hoping she
would melt like a huge dissolving peach into my mouth.
Then she was behind me, licking the bottom of my
spine. Then I was in her arms, her breath warming my
eyes. But we knew we were still too far apart. So we
climbed into the trees, rolling across the tepid branches,
our hands searching for the beehives hidden in the
secret limbs. Then our tongues sought out the honey
waiting for us in the deep cells and we supped.

This went on and on, day after day, until we were
glutted. Then, instead of going to bed, we would go to
the hairdresser's, or shopping, or to a museum or an
art gallery, or swimming or ice-skating, or just walking.
But toward evening our desire was usually rekindled
and, if we were too far from the hotel, we would have
to find a place to make love wherever we happened
to be.

Any cinema would suffice, providing the balcony

wasn't too crowded. This was only good for hands, though. Office building lifts were excellent. We'd simply open the door between floors and take turns on our knees. But this wasn't really reciprocal enough. And my legs became too wobbly when I was standing up.

Our favorite place, finally, was a Finnish sauna on the Kurfürstenstrasse. We ended up there almost every day. It was paradise! We would take a private bath for ten marks and spend eternities entwined together in the fog, ravishing each other gloriously. Steam gave our flesh rare tastes. Our derrieres and armpits became as succulent as clams and the insides of our thighs like wine vats.

Nights, of course, she spent with her husband. He had a heart ailment, so his demands on her body were not excessive. He wanted a child, so he just entered her, fired off his rifle into the salient, then retreated. He was incapable of any further voluptuosity.

It was through him, via Lisa, that I learned of the army's dire fear of the Brown Shirts. The general staff considered "Corporal" Hitler a mere figurehead and refused to take him seriously. But they saw in Ernst a reincarnation of Attila the Hun, ready to scourge German tradition in mustard-colored barbarianism. There was even talk—and this was dreadfully confidential; she made me swear on her head I wouldn't gossip about it—talk of a military putsch to neutralize the menace.

This made me laugh. Attila the Hun! Ernst? What shit! And I just could not see any of those general staff dandies soiling their impeccable uniforms and spotless gloves in a vulgar rumpus.

An entire month passed, and then it all ended. Lisa and the colonel were leaving for Portugal in ten days.

On our last meeting—like the first, in the hotel bed —we could only lie together like paralytics, biting each other's tongues, weeping on each other's cheeks, absorbing each other's misery.

We fell asleep, kissing. And when I woke up she was gone.

That same afternoon little Joseph returned from Obersalzberg.

If he was surprised to see me he didn't show it.

"Yes, Edmonde? What do you want?"

"I'd like a job in the embassy in Lisbon."

I knew this wouldn't be difficult to arrange. He was always sending people out of the country on missions. All he had to do was pick up the phone and I would be on my way.

Naturally, I would have to pay for it first. But that didn't bother me. A night or two in bed with a gnome wasn't the end of the world.

"Why?" he asked.

I had a reasonable story prepared. I explained that I'd gotten myself into a dangerous impasse with Eva. It could only end in disaster for *all* of us. I emphasized the plural. It included him. He was subtle enough to understand.

"I have to disappear for a while," I concluded. "Before it gets out of hand."

"But why Lisbon in particular?"

"I want to learn Portuguese," I lied.

He just nodded. I looked at him, waiting for the poisoned dart.

"You'll have to do something for me in exchange."

"Certainly." I pulled up a chair and sat down.

"Stand up," he growled.

I obeyed. He was the master of the situation, the

little pigfucker. Let him play the scene in his own way. And what a scene! Baron Scorpio and La Tosca!

"What do you want me to do, Herr Goebbels?"

He leaned forward in his chair and folded his hands on the desk. This was the moment to sing his aria. But he didn't. He just sat there, eyeing me. And when he finally spoke I almost toppled to the floor with surprise.

"I want you to go back to Munich," he said, "and find out what Ernst is up to."

I remained in Munich for the rest of the winter, once again an active member of the Sturmabteilung. I moved into a rooming house on the Haydnstrasse and I finished Books One and Two of *Anthony Adverse*. I began Book Three, Chapter 20.

Ernst fascinated foreign correspondents, and they flocked around him like pigeons. My title was press secretary, and my job was to see that his interviews with them didn't sound too foolish. An impossible task!

He was a bombastic clod and a fire-and-brimstone braggart. All his pronouncements were thunderclaps. He screamed and bawled and roared and shook his fist in the air. But despite all this, I was certain he was essentially harmless. I reported to little Joseph every day and tried to tell him this, but he wasn't convinced.

"He's a maniac!" he snarled. "And a revisionist!"

Ernst *could* have been dangerous, there was no doubt about that. The Brown Shirts worshiped him, and he had only to give the word and they would have marched joyously against Berlin, vast multitudes of them, brandishing their truncheons and singing the "Horst Wessel Lied."

But he didn't.

He staged rallies and parades, he browbeat newspapermen, he frothed at the mouth, he whirled around

Bavaria like a typhoon. But he didn't really *do* anything.

And then the poor dunce made that idiotic speech in Mannheim, letting drop the fatal word: "revolution." And—as my *Dictionary of American Slang* put it— "the cat was out of the bag"!

When I telephoned Berlin the same night, little Joseph was throbbing with tension.

"Find somewhere to hide," he hissed. "Stay away from Munich."

I realized immediately what that meant.

They were going to kill Ernst.

I did go to Munich. I had to. I'd left *Anthony Adverse* in my room on the Haydnstrasse. I wanted to catch the night train and just slip into the city, pack my things, then flee to Bad Tölz. But Ernst insisted on driving me back in his car.

It was a wild, horrifying ride. He hung on the steering wheel with a bottle of rum tilted to his lips, driving like a halfwit, singing and drooling and playing with the lap of his boyfriend, Hines, sitting beside him.

I huddled in the back seat, praying and whimpering.

We flew through Heidelberg, then Heilbronn, then Stuttgart.

Ernst fell asleep and there was an awful rending crash, then harsh gongs as if tin balls were bouncing on an iron stairway. I closed my eyes and bid farewell to Lisa, to Lisbon, to—

We stopped. I opened my eyes. We were off the road, in a muddy field. After that Hines drove, thank God.

At four o'clock in the morning I saw the armored car behind us. It followed us to Ulm, then Augsburg, like doom.

"Hines," I whispered. "They're going to murder us all."

He giggled. "Who is, Eddy?" He was a dense, giddy boy of about my age. Ernst made him wear a girdle.

"Hitler and the party," I was trembling, I couldn't control my jumping muscles. "They're following us now. Don't let them catch us . . ."

He looked back and saw the armored car. He accelerated, still giggling.

"Hitler is a ninny," he shrilled. "He couldn't kill a kitten. Right, Ernst?"

Ernst snored. Then he woke suddenly. "Where's my briefcase?" he sniveled. "My briefcase, Eddy . . ."

It was on the seat beside me. I handed it to him.

"Keep it." He took another gulp of rum. "Don't let anybody take it away from you." And he went back to sleep, his hand inside Hines's shirt.

I held the briefcase on my lap. And I think that's what saved my life.

We arrived in Munich at dawn. They dropped me off on the Goethe-Platz.

I ran up the Haydnstrasse toward my rooming house. I stopped and looked back. There was no sign of the armored car.

Was I being psychopathic again? Was it all a fantasy? I began to think so as the sun rose, pulling away the shrouds from the city.

They would expel Ernst from the party and disband the Brown Shirts. Nobody would be killed.

I went into the house, feeling much better.

A scarecrow was standing in the vestibule. It reached for me. I jumped back with a cry.

It was Anna, wearing a man's suit smeared with blood, her face a mask of stark, ugly panic.

"Hide me, Edmonde," she wailed. "They're shooting everybody!"

I took her in my arms to keep her from falling and made her tell me what had happened. It was insane! She had been at a party at the Rundfunk-Platz penthouse when Himmler and a dozen of his Schultzstaffel thugs came barging in with machine guns. They fired at the crowd, slaughtering everybody!

"They're all dead," she whined. "Sigi, Putzi, Hans, Rosa . . ."

"Hans? Hans is dead?" I couldn't believe it. "They killed Hans?"

"I was in the kitchen." She was ice cold, the blood on her smelled like old meat. "I ran out the service entrance. They're looking for me . . ."

A car drove up the street and stopped outside. She hugged me. "There they are!" I pushed her away and opened the door.

It was Hines and Ernst. Ernst was still flopped in the front seat, snoring. Hines jumped out to the sidewalk, waving to me.

"Ernst wants his briefcase, Eddy!"

I was still carrying the briefcase. I'd been holding it under my arm all this time.

I looked past Hines. The armored car was sitting like a squat fat bug on the other side of the street. Four men in black uniforms, carrying rifles, emerged from it and walked toward us. When Anna saw them she screamed and ran off down the pavement. One of them fired at her. I saw the bullet tear off the top of her head, saw the insides of her skull spray into the air like a fountain. She fell into the gutter.

Hines stared at the men, lifting his arm. "Heil Hitler!" he crowed. The four rifles fired into him, sending him dancing back against the house, pieces of his body

and face flying from him and sponging the wall bright
red.

Two of the men pulled Ernst out of the car and
began pounding and kicking him. He vomited all over
them.

The other two faced me, their rifles pointing at my
breasts. I showed them the briefcase.

"These are Röhm's private files," I told them.

They looked at each other. This was unexpected and
it baffled them. I pulled my comb from the pocket and
ran it through my hair. Why on earth I did that I'll
never know! They watched me, like two cows. One of
them reached for the briefcase. I held it away from
them. "No. My orders are to give it to Herr Goebbels
in person. No one else is to touch it."

The other two continued to beat Ernst with their
rifles.

They took him to Stadelheim Prison and shot him.
They drove me to the airport. Hitler, Himmler, Hess,
Bormann, and little Joseph were there, just boarding a
plane.

I flew back to Berlin with them.

I gave Joseph Ernst's briefcase. It contained a bottle
of rum, a pair of pink silk stockings, a brassiere, and
a German translation of *Tarzan of the Apes*.

4

THE STURMABTEILUNG DISAPPEARED overnight, like melting snow. The new Praetorian Guard was Himmler's Schultzstaffel—the SS. They wore black shirts instead of brown.

In August President von Hindenburg died and Hitler became both chancellor and president. He called himself Reichsführer.

Once Röhm was out of the way the army became docile. The opposition parties no longer existed. Freedom of the press was suspended and dozens of newspapers closed down. We withdrew from the League of Nations. Nazi Gauleiters ruled the provinces and Nazi Berlin ruled the Gauleiters. Germany was now the Third Reich.

And I didn't go to Lisbon.

Hitler turned down my request for foreign employment. I thought at first that Eva was behind it. But no. Hermann told me later that everybody connected with the Röhm putsch had to remain inside Germany until further notice.

I don't think I would have gone even if they had permitted me. In March Lisa wrote to me, announcing the birth of a son. She named him Eduard.

I asked Hermann for a job. He had recently been nominated Reichsmarschal and was commander in chief of the Luftwaffe. He appointed me personnel administrator in his new Air Building on the Wilhelmstrasse, a palace thrice the size of little Joseph's Propaganda Ministry.

I had an office of my own—a bright, bare cell with blue walls, a pale green desk, four telephones (black, tan, orange, and gray), and two scarlet armchairs. All I had to do was supervise a roomful of typists, drink coffee in the canteen, and look out the window.

One of my first "official" acts was to pick up the tan telephone and call the rooming house in Munich. I told the landlady to pack my things and send them to Bad Tölz, making sure she didn't overlook *Anthony Adverse*.

Then I checked out of the Grunewald hotel and moved into a flat in town, on the Pallasstrasse overlooking Kleist-Park.

So there I was.

Eva was living in Obersalzberg and I hardly ever saw her. When she came to Berlin, Hitler kept her locked up in one of the chancellery apartments. They invited me to dinner there one night. It was grisly! The Führer talked for three solid hours about nothing but autobahns and cement! I thought I would fall asleep. In fact, I did. He was a worse bore than Mercutio!

A whole year passed swiftly.

Then one afternoon Lucie Ibsen came into my office. She was about twenty-three, dark and superb, with eyes like mirrors. She was a stenographer looking for work. I hired her immediately. I gave her a desk just outside my office so I could see her every time I opened the door. She was unearthily lovely! The other typists were a herd of sheep. From nine in the morning until six in the evening they read magazines and ate candy and

painted their fingernails and jabbered about their boy-
friends and husbands and horses. They were all race-
track addicts and the place was a constant turmoil of
betting.

Lucie was quite different. She didn't bray or squeal
or chew matchsticks or smear lipstick on envelopes or—
She was—mon Dieu! She reminded me of someone
—who? Was it Greta Garbo in *Anna Christie?* No, but
somebody like that. A somber young woman in a raincoat walking in the fog.

I stayed awake half the night trying to recall who
she was. Just before I fell asleep I remembered. Inge
Hengl! Of course! She was one of Papa's favorite
actresses. I saw her in *As You Like It* in Frankfurt
when I was a little girl. And she made scores of silent
films, all putrid, except one great one, *Selig Sind die
Toten,* directed by Robert Siodmak. Like *Anna Christie,* it was the story of a whore trying to escape from
destiny or something. It was beautifully photographed,
misty and translucent. And her performance was glorious! Inge Hengl, yes.

Had I been a normal human being and not an in-
explicably complex paranoiac, I simply would have
walked up to her and said, "Good morning, Fräulein
Ibsen. Has anyone ever told you you look like Inge
Hengl?"

But no! Instead I watched her, committing to memory all her gestures and movements, every expression
on her face, the myriad tones of her voice and the
palette of her complexion. Her desk was next to a
window, and as the light changed, so did she, like a
chameleon. Once, in the late afternoon, sitting in a
halo of sunshine, she turned hazy crimson, then hay-
field amber, then iodine, then azure. On rainy mornings the window was a fjord and she, a pastel Norse

maiden in a seascape of emerald brine. At noon in the sun she was Italian vermilion and Indian copper. But in the evening she was Cleopatra painted by a madman in a riot of dyes.

> Give me my robe, put on my crown; I have
> Immortal longings in me; . . .
> I am fire and air; my other elements
> I give to baser life . . .
> Come then, and take the last warmth of my lips.

Oh, I longed to be a Hittite queen and capture her in battle. She would be brought before me in chains, a Nile goddess too arrogant to beg for mercy. And I would free her and bathe her and anoint her sacred limbs in balm. Then I would send her back to Egypt in a barge laden with treasure.

I studied her personnel file too. It didn't tell me very much. Name and address: Ibsen, Lucie, 98 Eosanderstrasse, Charlottenburg. Place and date of birth: Tangemünde, 1912. Former employer: Golan Ltd. 10 Paulsbornerstrasse, Wilmersdorf.

Golan. The name struck a tiny bell. Papa once made a film for a producer named—yes!—Absalom Golan!

During the lunch hour I walked to the Paulsbornerstrasse. Number 10 was a rococo nineteenth-century office building with a Babylonian entranceway. There was no Golan Ltd. listed on the name plates in the lobby. I found a janitor and was told that the office no longer existed. But it was the same Absalom Golan, film producer. He left Germany in '34.

He was a Jew.

All the Jewish talent was migrating. Fritz Lang had left, and Siodmak and Conrad Veidt and hundreds of others. The German motion picture industry had become as Aryan as *Parsifal*.

Back in the Air Building I used my orange telephone to call an old friend of Papa's, a director named Hoffmann who used to work for Ufa. He was making documentaries for the Wehrmacht now.

"Inge Hengl?" He became instantly wistful. "Of course I remember her. Lovely Inge. I made three pictures with her." He named them, I had never seen any of them. "MGM wanted us both to come to Hollywood, but she refused, and they wouldn't take me without her."

"Who produced those pictures, Herr Hoffmann?"

"Her husband, Ab Golan."

"She was Golan's wife?"

"Yes. He produced all her films."

I felt like Hercule Poirot solving *The Mystery of the Blue Train!* So, *mes amis,* we have now established a definite relationship, *n'est-ce pas?* between our three main suspects: Inge Hengl, Golan and Mademoiselle Lucie.

"He's in New York now."

"I beg your pardon . . ."

"Golan. He's in New York."

"And whatever happened to Inge, Herr Hoffmann?"

"She died in '28 or '29. Why do you ask, darling Edmonde? What is all this?"

"I'm checking a reference for the Luftwaffe. One of our employees is a relative of hers."

"What's his name?"

"It's a girl." I held my breath. "Lucie Ibsen."

"Lucie! Her daughter?"

"Her"—I swallowed—"daughter?"

"Ibsen is her married name?"

"I don't really know. Inge had a daughter named Lucie?"

"Sure. I doubt that it's the same girl though," he laughed. "A Jew working for Göring? That would be unheard of!"

I hung up.

Voilá! So that was it! I lifted my gray telephone and summoned Fräulein Ibsen into my office.

She stood before my desk, slim, dark, winsome, my captive Egyptian facing the Queen of the Hittites.

"Is Ibsen your real name, Lucie?"

Her eyes flashed like red coals in a stove. Supernatural eyes! The eyes of a sorceress ruled by the moon!

"Yes, naturally."

"Can I have your birth certificate for our files?"

"Yes. I'll bring it in tomorrow."

And she left, the poor girl, dismayed. I was too cruel! She thought she had found the ideal hiding place—Hermann's ministry, the very citadel of Nazism. By changing her name and coming to work here she would be beyond suspicion, perfectly safe forever! And she would have been too, if it hadn't been for me. Now she was unmasked. How she must have cursed me! The poor, poor girl!

I followed her home that night.

The U-bahn was Dante's *Inferno*, crowded and suffocating and rank. I was almost crushed to death; my lungs were poisoned. Hands wiped themselves all over me, Gorgon faces breathed garbage odors on me. Lucie stood at the opposite end of the car, leaning against the wall, as serene as a statue in a sewer. I watched her, envying her magnificent isolation. She seemed to transcend the claustrophobia, the mob, and the stink, adrift in some faraway hiatus of Jewish yoga.

I wondered what she would do.

We got off at the Wagner-Platz. I let her walk a half-block ahead of me, then fell in behind her à la Nick Carter tracking a—according to my *Dictionary of American Slang*—"footpad, depredator, freebooter, or crook."

She lived in a decaying old building on the Eosander-strasse. Its front door closed behind her.

I walked around the block, feeling extremely uneasy. *What would she do?* Why hadn't her father taken her to New York with him? Why had she remained in Germany? She surely knew that no matter how cunningly she was disguised, she would be in continuous jeopardy here.

I was suddenly afraid.

I went back to the house and entered the dank front hallway. There was a row of cards pinned to a wall. Her name was on one of them. She lived on the top floor.

I climbed five flights of stairs and found her name on another card on a door under the sagging rafters.

I knocked. I waited. I knocked again. I opened the door.

The room was a small dungeon with brick walls. A table, a chair, one window. There was a sleeping bag on the floor. The rope was tied to a beam of the ceiling. She was standing on a valise, slipping her head into the noose.

I made her move out of the dungeon that same night. We packed her valise and rolled up the sleeping bag and I put her in a small hotel on the Schillerstrasse.

Then we had supper together in a restaurant in the Tiergarten.

It was some time before her shock dissipated. When

it did, she couldn't tear her eyes from me. It was as if
I were the solution to some horridly complicated math
problem and she just couldn't understand the formula.

"Why did you choose the name of Ibsen?" I asked
her.

"Because of *Hedda Gabler.*"

She ate everything that was put in front of her, emptying her plate with the casual relentlessness of a
suction pump: salad, omelette, goulash, strawberries.

"You like *Hedda Gabler?*"

"Yes."

"Did your mother ever play the role?"

"Yes."

Conversation was like that for a while. Toilsome.

"She played it twice. Once in Vienna and once in
Budapest."

"Never in Berlin?"

"No."

"Why not?"

"I don't know."

"I was named after a character in a play."

"You were?"

"*King Lear.* Edmund."

"My mother played Rosalind in *As You Like It.*"

"I know. I saw it. It was beautiful."

"What will happen to me now, Fräulein Kerrl?"

"Nothing. Do you want some ice cream?"

"All right."

We each had a café Liègois and two cognacs. Then
we went for a walk in the park and she told me about
Wilhelm, Wilhelm Kongehl. He was thirty-two years
old, a florist with a shop on the Unter den Linden.
They were to have been married the previous spring.
He was a Jew.

"He went to, to Hanover," Lucie stammered. "To visit his uncle. He never came back."

She had been waiting for him to reappear for almost two years. That was why she didn't go to America with her father. The Unter den Linden shop was closed, and the uncle in Hanover was gone too.

She was alone in Berlin, abandoned by them all.

At the office the next day I made her a chief clerk and doubled her salary.

During the next several months, we hardly ever spoke to each other. I was content merely to watch her. Her fear of me gradually subsided and she even smiled occasionally. Her new duties kept her busy and she began to enjoy her work, blossoming happily in files and letters and invoices like a flower growing in manure.

She bought new clothes and went to the hairdresser's once a week. She became our ministry deity. The other girls adored her, but she never really joined their rat-pack, thank God. There was always a certain distance between them, just as there was between her office and mine. I enjoyed that most of all, her remoteness. It was like watching a film.

Then one morning she came to see me, dismayed again.

"The people at the hotel said the police were asking questions about me."

But that was nothing to get upset about. Everyone who lived in a hotel in Berlin was considered a transient, and the precincts like to keep track of them. Still and all, though, it would be awkward if some meddlesome inspector started an investigation.

I took her home with me to the Pallasstrasse that evening and introduced her to my landlord, who kept a list of every vacant flat in the Schöne area. But all he could offer us for the moment were basement caves and attic servants' quarters. He promised us we would have first choice as soon as something decent was available.

In the meantime, Lucie moved in with me.

I had two rooms—one overlooking the courtyard, the other on the street—a bath, and a kitchen as large as a telephone booth. Its nudity disconcerted her.

"Where's the furniture?" she asked.

"I hate furniture."

She just looked at me. I put her in the back room. The first night she slept in her bag on the floor. The next day we bought a small bed and a wardrobe for her clothes.

We spend a month studying each other like goldfish in a bowl. She was unobtrusive and I was undemanding. We fit perfectly into the confines and never collided.

Hitler was resolving a similar problem. He insisted that Germany needed living space—*Lebensraum*—and took over Austria, then broke the Locarno Pact and marched into the Rhineland. Now the prime ministers of France and England came to Munich and gave him the Czechoslovakian Sudetenland. The Third Reich became more gigantic every day.

On the twenty-fourth of December Eva invited me to tea at the chancellery. We sat all alone in one of the huge, drafty salons, dwarfed by the massiveness of the décor. The Führer was entertaining some guests in an adjacent suite, and we could hear the drone of voices and the tinkling of glasses. Eva was still ostracized from such gatherings and she was devastated with misery.

"I never go anywhere or see anybody," she moaned. "I haven't had an orgasm since forever. Even when I do it myself nothing happens. I'd leave him if it wasn't for my horoscope. He never even kisses me."

"What does your horoscope predict?"

"That I'll share the fate of a personage of importance."

"Why doesn't he just marry you?"

"He says he will, just as soon as the situation is stabilized."

"What situation?"

"Germany."

Himmler dropped in and ate some cakes with us. He had fattened since I saw him last. He looked like a seal. During the conversation he turned to me and remarked, *à propos de rien,* "By the way, I understand Inge Hengl's daughter is working in your office."

I almost fell through the floor. "How did you know that?" I babbled.

"Hoffmann told me you were checking on her."

Mon Dieu! That was unexpected, to say the least. I lit a cigarette, trying to minimize the catastrophe.

"Inge Hengl was only half-Jewish."

"Yes," he smiled. "And Conrad Veidt was only half-Buddhist."

He remembered that, the pigfucker!

"Please don't smoke, Edmonde," Eva said. "He'll smell the tobacco and make a fuss."

"Anyway"—I put out the cigarette—"I fired her."

Himmler ate another cake, brushing his lips daintily with a napkin. "You did?"

"I will." I was slithering now. "She's incompetent and . . ." I drank my tea. It tasted like bile. "Incompetent and sloppy and doesn't know how to type. I'm going to let her go after the holidays."

"Let's stop talking about Jews!" Eva wailed. "It's Christmas Eve."

I finally got out of the place and rushed across town to the Hohenzollerndamm. Lucie was waiting for me in a bar on the Günzelstrasse.

I didn't tell her because I hadn't decided yet what I was going to do about it. Shit! She had to leave the country. It was the only possible solution.

We went to the movies and saw *The Hurricane*, directed by John Ford. There was a colossal storm sequence at the end that perfectly depicted the upheaval I was going through. How could I get her out of Germany? It was impossible!

Then we went to a nightclub and drank a bottle of champagne and ate oysters and a lobster. Lucie had a gift for me, a jade bracelet that had belonged to her mother. I didn't want to accept it, but she took my hand and clipped it on my wrist. It was gorgeous. So was she! It suddenly occurred to me that I loved her with all my heart and that if I were to lose her I'd die.

Loss, loss! Always loss!

I had nothing to give her—except perhaps a concentration camp.

We walked home through the long, empty, frozen streets. Three soldiers tried to pick us up in the Barbarossa-Platz, but they were sozzled and we easily outran them. The radiators in the flat weren't working and the temperature was ten below. We fled into our rooms. I undressed, almost freezing to death, and put on a pair of ski pants and a sweater. I wrapped myself in Frau Frankovitch's mink coat and crawled under the covers, my teeth clattering.

At three o'clock in the morning Lucie came into my room.

"Edmonde!" she gibbered. "I can't stand this! I'll catch pneumonia!"

I pulled her into bed with me, buried her in blankets, hugged her like an octopus. She fell asleep, her icy nose on my throat.

An hour later the radiator pipes rattled and ding-donged and the heat came on, boiling us. We woke up in the Congo, steaming in our Eskimo costumes.

We kicked the covers to the floor and peeled ourselves nude, then fell back into each other's arms and slept on.

Her breath blew softly into my ear, murmuring inside my head, humming along the corridors of my body, calling to me, waking me.

Fiery lights began igniting all over me like candles on a Christmas tree. My breasts burned against hers, our stomachs fused together, my hands and her flesh coalesced.

Her eyes opened, blazing into mine.

"Edmonde," she whispered. "What are you doing?"

"Merry Christmas, Lucie." I kissed her. Her lips yielded, our tongues touched. Her hips melted into me, our thighs parted. And we exploded then and there, so joyously and effortlessly that we were stunned with bliss.

I would never lose her. I knew exactly what I was going to do.

When I told her about Himmler's prying she was terrified. But we had fifteen days' vacation before us and went to Bad Tölz. Once out of Berlin she was all right.

My plan just could not fail because it was so simple. It was based on Edgar Allan Poe's theory—expounded in *The Purloined Letter*—that if you wish to hide something you simply dangle it in front of everyone— and nobody will ever find it.

Once installed in the house I took her around to all

the shopkeepers, to the postmistresses and the mayor, even to the chief of police and the local party *Abteilung* boss, and introduced her as Lucie Kerrl, my cousin from Leipzig.

I chose Leipzig because there had been a train accident there a few months earlier, with scores of people killed. So if anyone asked I explained that her parents had been among the victims and she was an orphan now, and that I had invited her to Bad Tölz to live in Papa's house permanently.

It was as simple as that. My family spirit was admired, and she was accepted into the community without any difficulty whatsoever.

Papa's ghost was elated to have a lovely young stranger occupy the premises. The rooms glowed with peace and delight, the vibrations were *Adagio un poco mosso,* like the second movement of Beethoven's *Emperor* Concerto. He even permitted us to sleep together. But the first night we didn't sleep at all. We made love, over and over again, pulverizing each other.

I'd forgotten about the luggage my landlady in Munich had sent to the house after Ernst's murder. It was all there, piled in the garage. Including *Anthony Adverse!* I began to read it again, from the beginning— Book One, Chapter 1, page 1.

Then, on our third morning there, we were suddenly shocked out of our honeymoon complacency. A column of SS soldiers marched past the front yard, blowing bugles and pounding drums and waving glaring red ϟϟ banners.

We cowered at the window, watching them, thinking they were the vanguard of Himmler's army to drag us off to retribution. But no. We learned later that there was a cadets' school in the neighborhood, training officers for the elite Liebstandarte and Totenkopf brigades.

This was absolutely perfect as far as I was concerned. They would be Lucie's personal bodyguard. Fugitives were expected to be loitering suspiciously around the Swiss frontier and such places, not living tranquilly on the doorstep of the SS!

The fifteen days passed like Puck putting "a girdle round the earth in forty minutes."

On the last night we sawed a thick log in two and burned both halves in the salon fireplace. We sat on the floor before the flames, nude, and ate five liters of ice cream.

Then I took her to my breasts like a baby and nursed her. I stared at the fire, and the gentle bites of her lips on my nipples drew from me the last drops of all my tumult and confusion, drowsing me in beatitude. She fell asleep there and I sang to her:

> Zum Leiden bin ich auserkoren,
> denn meine Tochter fehlet mir . . .

I took the 6:30 train to Munich. The Berlin express didn't leave until ten o'clock, so I walked across the Bahnhof-Platz and had breakfast in a café on the Karls-Platz.

A voice hailed me: "Fräulein Valkyrie!"

It was a Luftwaffe officer sitting at one of the tables. I remembered him vaguely. He was Hermann's operations chief, a colonel named Bodenshatz. He joined me and paid for my coffee.

Meeting him was a stroke of luck, for he was going to Berlin himself—by plane. He invited me to come along with him. In the taxi driving to the airport I asked him what he meant by that "Fräulein Valkyrie" greeting.

"That," he laughed, "is what the girls in your office call you."

"They do? But why?"

"I suppose because you're so martial and warrior-like."

"Me?" I was dumbstruck. That was typical of that gaggle of hags! Fräulein Valkyrie indeed!

We boarded a Ju 52 and were at Tempelhof two hours later. During the flight Bodenshatz gave me a Luftwaffe flight pass. It entitled me to fly anywhere in Germany free of charge! It solved all my transportation problems in one fell swoop!

Back in the office I pulled Lucie's personnel card out of the file and stamped it DISCHARGED. Then I called in one of the girls and handed it to her—*martially*.

"Put this in the archives," I snapped.

She looked at it, surprised. "Lucie has been discharged?"

"Yes," I sneered—very *warrior-like*. "Fräulein Valkyrie is cleaning house, darling. So you'd better look sharp."

She ran out of the office to spread the word.

If they wanted a valkyrie, that was what they would get. I fired three others for inefficiency just for the hell of it.

The winter passed, then spring. I reread Books One and Two of *Anthony Adverse*. I flew to Munich every Friday night and back to Berlin every Monday morning. Every month I gave Lucie half of my salary. We painted the entire house—gray and yellow and orange and green and white—and pasted flowered paper on all the walls. The rooms looked like gardens. All except Papa's study. I left that as it was so that my poor neglected ghost would have a sanctuary to retreat to.

Lucie bought a phonograph and taught me to dance.
We made love in the cellar and up in the garret, in the
bathtub and in the kitchen, and many times sunbathing on the roof. One night we made love on the train
returning from Munich. And once, swimming in the
river, I made love to her under water and almost
drowned.

The summer passed.

There were little things, little signs, little clues, little
arrows pointing to the end. Little lies and little deceits.
Looks, glances, words, phrases, silences.

I drank deeply, but never saw the spider.

> Thou hast describ'd
> A hot friend cooling. Ever note, Lucilius,
> When love begins to sicken and decay,
> It useth an enforced ceremony.

And then one afternoon in September I flew to
Munich on Wednesday instead of Friday. The sun was
just setting when I arrived in Bad Tölz. The windows
of the house were closed. A bike was leaning against
a tree in the yard. The back door was open. I walked
through the kitchen and out into the dining room. There
was a black SS tunic on a chair. A pair of black boots
by the door. A black cap on the mantel. Black trousers
hanging on the doorknob. On one thigh Lucie wore a
⚡⚡ armband like a garter. That's all she had on. The
rest of her body was naked and damp and gleaming
with sweat. They were on the floor together. He was
naked too. A tall blond boy with pimples on his back.

They plopped apart and looked up at me.

Loss.

I went back to Munich. An agency on the Dachaurerstrasse was still open. I sold them the house. We couldn't discuss the price until they saw it, so I left them my keys and my phone number, signed a *Wohnort* sale permit, and caught the night flight to Berlin.

They called me up the next day and made an offer. I accepted it without quibbling. They asked me what they should do about "the person presently residing on the property." I suggested they kick her out on her ass. I suppose that's exactly what they did, because she came to Berlin that weekend and tried to see me. I told the landlord not to let her in the building.

She was arrested three days later on the U-bahn.

Himmler telephoned me.

"What is this fantastic nonsense?" He was smirking with mockery. "Lucie Hengl alias Lucie Ibsen alias Lucie Kerrl. Is she really your cousin?"

"Of course not!" Wearily, guiltily, I told him the whole woeful story.

"I ought to arrest you too," he drawled. "It's irresponsible people like you who make life a burden for the poor SS."

This gave me an idea. The office and the Luftwaffe and my telephones and my herd of girls were becoming more and more tedious. I asked him if he had a job for me.

He invited me to dinner.

Suddenly I remembered the song Mademoiselle de Marigny had taught us in the *sixième classe* at l'École des Jeunes Filles:

> Promenons nous dans les bois
> Pendant que le loup n'y est pas
> Si le loup y était
> Il nous mangerait.

I would go for a walk in the woods and meet the wolf.

He lived in a large, cluttered, bourgeois house on the Walchensee. Frau Himmler was a motherly, fussy, busy little woman who summoned her daughter and insisted I speak to her in English and French because her foreign language marks at school were "sadly disappointing." Himmler himself, out of uniform, wearing a woolen smoking jacket and slippers, poured me a large glass of Gewürztraminer. Then we all sat down and talked about the Russo-German nonaggression treaty.

"A masterpiece of diplomacy," Himmler pronounced. "The Führer and Foreign Minister Ribbentrop are paladins of statesmanship."

"They are," Frau Himmler agreed.

We went into the dining room and devoured an enormous meal of sauerbraten.

That night Germany invaded Poland and war was declared.

5

My ORDERS WERE to report to Obersturmführer Weiss in Trier and to proceed with him into occupied France. He was the new commanding officer of the Records Department of the SD and I was supposed to be his interpreter. But he wasn't in Trier. I waited for him for a week, then requisitioned a car from one of the infantry divisions and drove on alone.

I crossed the frontier at Saarbrücken and drove south through St.-Avoid and Pont-à-Mousson, then west toward St.-Mihiel and Bar-le-Duc. It was August. The countryside was lettuce green and the roads and village streets deserted. War and the Wehrmacht had come and gone, leaving a wake of silence and emptiness all across Lorraine.

At nine o'clock at night I stopped in a woods on the left bank of the Marne and took a nap.

"I swear to you, Adolf Hitler, as Führer and Reich chancellor, loyalty and bravery. I vow to you and to those you have appointed to command me obedience unto death, so help me God."

That was the oath I had to swear when I joined the SS. I received an Untersturmführer's pay and was assigned to the Communications Section of the Reichsicherheits Hauptamt (RSHA), first in Berlin, then in Warsaw.

Warsaw was nothing but rubble. I spent the whole winter living in a tent in a gutted park with four other RSHA girls. During the day we pedaled bikes through the ruins, delivering tons of directives to innumerable message centers.

Whenever I had a free moment, which was hardly ever, I read *Anthony Adverse*. I was now into Book Three, Chapter 21.

By the end of March I was the only girl in the tent who wasn't pregnant.

In April I was sent back to Germany and transferred to the Sicherheits Dienst—the SD. My pay was raised to an Obersturmführer's salary, which enabled me to throw away the black potato sack I'd been wearing and have a new uniform custom-tailored by a party couturier on the Kurfürstendamm. I also bought a pair of silver ϟϟ forks to pin to my collar.

I worked in the Records Department, filing dossiers—millions of them! One entire section was filled with Wehrmacht files, and just for the hell of it I looked up "HEYE, Richard." He was by then a general, on the staff of the Third Panzer Division, XIX Corps. And his wife was still "HEYE, Elisabeth, née Stieff." She was living in Kiel.

Lisa! She would be—mon Dieu!—almost thirty now, an old woman in a mauve dress, with romantic smudges under her eyes! I ran to a mirror and studied my own eyes, glowering at me out of a demented face. I looked ghastly! Eva and Anna and Lucie—and even Lisa— they all said I was beautiful. They were mad! I was appallingly repulsive! A haggard crone with a long fiendish neck! I looked like a condor! And in my funereal black uniform I was Medea!

Thank God she wasn't in Berlin! Suppose I were to

run into her on the street? She would bolt from me, nauseated!

But I still had my Luftwaffe flight pass. I could fly to Kiel that very day. I could . . .

Then the Hauptsturmführer in charge of the department, a man named Neumann, came back from Poland and killed himself in his office. (Later, I found out from his secretary that he had been in command of an execution squad in Bydgoszcz and it had been too much for him.) There was a terrible hubbub about it. Himmler assembled the whole section in the auditorium and made a speech.

"If you are unfit to perform your duties," he said, "then by all means let Herr Neumann's act be an example to all of you. I prefer a dead SD officer to an incapable SD officer."

There were all sorts of reassignments and I had been sent to Trier.

And so I came to be sound asleep in my car in a dark wood on the Marne.

"SS," a voice whispered.

I opened my eyes. It was five o'clock. The sun was rising through the trees in a misty orange blur. Two French soldiers were peering at me through the window.

"It's a girl!" one them yelped.

They opened the door and dragged me out to the bank. They were ragged and grimy and armed with bayonets. They looked like a pair of Syrian dacoits.

It suddenly occurred to me that I was about to be murdered. But first they wanted my body. They began fumbling at the buttons of my tunic.

I was seized with an insane determination to save my new uniform. I pushed them away and unbuttoned the jacket myself. I removed it, folded it neatly, and laid

it on the hood of the car. Then I unbelted my skirt
and stepped out of it à la Casino de Paris. They watched
me, agog, as I placed it atop the tunic. I faced them,
wearing only my underthings and boots. They stood
there, petrified. They smelled like a kennel. I pulled
off the boots and rolled down my stockings.

They dropped their trousers and out popped two
gigantic hairy Gallic pythons.

I told them to wait and took a blanket from the
rear seat. I shook it open and spread it on the ground.
They were grinning now, the pigfuckers. They threw
aside their bayonets and came toward me. I went to the
car again and leaned across the front seat, aiming my
derriere at them. I pulled the Lüger from my purse on
the floor. They both reached for me, pulling me against
them. I turned and shot the first in the stomach, setting
his shirt on fire.

He coughed and jumped up and down on one foot.
He tumbled to the ground, smoking like a bonfire. The
other backed away from me, neighing. I shot him in the
eye. His face parted asunder in a red mass and he
fell too.

I undressed and took a bar of soap and a towel from
my valise. I waded into the river and bathed. The water
was warm and thick with green foliage. Drumming
pulses of lust tingled up and down the insides of my
thighs. I dropped to my knees and opened my legs.
I leaned into the rushes, scooped up a handful of mud,
and wiped it against my longing, scouring the exquisite
itch. I looked at the two corpses on the bank and
geysers of pure rapture bubbled out of me. The Marne
flowed melodiously through my womb, rose to my
throat in a vortex, then ebbed, leaving me limp and
numb and glorified, sprawled in the muddy weeds like
a fossil.

For just an instant I was absolutely certain that in nine months I would give birth to an ondine.

Then I put on my clothes, climbed into the car, and drove off.

I arrived in Paris at four o'clock in the afternoon.

The SD Records office was on the Avenue Marceau, just on the circumference of the place de l'Étoile. Obersturmführer Weiss was already installed there, bleating petulantly because I was forty-eight hours late in reporting. We had received conflicting orders, as usual.

He was a burly, bovid clod with greasy wavy hair, and the idea of working for him immediately depressed me. He gave me a lodging billet entitling me to a room in any hotel in the eighth arrondissement. I picked the George V because that's where Papa used to stay when he came to Paris.

I was given a small room and bath overlooking the avenue Pierre 1er. I unpacked quickly and went out and took a walk.

All the shops and cafés were closed. The Champs-Élysées was as dead as Pompeii. Over the barred entrance of a cinema on the rue Marbeuf was a film poster, like an epitaph:

> Corinne Luchaire et
> Claude Dauphin dans
> CAVALCADE D'AMOUR

On the place de la Concorde one lone soldier was taking pictures of the Obelisk. I went into the Jardin des Tuileries. Hanging on a façade on the rue de Rivoli was a swastika flag. Floating in the scummy water of a fountain was a sailboat.

I sat down on a bench and smoked a cigarette.

A man was standing beside a tree, over by the Orangerie, watching me.

I beckoned to him to come and sit beside me. He walked off toward the quay. I jumped up and ran after him.

It was Papa, of course. He had been avoiding me peevishly ever since I sold the house. But if he had followed me all the way to Paris, perhaps he wasn't as angry as he pretended to be.

He crossed the Pont de Solférino to the Left Bank. So did I. When he saw me behind him he broke into a trot, wheezing and huffing along the bridge like a tired old elk. The idiot!

I lost sight of him on the rue de Lille. I walked down the rue de Bellechasse to the boulevard Saint-Germain, and lo and behold! there was a bistro open for business. I went into the place. A lugubrious old woman stood behind the bar, scowling at me with patriotic disapproval. Two men were sitting at a table, playing checkers. They didn't even bother to look at me. I ordered a pernod. The harpy pretended she didn't understand my French. The two men smirked. Shit! I didn't really feel like a drink anyway. But it was dim and cool in the bar, so I pulled up a chair, sat down in a corner, took *Anthony Adverse* from my purse, and began Chapter 22:

Icons and Iconoclasts

In times of great change it is a question whether the restlessness of the human heart is due more to individual dissatisfaction with experience than to the drag and flux of the age.

The Records Department's grueling mission was to compile racial dossiers on everyone in France of Jewish origin. It was dull, dull, dreary, plodding drudgery. I would have preferred working with the Intelligence branch or even the Political Bureau. I could never understand the Nazi obsession with Jews. A pigfucker was a pigfucker, regardless of his race or nationality. And a Jewish pigfucker was absolutely no different from a Gentile pigfucker. Hitler and Himmler just could not grasp that simple fact of life.

Neither could Obersturmführer Weiss. His anti-Semitic zeal drove me frantic. He actually signed warrants of deportation for Michel Simon, Sacha Guitry, Edith Piaf, Arletty, and Jean Cocteau, insisting they were "of doubtful lineal descent." I had to telephone Himmler in Berlin and beg him to countermand the order, otherwise they all would have been shipped off to Germany in a cattle car! Mon Dieu! What nonsense!

And Ohlendorf was worse.

On the twenty-seventh of August an RAF pilot was picked up on the rue Vavin in Montparnasse. His name was Flight-Lieutenant James Sanders and he had been shot down on the coast, near Fort-Mahon. He was obviously on his way to contact someone in the French Resistance.

The Gestapo phoned us, asking if there was anyone in our department who could speak English well enough to interpret an interrogation. Weiss recommended me for the job. Ugh!

He must have known what I was in for, the swine, because he was snickering when he called me into his office.

"Report to Ohlendorf," he said. "Rue Galilée, just around the corner."

I knew the address. So did everybody else in Paris. It was known as la Fosse aux Serpents.

"Who's Ohlendorf?"

"You'll find out."

Feeling a bit queasy, I walked down the avenue Marceau to the rue Galilée. The Gestapo bureau was just another building, but it looked as sinister as a pesthouse. In the lobby, a little man with a morgue face, wearing a shabby suit of civilian clothes, was waiting for me. We both lifted our arms.

"Heil Hitler!"

"Heil Hitler!"

"Ohlendorf."

"Kerrl."

He led me through a long dark passageway, then down a flight of steps into the basement. There two giants in leather aprons were standing over a boy lying naked on a table. Ohlendorf introduced him with a sneer.

"Flight-Lieutenant James Sanders."

He was no more than nineteen or twenty, redheaded and lanky, with a small penis and bushy pink eyebrows.

Ohlendorf sat on the edge of the table and struck a match. He leaned over and carefully singed Sander's pubic hairs.

"I want to know where he was going when he was arrested," he said.

I put the question to Sanders, in English. He smiled at me idiotically.

"Balls to you, miss," he chirped.

"Tell them," I whispered. "They're just waiting for an excuse to do all sorts of nasty things to you."

"Balls to them too."

"What does he say?" Ohlendorf asked.

"He says he was on his way to the Gare d'Austerlitz," I lied. "He was going to try to catch a train to Vichy."

This was reasonable enough. Vichy was the capital

of the unoccupied zone. But of course Ohlendorf didn't believe a word of it.

"He's lying."

They tortured him. First one of the huge brutes clamped an iron fork around Sanders's knee and twisted it slowly, breaking his leg. The bones snapped like ice. Then they smashed one of his hands with a stonecutter's mallet, tap-tap-tapping on his fingers and knuckles until there was nothing but pulp hanging in shreds from his wrist. Then they rolled him over on his stomach and burned his anus with the flame of a candle. Then they hammered nails into the thick flesh of his derriere. Then they turned him over on his back again and squirted terebinthine into his nostrils with a nosedropper. Then they—

And all the while he screamed, or rather mooed, lowing like a desolate foghorn: "Hoooo-oooo-uuu!" He covered the table with his blood and filth. He broke the straps holding him prone and jumped up. He hobbled across the room, Ohlendorf and the two giants lurching after him. It was unbearable. The four of them lunged and bounded about as if they were dancing a polka in a beer garden.

I ran upstairs and opened a window. I thought I was going to vomit. Two men in their undershirts were standing out in the courtyard, bouncing a ball against the wall. They stared at me blankly.

"Kerrl!"

I went downstairs again. The session went on and on and on, all afternoon. They crippled his other hand with the mallet, then poked out one of his eyes with an icepick. I pleaded with him to put a stop to it.

"Tell them who you were going to meet, Lieutenant, for God's sake! This is absurd!"

"Mad," he whimpered.

"What does he say?" Ohlendorf asked, panting with fatigue.

"He says you're mad." I agreed with him whole-heartedly. They had to be stark raving mad to be capable of this sort of thing. Not only that, but they were actually enjoying themselves, the pigfuckers.

"Break his other leg," Ohlendorf grunted.

Later they left me alone with him while they went off to have something to eat. I tried again to reason with him. I bent over his battered face and whispered in his ear. "You have to tell them, Sanders, you *have* to." I put my hand on his penis, stroking it gently. It stiffened under my touch. I glanced down at it. It was yellow and spotted, like a mushroom.

"Mad," he croaked.

"Yes, I know. It's completely insane. Tell the bastards what they want to know."

"Chaise Mad."

"What?"

I continued to fondle him, the poor wretch. It grew in my hand, its length trembling and trebling.

"Chaise Mad," he repeated. "Mad . . ."

It was an oak tree, mighty and solid. I squeezed it, tugged it clemently, rowing him slowly and leniently. It spurted into the air, sending rosy froth flying across the table.

Then he died.

It was after five o'clock when I finally got out of the dreadful place. I walked down to the place d'Alma, feeling utterly dismal. Papa was standing on the other side of the avenue, peering at me out of a doorway. I pretended I didn't see him, but watched him out of the corner of my eye as he followed me.

I leaned against a lamppost on the quay and let the sun warm me.

Hanging on a kiosk before me was an *affiche* depicting a young woman in a tuxedo smoking a cheroot. The smoke curling out of her lips formed the caption: "Chez Mad Cabaret Féminin Boulevard Edgar Quinet Paris 14."

I stared at it, suddenly thunderstruck.

Chez Mad.

Of course! That's what poor Sanders had been trying to tell me. I thought he had been raving inanely about the madness and insanity of what they were doing to him. But no. He'd simply been mispronouncing a name. His "Chaise Mad" had meant Chez Mad! That's where he was going when they picked him up!

It never occurred to me to rush back to the rue Galilée and tell Ohlendorf. Balls to him.

The boulevard Edgar Quinet was a mournful, funereal land lined on one side by the display windows of mortuaries and on the other by the wall of the Montparnasse Cemetery. At its more cheerful extremity, past the rue de la Gaité, was a row of nightclubs.

Chez Mad was tucked between Le Cendrier and Le Tamtam.

I felt the chill of disapprobation the moment I went through the door. Although I wasn't in uniform, I had been immediately identified. I was *l'Envahisseuse*.

It was a small, ornate, murky place à la Joseph von Sternberg, with blue velvet walls, golden tables, and a stunning barmaid wearing Hamlet tights and a bow tie.

Women sat at all the tables, staring at me with lovely baleful faces. There were no men present.

I went over to the bar and ordered a Mokkei. This disconcerted Mademoiselle Hamlet completely. She had no idea what a Mokkei was. In fact, neither did

I. I'd come across the name in one of S. S. Van Dine's mystery novels. I drank a champagne cocktail instead.

All the lamps went out. Then a ruby light illuminated a young woman sitting at a piano. She wore a dark silk dinner jacket, a white lace shirt and cravat, and trousers as tight-fitting as stockings.

This, to be sure, was Mad herself.

She sang, or rather purred, a cynical and debonair song about lovers saying adieu. Everyone laughed and applauded.

I thought it was all rather chichi.

"My next number," she announced, "is dedicated to that ravishing Boche doll sitting at the bar."

And she sang,

> Voisin, d'où venait ce grand bruit
> Qui m'a réveillé cette nuit
> Et tous ceux de mon voisinage . . .

She warbled on, then played a Wagnerian flourish and ended with a cry of "Seig Heil!" All the girls clapped merrily.

Ugh!

Later she came over to the bar and sat down beside me. "I hope I didn't embarrass you," she cooed. "I know how sensitive Germans are."

"How did you know I was German?" I asked.

She dipped her finger into my champagne and licked it. "Because of your Götterdämmerung eyes," she whispered.

I wondered how one went about smuggling RAF pilots out of the country. It must have been a tremendous enterprise, involving scores of people.

"What do you want here? This is a private club."

"That's what I'm looking for," I told her. "Privacy.

A place where I can hide from time to time. A . . ."
I thought at first that I was just bantering with her. But
I wasn't. It suddenly occurred to me that I was sincere.
That was exactly what I was seeking—a haven.

"I'm Mad. Who are you?"

"Edmonde."

"What are you hiding from, Edmonde?"

What indeed! I laughed. "Phantasmagorias," I said.
I was being flippant again, although there was a lump
in my throat. "Gypsies."

"Gypsies?"

"When I was a little girl the gypsies used to come
through our village every year, in the spring, and camp
in the woods. They would arrive at twilight and leave
at sunrise, and during the night they would steal everything they could get their hands on. But they would
only take little things. Doorknobs and lumps of coal
and sticks of firewood. And the nozzles from hoses and
lamppost bulbs and ashcans and flowerpots and hub-
caps from cars and clothesline ropes. And the next day
everything would seem to be the same as it always had
been, but if you looked closely you would see that all
the tiny pieces of the town were missing, as if a horde
of soldier ants had passed in the dark and each one
had eaten a small mouthful of the world. And only the
remnants of things remained."

I blinked at her, astonished by my loquacity. Mon
Dieu! It was an aria! What on earth had dredged all
that out of me?

She smiled. "You're delightful. How could I possibly
turn you out?" She took my hand. "Consider yourself
a member of our coven." And she leaned forward and
kissed me on the lips. "There. Now you've been ini-
tiated!"

All the girls cheered. Mademoiselle Hamlet refilled my glass. I turned toward the door.

A girl in white slacks and a violet sweater was leaning against the wall, watching me. She had pale green eyes, thin inky arched brows, and Aztec hair cut short in a Jeanne d'Arc bob. And she was there to meet Flight-Lieutenant Sanders.

I knew it instantly. And she knew I knew.

Mad called to her. "Marie-José, come and meet Edmonde!"

She came toward me like an Apache Montezuma approaching a sacrifice. Her eyes overflowed, tinting all the other colors in the room with jade greenness. She stood before me, dazzling, blinding me with her stare.

Jade green, yes. Where had I seen that rare color before? In Berlin . . . one freezing Christmas . . . Lucie's bracelet, yes! It was exactly the same shade of warm smoky verdigris, glinting with dots of glass.

Then she was gone.

I raced after her, panic-stricken at the idea of remaining a whole night away from her. She was waiting for me out on the boulevard Edgar Quinet.

We walked along the rue Delambre toward Vavin.

"I'm sure Hitler has done something about those gypsies," she said.

"Yes. He put them all in concentration camps."

"But don't you think"—she stopped and opened a pack of cigarettes—"that by stealing only insignificant things, they were trying to express their gratitude?"

"Gratitude?"

"For your hospitality."

"That seems to me to be a rather peculiar way of looking at it."

"Oh?" She lit a cigarette and offered me one. "It

seems to me, on the contrary, to be a perfectly logical explanation."

We walked on, crossing the boulevard Raspail. What in the world was I doing, walking through dark streets with this outlandish girl? I had the strangest feeling—it was as if I had come all the way to Paris just to meet her. *Dear Edmonde, I'll be in Chez Mad's at ten o'clock on the 27th of August, 1940. Chère Marie-José, D'accord, j'y serai.*

"Do you go to that place often?" I asked.

"She pays me a hundred francs a night just to sit at the bar and let the girls buy me drinks." She stopped and looked at me. "There are now . . ." she counted on her fingers ". . . four of them in love with me."

"Five," I said.

Sapphire pinpoints blazed in her eyes. She slipped off into the blackness of the boulevard Montparnasse. I followed her white-clad legs. Her heels rapped on the sidewalk—*tap-tap-tap-tap*—like the mallet hammering nails into poor Sanders's derriere. I would get even with that pigfucker Ohlendorf. We went down the rue de la Grande Chaumière, then through a doorway, then up a flight of stairs.

We were in a grubby studio filled with half-undressed boys and girls dancing. A phonograph was playing an American folk song:

> All the world is sad and dreary
> Everywhere I roam . . .

In all the shadows couples and trios were making love noisily. They sounded like waves lapping a pier.

Marie-José took a plate of grapes from a table and led me into a corner. A boy with a beard, wearing only his undershorts, came up to her. They moved off into the obscurity, whispering together, eyeing me.

I sat down on a bench and ate a handful of grapes. She came back and sat beside me. "If you wish to remove your clothes," she suggested, "do so." I sniffed the air. "You disapprove of the odor?"

"It smells like a locomotive."

"It is *kef*. Do you want to smoke some?"

"No."

"What do you want?"

"Just to sit here next to you."

Her absinthe eyes flared at me again. It was marvelous. Being with her was a constant green thrill!

On the floor nearby a boy and a girl were locked together, thumping up and down, while a second boy sat on the girl's face. Farther on another girl was on her knees, with a penis in her mouth.

"Marie-José, are you clever? Or are you stupid?"

"I'm reasonably intelligent."

"What do you do?"

"I paint."

"Will you show me your paintings?"

"Yes, if you like."

We ate the grapes. Two naked boys danced past us.

"When you look at me, Marie-José, what do you think? What are your thoughts?"

She crossed her legs and leaned on her elbow. "When I saw you in the bar, I said to myself, 'She will pretend to be Swedish, or Swiss, or something.' But you didn't. You didn't pretend to be anything. And when I look at you now"—she blazed at me again, coloring our corner jade—"I think, 'Now she will say this, or perhaps that.' But you do not. You ask unexpected questions. And you make unexpected statements. Like, 'Five.' And you bewilder me. So my thoughts, in consequence, are not clear."

"A French doctor once said I was a German mystery."

She smiled. "What have other people said about you?"

"A dentist called me a Munich bitch. A judge said I was a dangerous criminal. The girls in an office where I worked called me Fräulein Valkyrie."

Someone had put a German record on the phonograph. A woman's voice trilled in the darkness:

> Du Armste kannst wohl nie ermessen
> wie "zweifellos" mein Herze liebt,
> Du hast wohl nie das Glück besessen
> das sich uns nur durch Glauben gibt?

"Marie-José."

"Yes?"

"What will you do with my corpse?"

She sat up straight. *"Hein?* Your corpse?" But she didn't look at me.

"You brought me here to kill me, didn't you?" She didn't answer. "Look at me." She turned slowly, her eyes shining like wet quetsches. "What are you waiting for? Is it because there are too many people around? Or are you worried about Chez Mad? You needn't. No one knows I went there tonight. And when I don't report to work in the morning, the SD won't even know where to search for me."

"You work for the SD?"

"Yes."

She rose to her feet. "Come, we will leave now." I followed her out the door.

We walked around the corner to the rue Notre-

Dame des Champs. We went through a gate into a courtyard, then along a passageway to a door. She unlocked it, opened it, turned on a lamp.

It was another studio, much smaller than the other. And much cleaner, thank God! In fact, it was spotless. There were no windows, just a skylight. The high walls were painted turquoise. Her canvases, seven or eight of them, were leaning against a coffer, their backs to the room.

There was no bed.

"There is not enough light to show you anything. Just this perhaps."

She unrolled a large drawing and held it before me. It was the elaborate sketch of some sort of mechanism, all coils and springs.

"What is it?"

"The inside of a lock."

"And where is the . . . ?" I looked around.

"Where is the what? The cabinet is outside."

"I was wondering where you slept."

"Upstairs." She lit a cigarette. "In Mad's apartment."

"Oh? Mad lives upstairs?"

"Yes." She sat down on the edge of the coffer and smoked. She pointed to a stool. I sat on it and stared at my shoes. At least fifteen minutes passed in silence.

"You were right," she said finally. "I did intend to kill you. I changed my mind. I hope I will not regret it."

"It's still not too late."

"It is. Far too late."

" 'Kill me tomorrow; let me live tonight. But half an hour. But while I say one prayer. A guiltless death I die. Commend me to my kind lord.' " She looked at me, her eyes expanding to vast green diameters. *"Othello,"* I explained. "Desdemona's death scene."

She shook her head and threw up her hands.

Then she laughed. So did I. Then we fell silent again.

"Mon Dieu, Marie-José," I pleaded, "please *do* something!"

"Yes." She unstrapped her sandals, got up, opened the coffer. She lifted out a heavy folded quilt and opened it on the floor. Then she turned out the lamp.

I watched, my insides tightening, as she stood beneath the skylight in a bright avalanche of moonlight and removed her white slacks and violet sweater.

One of her ankles glittered with silver. I stared at it. "What's that?"

Clothed only in pearly shadows, she lifted her leg and put her foot on the coffer. She bent over and unclasped a chain from her ankle.

"It's platinum. My father gave it to me when I passed my bac." She set it on a shelf.

I rose from the stool and took off my dress, my shoes, and my stockings. Her arms opened and I moved into her. Our thighs and our breasts touched, then our noses, then our lips, then all of us, our bodies merging entirely. She was warm as a furnace. Her kiss was sweltering. Her eyes, pressed against mine, became a single giant orbit of sulfurous beryl.

We separated, our nostrils seeking out our odors, our hands descending between us, out toes mingling. We lifted our arms and our tongues lapped our perspiration.

She glided away from me. "Do you like to play games?" she whispered.

"No, yes. I don't know. What games?"

"This, for instance." She floated off into the milky darkness. She came back to me, carrying a whip.

*　　*　　*

I returned to the George V at eight o'clock in the morning. I could hardly walk. My back was broken and my derriere throbbed. I wanted only to fall into a bathtub filled with boiling water and die. But there wasn't time. I took a shower and put on my uniform. I was at my desk in the office by nine.

Obersturmführer Weiss arrived angrily at nine-fifteen. "Ohlendorf wants to see you again," he snarled. "You might remind him that you work for me, not the Gestapo."

"Yes, sir."

The very idea of going back to that zoo on the rue Galilée chilled me. I couldn't bear another interrogation.

Instead of going down the avenue Marceau, I took the long way around, via the Champs-Élysées, the avenue George V and the rue Vernet.

It was a divine, Olympian morning. Paris was still dead, but here and there resurrections were visible. Window shutters were open, there were flowers on some balconies, waiters were sweeping the terraces of cafés, natives on bikes were beginning to come out of the woodwork.

My back was pleasantly numb by then and I was certain I would survive.

What a night it had been! Incredible!

I had whipped Marie-José first, very gently to begin with, but then, as she flung herself about the floor beneath me, railing and gibbering, licking my feet and caressing my knees, I had been seized with a frenzy of lust—possessed! overwhelmed by raging wantonness —and had thrashed her as hard as I could.

Then we rolled on the quilt and made love until we were wrecks.

Then it had been my turn! Mon Dieu! Even then,

thinking about it, the hairs under my skirt bristled and my derriere swung back and forth lewdly.

I had been asleep when the lash woke me, biting my spine with crocodile jaws. A thousand asps stabbed their fangs into my back, paralyzing me with ecstasy. Cobras coiled around my hips and gnawed my anus. Lascivious hornets flew between my legs and stung me in spots I never even knew existed, turning my blood to lava, stunning me, splitting me open like a melon and splattering my dripping lushness all over the studio.

And we had made love again, squeezing the last needlepoints of rapture out of each other. After that, we had been two empty hulks.

And strangely enough, walking now in the sun, I was suddenly ready to begin again. Sweat dripped sweetly under my arms, and my thighs, scraping together, itched and burned with hunger. I felt like slipping into a doorway and touching myself.

Even the Gestapo basement no longer frightened me.

On the rue Galilée Ohlendorf, the evil cock, was just coming out of the building, followed by two flunkies carrying suitcases. He greeted me happily, all smiles, like Richard III:

> Why, I can smile,
> And murder while I smile.

He was on his way to Leipzig and wanted to thank me for my "wonderful wonderful cooperation" before he left. He opened one of his bags and fished out a bottle of perfume. He presented it to me and kissed my hand gallantly. Then he was gone. Auf Wiedersehen!

Shit! There went my vengeance! I would probably

never see him again and poor Sanders's death would remain unrequited.

Tant pis! I would punish Obersturmführer Weiss instead. One SS pigfucker was as bad as another.

Mad lived in an immense apartment on the rue Notre-Dame-des-Champs. That's where Marie-José and I would go for our orgies, every night, night after night, from ten o'clock until dawn, while Mad was at the club.

I would reel back to my hotel at six or seven in the morning, then go to the office and doze all day at my desk.

Saturdays and Sundays we would spend the whole day together. We went to Versailles twice and once to Fontainebleau. We saw all the films and plays. And, of course, we walked all over Paris, roaming tirelessly through every one of the twenty arrondissements.

And we spent entire afternoons in cafés in Montparnesse and the Champs-Élysées, in Saint-Germain-des-Prés and Pigalle and the Latin Quarter. Marie-José knew everybody, and I met thousands of actors and actresses and directors and poets and painters.

When we had enough of whipping each other, we played other "games." She took me to her coiffeur and had my hair cut even shorter than hers. Then she would dress me up in one of Mad's masculine suits and we would go out dancing, or to a restaurant. Or we would both disguise ourselves as boys and try to pick up girls on the Métro. One night we succeeded and took two charming secretaries to a *hotel de passe* on the rue d'Odessa. We made love to them, side by side, on a stained and stinking bed. Then we unveiled ourselves dramatically and told them we were policewomen from the Brigade des Moeurs. We threatened to have them arrested for "indiscrimination" if they didn't return our favors. The poor terrified things complied, committing the act with surprising dexterity. It was terribly hilarious and exciting.

But the strangest "game" of all took place one night in October. We had been in the studio all evening, drinking cognac and smoking *kef*. Marie-José was painting my portrait on the door, a full-length nude, posed in a ballerina's classic *cinquième position,* wearing only sandals strapped to my calves. I was exhausted from standing with my feet pointing in all directions and stretched out on the quilt to take a nap. I was also sozzled. I slept—according to my *Dictionary of American Slang*—"like a log." I dreamed of Anthony Adverse sailing to Cuba on a ship haunted by the ghost of a little girl.

And I woke up to find Marie-José lying on top of me. She was deep, deep, deep, *inside* me. I couldn't for the life of me understand how her tongue could be in my mouth and, at the same time, away down there between my legs. And what a tongue! It stretched on and on and on, unwinding for kilometers!

"It's Mad's," she whispered. "Lift your hips higher." She rose into the air. "Look." I peered down between our bodies. It was a *penis!* "How does it feel?" She sank into me again, growling in my ear.

It was strapped to her waist, burrowing within me like a supple mole, rending me, tunneling me, battering me open, bouncing me up and down, and, finally, lifting me to the ceiling and flinging me out the skylight over the rooftops, smashing me to smithereens against the dark sky.

After that, no one could ever again call me a virgin.

* * *

One morning Weiss came lunging into my office, pale with shock. "The Führer!" he blubbered. "Line two!"

I picked up my phone and pushed the second button.

"Hello."

"Edmonde?"

I almost fell out of my chair. It *was* the Führer! He was calling me from Le Bourget airfield.

"I'm only in Paris for the day," he announced in his familiar Hofbräuhaus rasp. "I'm going to do some sightseeing. Care to join me?"

"Is Eva with you?"

"Certainly not."

I met him an hour later on the steps of the Opéra. He was with an entire flock of Very Important People, all packed into three Mercedes sedans. We saluted and he shook my hand formally, clicking his heels à la Erich von Stroheim.

He took me by the shoulders, beaming. "You look very handsome."

"Thank you, my Führer. Your victories are responsible for that." He barked with puppy delight and actually kissed me on the cheek! Mon Dieu! What lechery!

We went into the building and spent an hour trooping through all the foyers and corridors. I found the décor baroque and hideous, a nightmare of gingerbread ornamentation and nouveau riche bad taste. But he gushed with pleasure, swooning over everything. The grand stairway made him dance with glee.

"I'm glad I didn't have Paris destroyed" he crowed. "I thought seriously about doing just that, Edmonde."

"No! Destroying Paris?"

"Yes indeed." He rubbed his hands. "Leveling the whole city. Like Carthage."

"But why?"

"You're right. Why bother. After I rebuild Berlin, all this will be a mere shadow of greatness. Remind me to show you my blueprints the next time you visit the chancellery."

We all crowded into the sedans and drove down the boulevard de la Madeleine into the rue Royale, then across the place de la Concorde.

"How is Eva?" I asked.

"Fine, fine. She often speaks of you. She misses you. You are her dearest friend, you know."

I thought of the *thing* strapped to Marie-José's waist. Mon Dieu! Eva would go wild! "My Führer, could she come to Paris and visit me?"

"No, I'm afraid not." He looked at me. His eyes were two morgues. I froze, my guts turning to frost. *Did he know?* No, certainly not! How could he? And yet . . . He turned away and leaned out the window. "Is this the rue de Rivoli?"

"No." I tried to swallow, but there was an ice cube in my throat. "The Champs-Élysées."

"Ah, yes."

We alighted from the cars on the place du Trocadéro and walked across the esplanade. We lined up like a firing squad and gazed across the river at the Tour Eiffel.

Hitler was impressed. He folded his arms and tilted his head, muttering to himself. I told him the old, old joke about the American tourist from Texas who thought it was an oil well. He didn't laugh. "Don't try to be too French, Edmonde."

A photographer took our picture and the following week I found myself in *Signal* magazine.

Then back into the cars. The next stop was Les Invalides. We marched into the crypt and looked upon

Napoleon's sarcophagus, everyone appropriately solemn and ghoulish.

"I want nothing like this when I die," Hitler stated flatly. "A soldier's simple plot of earth will do very nicely for me, thank you. In a military cemetery, among my fallen comrades-at-arm. I want no shrines. No pyramids, no domes. The Third Reich itself will be my memorial. Edmonde?"

"My Führer?"

He took me aside. "Is there a men's room here?" he whispered.

I led him off into the depths of the monument, looking for a *pissoir*. We couldn't find one. He finally urinated on the floor of an alcove.

After that we visited the Panthéon, the Place des Vosges, and the Sainte-Chapelle.

In the car he held my hand. "This has been the happiest day of my life." He glowed. "I've always dreamed of coming to Paris."

I suddenly had an insane inspiration. "Come to Montparnasse. We'll sit on the terrace of a café and drink beer." Then I remembered that he didn't drink. "Or lemonade. Or Vichy."

"No, my dear."

"Or—I know! An artist is painting my portrait. Come to her studio and I'll show it to you."

"I have no time for that sort of thing, Edmonde."

"Why not? You must find time, otherwise what's the point of conquering the world?"

He smiled and said, "The world isn't conquered yet." He patted my arm. "Not quite. But I promise you we'll have a cup of tea together, next year, in a pub in London."

I glanced out the window and saw Papa on a bridge. I gasped.

"What is it, Edmonde?"

There he was, wearing his shabby brown raincoat—
I hated that coat, it made him look like a hoodlum—
just standing there . . .

"Someone you know?"

"No. I thought it was . . . he looked like . . ."

"Why are the streets so filthy? Are there no garbagemen in Paris? When the British bombed Berlin last
month, all the citizens assembled with brooms and
shovels and had the mess cleaned up in an hour." I
knew the symptoms. He was off on one of his tirades.
"I'm convinced we must keep a very cool head in our
dealings with the French, both now during the armistice
period and later when the peace treaty is formulated."
I leaned back and closed my eyes. "And we must bear
in mind all historical precedents and make decisions in
which sentiment plays no part. We must not be content
with the control of the Atlantic islands. If we are to
ensure the hegemony of the Continent, we must also
retrain strongholds on what was formerly the Atlantic
coast." He droned on and on. "We must further not
forget that the old kingdom of Burgundy played a
prominent role in Germany history, and that it is from
time immemorial German soil, which the French
grabbed at the time of our weakness. Not only that,
but . . ."

At four o'clock the convoy drove back to Le Bourget.
In the airport lounge he left me alone while he chatted
with his fawning toadies. Then, abruptly, he beckoned
to me. I walked over to him. He was visibly upset.

"I really should take a present to Eva."

"Yes, you must."

"What, though? Where can I buy something?"

I took Ohlendorf's bottle of perfume from my purse.
I'd never even bothered to open it. "Give her this."

He accepted it gratefully. "Perfume! Perfect!" He kissed my hand. "Thank you, dear Edmonde." He called to one of the officers, "Colonel Speidel, please drive Comrade Kerrl back to Paris!"

And then he flew away, off to Cloud Cuckooland. Colonel Speidel dropped me at Vavin and I went to the Dome and drank three pernods.

Mad caught us, of course. It had to happen sooner or later. Instead of returning home at dawn, she came sauntering in at eleven o'clock one night and found us in bed together.

We didn't play the usual *"Ciel! mon mari!"* scene. She wasn't even angry. And there wasn't the agony I had endured when I'd discovered Lucie on the floor with her pimply SS lout. On the contrary. Mad just laughed, removed her tuxedo, and climbed in between us.

"Very well, little girls," she drawled. "You will now pay the landlady." She grasped the backs of our necks and pushed both our faces down upon her and we alternated kindling her to lunacy. She thrashed and brayed and kicked, beating our shoulders with her fists. It was like eating a whirlwind. And when she ignited the bed almost capsized.

Then we opened a bottle of whiskey and sozzled ourselves into oblivion. Marie-José put a record on the Victrola and I danced with her. Then with Mad. Nude, Mad was far more alluring than she was in her ridiculous maître d'hôtel suit. In fact, she was Juno! She was as lithe and slim as an athlete, with freckled shoulders and an insolent Folies-Bergère bosom, and her arms were covered wth blond fuzz.

When the bottle was empty she sat down at her dressing table and donned all her jewelry, wrapping

scores of necklaces and bracelets around her throat
and arms and ankles and thighs. She made us kneel
before her. Marie-José took her left foot and I her
right, and we had to suck her toes and demand her
pardon.

After that the night became a weird hodgepodge of
stomachs and diamonds and hips and tastes and emer-
alds and nipples and armpits and pearls and navels and
gloriously swelling oceanic cataclysms.

Knees kept descending on me and wrapping themselves around my head. I had no idea who they belonged to. I simply mouthed everything that came my
way, like a blind glutton submerged in a gigantic pud-
ding.

Once, crawling through a forest of legs, I suddenly
came face to face with Marie-José and we kissed ten-
derly, like chaste sisters. It was so exquisite we wept.

Teeth ravaged me, bogs of hair smothered me, ant-
eaters' tongues licked me raw. Then Mad strapped on
the *thing* and jumped on my back, stabbing me in the
derriere. Marie-José whipped us both, yelling like a
savage. And then . . .

And then one morning I pulled back the curtains and
looked out the window and saw that it was spring. An
entire winter had passed.

I hadn't read a single page of *Anthony Adverse* for
months and had been neglecting my work shamefully.
My files and lists were a shambles. Obersturmführer
Weiss was very patient with me and even polite occasionally. The truth of the matter was that he was a bit
afraid of me. That telephone call from Hitler had put
him on his guard. But then the pigfucker was promoted
to Hauptsturmführer and started to turn obnoxious

again. He canceled my weekend leave and gave me
forty-eight hours to clean up my office.

I decided to slap him down.

Marie-José, Mad, and I were having lunch one afternoon in a black-market restaurant on the place Denfert
when I lit the fuse.

"I hope you aren't members of the Resistance," I
remarked casually.

"The Resistance?" Mad dropped her fork. "What
an idea!"

Marie-José's magnesium green eyes exploded. "Why
do you say that, Edmonde?"

"Because there's an enormous raid coming soon." I
lowered my voice. "Scores of people are going to be
arrested."

"Who?" they asked, awed.

"I've no idea. Hauptsturmführer Weiss keeps the list
in his briefcase. It's so confidential he won't even leave
it in the office."

They wanted to know who Hauptsturmführer Weiss
was. I told them. Three nights later he was shot in his
apartment on the rue Copernic in the sixteenth arrondissement.

I rushed to Chez Mad to celebrate. The club was
closed. I walked over to the rue Notre-Dame des
Champs. There was no one in the apartment either.
I went down to Marie-José's studio. She wasn't there.

I waited for her all night, prowling up and down
the boulevard Montparnasse like Ophelia:

> O heavens! is't possible a young maid's wits
> Should be as mortal as an old man's life?

At three o'clock in the morning Papa came out of
the rue Bréa and went down the boulevard Raspail. I

wandered after him, moving just behind him until I was almost at his side. And we walked together across the Maximilians-Platz and up the Briennerstrasse to the Hofgarten. We walked through the Bad Tölz woods and we walked into the meadows and the lanes and we walked along the river past all the familiar centimeters of everything I'd lost.

Then we were on the boulevard Edgar Quinet and he entered the cemetery. When I tried to follow him the gate was closed.

The Gestapo telephoned me the next morning. They wanted me to come immediately to the rue Galilée.

Ohlendorf had been replaced by another pigfucker, a Cro-Magnon specimen named Roesch. I marched into his office and saluted.

"Heil Hitler!"

"Heil Hitler!"

He snickered. He looked like a bison. He pushed a pad in front of me. My heart sunk to my intestines. It was Marie-José's sketchbook! Shit! It was filled with drawings of me! "Is this *you*, Kerrl?"

"Yes, sir."

"You know Marie-José Carré?"

"Yes, sir."

He sat back and lit a cigar. "Where did you meet her?"

"In Montparnasse. She's an artist. She's painting a portrait of me."

He glanced at several sketches, grinning. They were nudes, naturally. "Without your clothes on?"

"Yes, sir."

"You posed in the nude, Kerrl?"

"Yes, sir. It's for the Führer."

"The Führer!" His buffalo mouth opened. "For the Führer?"

"Yes, sir. A painting for the museum he's building in Linz. In fact, he suggested it himself, when he was in Paris."

He believed it. He knew about my accompanying Hitler on his famous sightseeing tour. Everybody in France knew.

"Have I done anything wrong, sir?"

He put out his cigar. "No, certainly not. But . . . uh . . . " He looked almost embarrassed. "Your friend has been arrested."

"Arrested?" My knees buckled. "Marie-José? What is she charged with?"

"Murder."

He took me down into the basement. Poor Mad was sprawled on the floor like a heap of rubbish, sobbing and twitching.

And lying on the same table, Sanders's table, guarded by the same two butchers in leather aprons, was Marie-José.

She was naked, both her legs were broken, and one of her lovely green eyes was missing.

A little bald man was leaning over her, holding a stethoscope to her heart. "You're worse than Ohlendorf," he grumbled. "You're supposed to interrogate prisoners, not demolish them."

"Is she dead?"

"Of course she's dead."

Roesch shrugged and lit another cigar. "It doesn't matter. We'll get what we want to know out of the other one." He caught me as I fell. They carried me upstairs, and the little bald monster gave me a pill.

Later, I went into Roesch's office and asked him

if I could claim the body. He gaped with surprise. "What for?"

"The funeral, sir."

He looked confused for a moment, then he consented. I went down to the basement again.

One of the brutes was on the floor with Mad, sodomizing her.

The other was stretched out on top of Marie-José, raping her corpse.

I sat down on the steps and waited until they were finished.

I WAS WITH OTTO KASPER in a bar on the Kurfürstendamm when little Joseph read the Führer's proclama-
tion on the radio:

Burdened with heavy cares, condemned to months
of silence, I can now speak freely to my beloved
German people. At this moment a march is under-
way that, for its extent, compares with the greatest
the world has ever seen. I have decided again today to place the fate and future of the Reich and
our people in the hands of my soldiers. May God
aid us and assure our victory.

"God in heaven!" Otto muttered. "We're going into
Russia!" He drank another martini.

I hadn't seen him for years, not since the Munich
days. He was a Standartenführer now, working with
the SS Wirtschaft-und-Verwaltungs Hauptamt. I had
met him at lunch at the Himmlers'. And naturally no
one there had mentioned an invasion of the USSR.

"Do you think Heinrich knew about it?" I asked
him.

"I'm sure he did. After all, he's the Führer's right
hand." He was still a zealot and still an ass.

"Speaking of right hands, what happened to Hess?"

"Hess?" He aimed his monocle at me. "What do you mean? He's in England, isn't he?"

Hess had suddenly disappeared the year before. We all thought he'd been "eliminated"—like Ernst. But then the British announced that they were holding him captive in London. The official version of the mystery was, as usual, obscure.

"What was he doing in England, Otto? How did he get there? And *why?*"

"Oh, who knows." He squirmed irritably. "How? Why? What? Everything was so simple and straightforward in the beginning. Pure and limpid, like Bach. Now nothing makes sense! Russia! When I conducted my political science course at Bad Tölz I went to great lengths to teach the cadets that Stalin was our ally and that communism and Nazism were exactly the same ideology. Now . . ." He drank my martini.

"That's my drink."

"I'm sorry." He ordered two more.

I was waiting for him to ask me to go to bed with him. I was looking forward to the pleasure of telling him to go to hell. But he was completely asexual now, having neither pistils nor stamens.

"You should see the orders I received this morning," he began. "They . . . Well, never mind."

The Wirtschaft-und-Verwaltungs Hauptamt—WVHA for short—was, as its name indicated, the SS's economic and administrative section. But rumors had been circulating that it also indulged in extracurricular activities that were even more repulsive than the Gestapo's ridottos. Poor Otto!

We went to bed anyway. I was too weary to go all the way back to my hotel in Steglitz and he was staying at the Bristol just around the corner.

We crawled between the covers, naked, but nothing happened.

"You don't really feel like it, do you, Eddy?"

"No, Otto." I had no idea that he was that perspicacious.

"Eee!" he yelped. "That's cold! What is it?"

"Platinum."

"Let me see." I lifted my leg into the air. "Why do you wear it on your ankle?"

"C'est comme ça. It belonged to a friend of mine in Paris. She died."

"You have beautiful legs."

"Do you want me to tell you about her funeral?"

"If you like."

"The undertaker didn't have any gas for his hearse. And no horses to pull it either. He sold them on the black market. Horses are worth a fortune in Paris. Butcher shops buy them. So we put her coffin on a *voiture-des-quatre-saisons* and pushed her down the rue Delambre and the boulevard Edgar Quinet to the Montparnasse Cemetery. But the grave wasn't deep enough. I had to pay an old pigfucker with a shovel an extra five hundred francs to dig another two meters. Then, when the box was in the hole, he didn't want to cover it with dirt because it was after six o'clock and the place was supposed to close at five-thirty. So I took the shovel away from him and filled it myself. The next day I went to a stonecutter's shop and had a verse engraved on a piece of marble. It cost me seven thousand francs. It read: 'I would give you some violets, but they wither'd all when my father died.' That's from *Hamlet.* Act Four, Scene Five."

"Good night, Eddy."

"Good night, Otto."

*   *   *

Papa was certainly glad to be back in Germany. He danced around the room all night like an elf, tapping the walls and kicking chairs and clanging ashtrays.

I switched on the light to try to surprise him, but he skipped off into the bathroom and hid behind the shower curtain.

I learned the next day, from a friend working at OKW, that General Heye was commanding a motorized division with von Kleist's First Panzer Army in Army Group South. Lisa was in Dresden, visiting her parents. I flew there two nights later, but she'd already left. Her mother told me she was in Potsdam. I flew back to Berlin, intending to visit her as soon as I landed. But in the meantime my new orders had arrived. I was assigned to something called the Rass-und-Siedlings-Hauptamt. Originally it had been the SS's official marriage bureau. God alone knew what the hell it had become! But its acronym, appropriately enough, was RUSHA.

I left for Russia the same day.

The Ukraine was an endless yellow tablecloth covered with sunflowers and butterflies. It went on and on, day after day, in everlasting xanthous suffusion, turning giants to dwarfs and making tanks look like matchboxes floating in the ocean.

Hitler could never conquer this immensity. I knew that the instant I saw it. Our guns couldn't shoot far enough and our iron was too fragile to outlive the kilometers. We couldn't even invade it. If every woman in Germany had twenty sons and all of them were soldiers, there still wouldn't be troops enough to fill one road between Kharkov and the River Bug.

Sixty-seven infantry divisions and four Panzer Corps divided into eight colossal armies became a little dot, a speck of fleashit, on the bottom of a blank saffron bedsheet.

This was going to be our Parthia, I felt it in my bones.

> I have an ill-divining soul:
> Methinks I see thee . . .
> As one dead in the bottom of a tomb.

I drove through Brest Litovsk in a truck, crossed the Dniester in a halftrack, and bounced into a place called Zhmerinka in the sidecar of a motorcycle.

Here I presented my credentials to a certain von Rundstedt, commanding general of Army Group South. He read the orders, dumbfounded. "I don't understand. What does this mean?"

"I am assigned to the Army Group, sir, for the purpose of selecting from fifty to a hundred Russian females for immediate shipment to Germany."

"Russian females? What for?"

"They are for the Waffen-SS brothels, sir, in occupied Europe."

"Are you joking?"

"No, sir."

He was speechless. He rose from his desk, walked to the door, opened it, and bowed. "Get out."

His adjutant was more sympathetic. He sent me to the commander of the SS Leibstandarte Panzer Reserve, who loaned me a car and suggested I contact the GBA in Balta. He also gave me a Russian map and, following its contortions, I drove south along the Dniester. Five hours later I found myself in a bleak ghost town in the middle of nowhere. I think it was Kamenka.

Since all the buildings were more or less intact, I

decided to spend the night there. I parked the car in a grange, unpacked my bedroll, and moved into the waiting room of the railroad station. I went to sleep on the floor beneath a portrait of Stalin glowering down at me from a wall. He looked vaguely like Warner Baxter.

At two o'clock in the morning I was awakened by the neighing of horses. I crawled out of my sleeping bag and glanced out the window. The streets were swarming with cavalry. I was on the point of going outside to hail them when it occurred to me that I'd never seen horses like that before—stunted, shaggy beasts with ugly little heads. And their riders were carrying spears.

They were Russians!

I folded the bedroll and dragged it into the back of the station. I hid it under a bench and climbed up a drainpipe to the roof. I crept behind a chimney and looked down at the square below.

They had fifteen or twenty prisoners with them, ragged Rumanians from Dumitrescu's Third Army. They were kneeling in a cluster of misery on the ground, their hands tied behind their backs. The cavalrymen stood around them smoking cigarettes, contemplating them glumly.

Then they all pulled out their spouts and urinated on the captives, inundating them. The Rumanians howled with terror and tried to flee from the flood. They were unable to. The ropes that bound their hands held them linked together and they could only splash and flounder.

One of the Russians stood on a barrel and made a speech. The others cheered him. Then they all scurried off into a building. They came back to the square carrying kegs. They pried them open and emptied them on the prisoners' heads, covering them with thick yellow flour. The stink of rotten eggs filled the town.

It was sulfur!

They buried the screaming Rumanians in it, smothering them in a huge mound. They watched them die, then jumped on their horses and galloped away into the night.

I climbed down from the roof, retrieved my bedroll, and ran back to my car.

I drove all night. Then the road disappeared. It just stopped dead and became a plain of wildflowers. I studied the map. I calculated that I was somewhere between Moldavia and the Black Sea. Shit! I ate a bar of chocolate and longed for the boulevard Raspail. I tried to drive back to the "road" but I was out of gas!

I slept. Then I read Chapter 24 of *Anthony Adverse*. A recon squadron from the Eleventh Panzer Division found me there in the late afternoon. They roped the car to a Mark III and towed me into Balta, forty kilometers to the east.

The GBA—Generalbevollmächter fur den Arbeitessinsatz—was installed in a former barbershop on the edge of town. It was a brand-new organization, responsible for recruiting Ukrainian slave labor for German war industries. The man in charge was a hysterical little pigfucker named Fritz Sauckel. When he read my orders he screeched with pique.

"No, no, no!" He stamped his foot. "The SS has no right to come here and requisition females for their whorehouses! I need every able-bodied Russian I can get my hands on for our factories and our shipyards!"

"But the population of the Ukraine is over thirty million people," I protested. "Surely you can spare fifty or a hundred women."

"I can't spare anybody! Go back and tell Himmler to mind his own business!"

So that was that. I decided that wandering around like a vagabond would get me absolutely nowhere. I had to have an office of my own.

On a side street off the main square I found an abandoned grocery store with an adjoining garage. I swept it clean, painted a swastika and RUSHA on the front window, and moved in.

A regiment of the Twenty-fifth Motorized was stationed in Balta. I went to see the mess officer and asked him if I could take my meals in his kitchen. The smug bastard refused. The Wehrmacht wasn't authorized to share rations with the SS, and vice versa. I'd need a special permit from the Division CG/Hq.

The Twenty-fifth's headquarters was in a collective farm three kilometers outside town. I borrowed a can of gasoline from some engineers and drove out there. The commanding general's name was Heye.

He invited me to lunch at the officers' mess.

The last time I had seen him—in Berlin, that night at the opera, a million years ago—he had been lean and forty. Now he was in his fifties, skeletal, completely bald. He'd been wounded twice and his left arm was useless and he wore a patch on one eye à la Lord Nelson. He looked like a weathercock.

When I told him what I was doing in Russia he was shocked.

"When we crossed the frontier," he said, "the people cheered us as liberators. Girls used to throw flowers at our halftracks when they passed. Now they're throwing Molotov cocktails at us. You people are responsible for that—you and that madman Sauckel and the rest of the Ostministerium vultures. You are going to turn our rear echelons into a charnel house."

"When war was declared in '39," I told him, "Goring said, 'God help us if we lose this one.' "

He and the other officers at the table were silent. The fetid winds of the Styx blew through the mess hall.

"We must not lose," he muttered.

"Hitler is making all the same mistakes Macbeth and Richard the Third made," I went on. "And every tyrant. They go too far and 'on horror's head horrors accumulate,' upsetting the balance of things and betraying life to chaos."

They all looked at me, jolted.

"That's treason," Heye whispered.

"No," I laughed. "It's just Shakespeare." He smiled. For dessert we had ice cream and strawberries. We talked about Lisa.

"She'll be astonished when I tell her you're here," he said. "She thought you were in Paris. As a matter of fact, she's been insisting for months that I ask for a transfer to France so she can come with me and look you up."

I couldn't answer. That old familiar lump had risen in my throat. How did she know I was in Paris? She must have made inquiries. She wanted to see me again! Mon Dieu!

"I'll visit her." I managed to swallow. "When I return. If I return. Is there any way to escape from this ghastly country?"

"We shall see," he replied.

He signed a pass authorizing me to eat in any of the Twenty-fifth Division mess halls, including the headquarters dining room.

I went back to my "office," took off my uniform, and stretched out on a blanket on the floor. I tried to take a nap. It was boiling hot and Lisa kept tiptoeing through my thoughts. My body was seething. I hadn't made love since I'd left Montparnasse.

I went into the garage, naked, and sat in the car. Everything smelled of lust—the gasoline, the heat, the dust, the sunlight, the shade. It was unbearable. I smoked a cigarette. Flies buzzed around me, crawling up my arms and tickling my throat. I leaned back and let them invest me, let them wade in my sweat and frolic on me like children playing on a hot beach. I was numb with yearning. My derriere itched. The cauldron between my thighs bubbled. A fly explored my nipples, droning sluggishly from one to the other— back and forth, as heavy as a crab, as delicate as a fingertip—a demon driving me mad with desire. He made love to my breasts, covering me with drool and electricity.

How now, you secret, black, and midnight hags!
What is't you do?

A deed without a name.

And then—O miracle of rare delight!—a divine girl named Edmonde came in and sat down beside me. She was as nude as I, just as flushed and tempting and dripping. And, like me, she wore a chain on her ankle. She put her hands on my knees and pushed the tip of her nose under my arms.

We sat there a moment together, beguiled and throbbing.

I couldn't believe two girls could be so alike, so attuned, so homogeneous! We were a concerto. I was the orchestra, simmering with music, and she was the soloist, rich with themes. *Allegro maestoso pour deux Edmondes en mi bémol maj.*

I tried to bend over and kiss her hips, but she was too far away. Everything was too far away in Russia. It was infuriating. I wanted to dance with her, to hug her, to take her between my legs, to put my cheek against her warm spine. But I was on the Dniester and she reclined on the distant bank of the Don, and between us was the Mare Foecunditatiis.

Fists pounded on the front door.

She—we—I jumped out of the car. I pulled on my skirt and shirt and went out to the street. Sauckel was there, frothing at the mouth.

"Where is she?" he barked.

"Who?"

"What have you done with her?"

"With who?"

He shoved me aside and hurled himself into the building, shouting, "Vera! Vera!"

I followed him. "Who are you looking for, Sauckel?"

He finally told me. "Vera" was his Russian housekeeper and she'd disappeared. He thought I had her. He barged off, swearing to bring the wrath of the Führer himself down on all our heads if he didn't find her.

I went back into the garage and looked around for the other Edmonde. But I was alone.

The evening news was triumphant. Army Group Center was past Smolensk and Army Group North was at the gates of Leningrad. In the South, von Rundstedt was about to take Kiev. The war would be over by September.

But I really didn't feel like waiting that long. I wanted to get this job over and done with as quickly as possible so I could go home.

I learned the next day that the new Gauleiter of the

Ukraine had arrived in the area. His name was Erich Koch. I'd met him in Munich years ago—he'd been a friend of Bormann's—and decided to look him up. If anybody in Russia could help me accomplish my absurd mission, he was the man.

His office was in a tractor factory on the Kotovsk road. I drove out there in the afternoon and found him sunbathing in a field.

He was plump, rosy, and soggy, smeared with lotion, and lying on a mattress in the grass wearing only a pair of trunks that bulged with an erection. He looked like a chubby, obscene, oily lizard. Ugh!

He listened to my problem, chuckling. "Splendid!" He stared at me, fingering himself. "I'm all for it. A hundred proud Communist virgins marching through Berlin in chains. I can see them now. Look! The very idea arouses me!" His bulge swelled. He lowered his shorts, coyly, releasing the monster. "Watch." He took it in his hand, "Just watch, girl." And he began to masturbate.

I gaped at him, petrified, as he tugged himself back and forth across the mattress, flopping up and down, gloating, "Watch me, watch! Isn't this something!" He foamed like a beertap, covering his stomach with a puddle of slush. "Go and see Bach." He laughed. "He's in charge of rounding up civilians."

SS Oberführer von dem Bach-Zelewski was in command of the Special Police Brigade. I'd heard about him in Poland. He'd made quite a name for himself "pacifying" villages behind the lines. I found him in an adjacent field, just across the road from the factory. He was a massive, hound-faced young man, dressed like a combat officer in a grassy camouflage smock, wearing field breeches and high boots. With him was a company of his hatchetmen, looking very warlike in steel helmets, and carrying MP 40s.

Lined up before them, digging a slit trench, were twenty or thirty filthy Russians, men and women. Several of the girls were rather good-looking. I asked him if I could take them off his hands.

"Absolutely not!" His canine snout snorted at me angrily. "They're commissars and Communist Youth swine. They're going into the ditch."

"Just a couple," I pleaded. I pointed to a pair of frightened girls, no more than eighteen. "Those two there."

"No."

"Please, Oberführer. I need them."

"Did Sauckel send you here?"

"Sauckel? No."

"You don't work for the GBA?"

"Certainly not."

"Who are you with?"

"The SS."

"What branch?"

"RUSHA."

"RUSHA? What's that?"

I thought fast. The pigfucker was obviously a raving maniac. I had to excel him. "It's a new department," I confessed, "created by the Reichsführer. We're in medicine. Our specialty is," I whispered, "vivisection."

He was impressed. "Vivisection?" That evidently appealed to him. "Very well. Take them." He beckoned to the two girls. They came toward him, cringing. He slapped both of them across their dirty faces with the back of his hand. "Sluts!" he growled. "Get them out of here before I change my mind."

I saluted and thanked him. Shit! What a ghoul! We were halfway across the field when the MP 40s roared.

I looked back and wished I hadn't. The Russians were toppling into the ditch, shrieking, tumbling one on top of the other like colliding ice skaters. Shit! It was sickening.

And over in the other field was Gauleiter Koch, sitting on his mattress, scratching his balls, waving to me! Ugh!

I drove my two damsels to Balta and put them in the garage. There was a well in the yard, and I filled a tub with water and told them to wash themselves, for they smelled like hyenas. They spoke no German whatsoever and I didn't know a word of Russian, so we just grunted at one another and pantomimed à la commedia dell'arte.

They were angels. Both were flaxen-haired and tan, with daisy eyes and long slim bodies. Naked and bathed, they were as fragrant as lawns.

The Nazis called these people Untermensch. What nonsense! *I* called them Mopsa and Dorcas, after the two shepherdesses in *The Winter's Tale*.

I went through the town like a vandal, looting all the hovels of everything I could carry off. The haul was considerable because the population had decamped en masse in a hurry, leaving all their belongings behind. I found trousers, jackets, dresses, coats, shoes, sandals. In a cellar I came across over two hundred jars of cherry jam. I lugged everything back to the "office," then went out to the 25th Motorized again. I needed a truck, and in one of the barns of the collective farm I'd seen several captured American Fords. Perhaps General Heye would give me one.

He wasn't in the headquarters building. I went to his living quarters, in a dairy farther down the road. He wasn't there either, but sitting on a cot in his room, polishing his boots, was a ravishing blonde wearing only her stockings.

I apologized for the intrusion. She smiled at me and answered in beautifully massacred German. "General he gone him to the river swimming."

"When will he be back?"

"Yes."

"Are you his, uh, batman?"

"I am Vera me."

Vera! Mon Dieu! Could this be Sauckel's missing housekeeper—nude, in the general's bed? I asked her.

At the mention of his name she recoiled with revulsion. "Sauckel a hog Sauckel him!"

"He's looking for you."

"I no go back there no!"

"The general will take care of you, I'm sure."

She laughed and put her hands to her face, blushing. "General he no not no." She shook her head. "No."

"I beg your pardon . . ."

"Me to take care of." She turned more and more scarlet. "Not."

"I don't understand, Vera."

She showed me her finger and bent it significantly. We both howled.

Poor General Heye! He was not only unfaithful, he was unable. I wasn't surprised. Lisa had hinted as much often enough. No wonder it took them so long to manufacture a child.

To hell with him! I would take a truck without his permission. Not only that, I would take Vera too.

"Vera, to Germany with me come you."

"Germany? Yes." She jumped up and pulled on her dress. We went outside and I showed her the car. "Can you drive?" She nodded eagerly. I went into the barn and boarded one of the Fords. I drove it back to Balta. She followed in the car.

On the road we passed von dem Bach-Zelewski, speeding along in a shining spotless halftrack. I tipped my cap at him. He just glared back.

At midnight a storm woke me. Through the open back door I could see the sky. It was exploding in lightning, clamoring like a dynamo, pounding the village with thunder and rain.

The four of us were sleeping on the garage floor, and I looked over at Mopsa and Dorcas and got the surprise of my life. They were lying together, *tête-bêche*, merrily gorging themselves on each other.

Vera woke too and we sat watching them, amazed at first, then amused, then . . .

They continued, unaware of their audience, their carnality like lightning rods, grounding all the voltage of the storm into their bodies. The sight lit an oven somewhere in my bowels and I began to roast.

"They doing that," Vera whispered. "Should not."

My vampires, thirsty from long fasting, came out of their crypt between my legs and searched for victims.

"You never tried it?" I crawled toward her.

"Is not for girls," she laughed softly, "doing."

"It's very agreeable, Vera." She sat wrapped in her blanket. I reached for her, unbundling her slowly. A shoulder gleamed at me. It was the most exquisite sight I'd ever seen. Maces of wanting beat my abdomen, making me giddy with pain.

"What?" she murmured. "What?"

I uncovered her breasts. Their irises stared at me, startled. I whimpered, my mouth filled with syrup.

Beyond us, Mopsa and Dorcas scraped together, jostling and squirming.

The blanket fell from her and I took her in my arms and kissed her throat. "No"—she tried to push me back—"not not." I lowered my face to her nipples and put them in my eyes. My hands found her waist and her hips, her thighs and navel. "Not not." Her resistance was sadistic and maddening! Her body rolled away from me, her legs locked. I squeezed against her, my groans begging for alms. How could she be so cruel? She tried to get up; I held her fast. I turned her over on her stomach and put my tongue into all the defenseless crevices, licking and biting her. She moaned and sang, melting. Her knees parted, her hands clasped my hair, pushing me into her. I twisted about, lowering myself on her mouth as my lips entered her. A moment later her own tongue cut into me like a saber, slicing me open all the way to my lungs.

She touched all my chords at once and the healing vibrations throbbed me to sleep. The last thing I heard was the thunder.

Just before dawn I woke again. The storm had passed, the moon was up—an autumn hunting moon, the herald of the north wind.

We were all piled naked on the floor, chilled. I unwound myself from Vera and covered her with a blanket. Then I threw a heap of coats and jackets over Mopsa and Dorcas.

I walked to the window.

If poor Papa had followed me to Russia, he was out there somewhere in that vast dark vile immensity, looking for me.

In the morning I went out to scrounge for rations. The tempest had turned the whole Balta sector into an endless swamp, and horses and wagons and guns were stuck in the mud for miles around.

Rumors were flying back and forth like mad canaries. A platoon of Hungarian infantrymen had drowned in a trench, eight tanks from the Sixteenth Panzer had disappeared in quicksand, the commander of the S.S. *Viking* had been struck by lightning, the entire recon squadron of the Seventy-fifth Infantry was missing, Sauckel had gone crazy . . .

This last proved to be true. He had set up roadblocks at both ends of town, guarded by GBA policemen. He was determined to find Vera and was searching every vehicle leaving the area.

I ran back to the garage to make sure she was keeping out of sight.

When she saw me she blushed and hid her face in her hands. I found a pair of scissors, sat her down on a stool, and, while Mopsa and Dorcas looked on, aghast, I cut her hair, clipping her almost to the skull. Then I dressed her up in odds and ends of the clothing I'd looted—trousers, shirt, jacket, cap. When I was finished she looked like Igor Voroshilovsk, average Ukrainian *male* truck driver. No one would recognize her.

To prove it we climbed into the Ford and drove to Ananyev. We passed the roadblock with ease. Sauckel himself was there, trudging through the mud in hipboots, peering at everybody suspiciously.

I called to him, "Have you located her yet, Herr Sauckel?"

He came over to the truck, fuming. "No! But she couldn't have gotten far."

"Maybe von dem Bach-Zelewski shot her," I suggested.

"If he did, I'll have his ass!"

We drove on. When we were safely away from the village Vera and I burst out laughing. "Is he in love with you or what?" I asked her.

She put her arm over my shoulders. "Love very very is doubtful," she sighed. "War also is."

She was adorable! In bits and pieces she told me the story of her life. She was twenty-three years old. Her father was a major in the Ninth Mechanized Corps of the Southwestern Front Army. She was in her last year at the Agriculture School in Kiev. When the Germans came she'd been on vacation in Zhdanov on the Sea of Azov. She had tried to return to Kiev by train and had gotten as far as Balta when she was picked up in a GBA sweep and taken before Sauckel the Abominable. He had raped her and made her his housekeeper. Then one day General Heye had spied her on the road, invited her into his staff car, and driven her back to his cot. He had tried repeatedly "into me to put it him" but he was hopelessly impotent and "always unready was."

Our troubles weren't over yet. Five kilometers farther on we were stopped at *another* roadblock, this one manned by 25th Motorized Division riflemen. They checked the truck and examined our papers.

I asked the sergeant in charge what the trouble was.

He shrugged with disgust. "The old man's Russian whore ran away," he told us. "He says he'll transfer us all to the Waffen-SS if we don't find her."

Mon Dieu! Heye was looking for her too! Vera was becoming more dangerous to the German war effort than a full Soviet army marching under flying banners!

The sergeant pointed his pistol at her. "Is he an Ivan?"

"Yes. He's my chauffeur."

"Aren't you afraid of driving on these lonely roads with an *enemy?*" he asked incredulously.

"No danger. He's subhuman."

*   *   *

In Ananyev the Eleventh Panzer had a prisoner-of-war cage. The corporal commanding the guard was only too glad to get rid of as many of them as he could. He told me to take my pick.

Among the seedy mob were three girl snipers—splendid, bestial creatures, like lionesses. They reminded me of Mad—except for their hangman eyes. There were also five young nurses and two female doctors from a medical battalion and a half-dozen clerks and whatnot from some headquarters unit.

I took them all. We loaded them in the truck and drove back to Balta. Passing through another hamlet, I saw a whole flock of girls in nightgowns sitting around the yard of what appeared to be a school or something. We stopped and I beckoned to them. They ran toward us, smiling and chattering.

Vera translated: "Crimea women they. From Sevastopol."

"What is this place?"

She questioned the crowd and then laughed. "Is insane clinic."

"Tell them to get in the truck."

"But crazy all of them they are!"

"Who cares?"

They climbed in with the others and we drove on. I counted them. Eleven nightgown girls plus the sixteen prisoners from the cage—twenty-seven. Plus Mopsa. Dorcas, and Vera—thirty. Not bad at all.

There was a message from General Heye waiting for me when we got back to our hovel. He wanted to see me as soon as possible.

I drove out to the farm immediately, expecting the worst. He received me in his quarters, visibly peeved.

"I want that truck back," he snapped. His voice was like an icepick. "Right away."

"You want Vera back too, I hear." Who did the pigfucker think he was talking to? I didn't have to take any shit from this Wehrmacht dolt.

He scowled at me, *très* general staff. "Vera?"

"I met her when I was here yesterday. She told me about your problem." His mouth fell open. "If you try to cause any trouble about that goddamned truck I'll make certain that everybody in Army Group South knows you're a eunuch."

He came toward me, his hands outstretched to seize me. I jumped quickly behind a table. I was horrified. He looked as if he was going to tear me to pieces.

"You . . ." he sputtered, too outraged to speak.

I suddenly remembered something Lisa had told me about him. "I know how to give you an erection," I whispered. He looked at me, taken aback. I walked over to the door and bolted it. "Sit down," I ordered. He dropped to the cot like a felled tree.

I unbuckled my belt and threw it on the floor. Then I unbuttoned my tunic and pulled it off. "Take it out," I said. He didn't move but just sat there, bug-eyed. I took off my shirt. I wasn't wearing a brassiere. It was too hot. I didn't have anything on under my skirt either. I removed it. "Take it out," I repeated, trying to imitate Greta Garbo in *Camille*.

He fumbled with the front of his trousers and Prometheus Unbound emerged timidly, flabby and wrinkled. I kicked off my shoes. Wearing only my stockings, I walked over to him, swaying my hips à la Carole Lombard, and put one knee on the cot beside him. Prometheus lifted its head and gazed at me tiredly. "Touch me." He reached for me, hesitated. "Go on." He caressed me awkwardly, the tips of his fingernails just brushing my hair. Prometheus stiffened like a beet. I leaned down and slapped it playfully. It deflated instantly. I laughed. "Pull off my stockings." He obeyed quickly, caught up in the game now. His breath spurted on me. He had had garlic for lunch. His rough hands on my thighs, then my calves and feet, had no effect on me at all.

I stepped back, lifted my leg, and put my foot on his lap. Prometheus stood at attention, beaming. I marched up and down it, trying to grip it with my toes.

"What about the truck?" I asked.

"Yes," he gasped.

"I'll need gasoline too."

"My . . ." He made sawing noises deep in his throat. ". . . my quartermaster . . . tomorrow . . ."

Prometheus grew fat and red. I flattened it with my heel. Marie-José's chain glittered at me from my ankle. I lowered my foot.

"No, no, *no* . . ." he whined. "Please."

I changed feet and squashed him under my instep. He gurgled. "Did you ever do this with Lisa?"

"No!" He emitted a high soprano note.

"You're a liar. You made her do it every time you were drunk. She told me." I wiped my toes on him. "But then she stopped doing it because it turned her stomach. That's why you're so anxious to find Vera, isn't it? You want her to do it too. A Russian slave to walk on you submissively whenever you like."

His mouth opened and closed, biting the air. Ugh!

I wondered . . . If Papa had lived, would he have become this repellently pitiful? God in heaven! If I ever caught him like this with a girl I would chop off her legs with a meat cleaver, the bitch! Then I would do it to him myself, to appease him, the poor man . . . Yes, that was it. I would pretend this elderly lout was my father.

I trod more gently upon him and didn't look into his

awful, driveling face. I stared at the ceiling instead. It was covered with cracks and smeared with filth, forming a mosaic of faces and profiles and silhouettes. There was a row of children standing in the clouds, and there, the seven gates of Ilium on the ringing plains of windy Troy. Farther on was a Norseman's dragonship. And just above me was a gypsy stealing mist.

Prometheus drenched my foot and the old man cackled rapturously.

The garage and the store were filled to the brim with Russian females. I put Vera in charge of them and she saw that they kept bathed and tidy. Happily, they were all docile and silent, otherwise it would have been a shambles.

I drew enough rations from the Twenty-fifth Motorized and the S.S. *Viking* to keep us fed. And we also had the cherry jam to fall back on.

The eleven mad creatures from Sevastopol were no problem. They played in the yard and picked flowers or just sat around grinning. But the three amazonian snipers were insufferable. They never said a word, never smiled, never complained. They just *stared* at me, like muzzles. They gave me—according to my *Dictionary of American Slang*—"the jitters."

I decided that forty or forty-five girls would be quite enough. The truck and the car between them couldn't hold any more than that. I toured the countryside and found two more in Pervomaisk and another one in Voznesensk on the southern Bug.

I took Vera with me on these trips because we no longer had any privacy to make love in Balta. But alone in the wilderness we could do what we liked.

We would tear off our clothes and race through the sunflowers, tumbling and somersaulting and leapfrog-

ging. We wrestled and boxed and danced. We basked
in the sun until we were both ebony from head to toe.
And, to be sure—ah!—we possessed every conceivable
centimeter of each other, merging so harmoniously that
we exchanged flesh, rhyming our delight for hours on
end.

We did extraordinary things!

Once we found a bog and wallowed in it all afternoon, head over heels, seasoning our greedy mouthings
in rich, deep, grassy mud. Once we made love on an
anthill, burying ourselves in hordes of scampering
monsters fraying us alive. Once we captured a grazing
horse and tried to masturbate him. Once . . .

And in the meantime, von Kleist advanced from the
south and Guderian from the north, cutting off Kiev
and encircling hundreds of thousands of Russians. Then
all the German tanks rolled toward Moscow.

I wasn't impressed. We were only conquering an
abyss. I wanted to leave more than ever.

A motorcyclist from the *Viking* told me he'd seen
several girls living in a *kolkhoz* in Olgopol. Vera and
I drove there the same day and discovered five gorgeous
maidens hiding in a silo. We requisitioned them without further ado. That brought the total to thirty-five
girls. My quota was almost filled.

As we were driving off, Oberführer von dem Bach-
Zelewski's elegant halftracks came storming into Olgopol. We pulled up to the side of the road to let them
pass. There was a prison in town and that was their
destination. They stopped in the square and von dem
Bach-Zelewski jumped smartly out of the command
vehicle. He looked very dashing with binoculars hanging around his neck, stick grenades thrust in his belt,
and an MP 40 cradled in one arm. He sauntered into
the building, followed by his natty killers.

A Hauptscharführer turned and saw us. He strutted over to the truck and checked our papers.

He eyed me sourly. "You're Kerrl?"

"Yes."

"With RUSHA?"

"That's right."

"Stay here."

He went back across the square just as von dem Bach-Zelewski and his warriors escorted a column of convicts out of the prison—at least a hundred of them, all civilians.

When his underling reported our presence, von dem Bach-Zelewski beckoned to me. I climbed out of the truck and walked over to him, my knees shaking.

"Heil Hitler!"

"Heil Hitler. How are you, Kerrl?"

"Fine, thank you, Oberführer."

He turned to the convicts. Several of them were standing apart from the others, protesting violently. "What language is that?"

An interpreter addressed them in Russian. They didn't understand him.

"They're not Russian, Oberführer."

"What are they?"

"I don't know, sir."

I walked over to the group. There were six of them, quaking with fear. I spoke to them in English. They just gaped at me vacantly.

"Parlez-vous française?"

One of them could and began blaring at me in broken French. I went back to von dem Bach-Zelewski and snapped to attention, *très* girl scout-like.

"They're Polish, sir. Voluntary workers attached to the GBA."

"What are they doing in prison?"

"They were billeted here last night, sir, because no other lodgings were available."

He looked puzzled. He turned to the Hauptscharführer. "How many names are on your list, Schobert?"

The Hauptscharführer consulted a clipboard. "One hundred and five, sir."

"And how many convicts do we have here?"

"One hundred and five, sir."

"So the inventory is exact, isn't it?"

"Yes, sir."

"Then what are you waiting for?"

The soldiers closed in on the convicts and began jabbing them with bayonets and clubbing them with bats. A frightening din of screams ensued, like a hurricane of hogs squealing. The sudden stink of raw blood made me choke.

Von dem Bach-Zelewski took me by the arm and let me into the shade. "Listen," he growled, "I had orders to dispose of eleven inmates in an asylum over in Ananyev. They aren't there. Did you take them?"

I was watching the Poles. They were being slowly beaten to death, still protesting loudly.

"Kerrl?"

"Oberführer?"

"Did you take those maniacs out of that asylum?"

"No, sir."

"Get that one!" he shouted.

A convict was limping off across the square. A soldier followed him and shot him in the back.

"No shooting!" von dem Bach-Zelewski barked. "Save your bullets!"

The convict was rolling in the dust, kicking and braying. The soldier pulled a knife from his belt and cut his throat.

I saw Vera jump out of the truck and vomit.

Papa, I whispered. *Keep out of this. Cover your eyes. Don't watch.*

Von dem Bach-Zelewski cursed. "Then it must have been Sauckel," he snarled. "That meddling bastard is picking up everything that walks. How am I supposed to do my job here if the GBA keeps stepping on my toes? And the Wehrmacht is no better! Always interfering and sending off official protests to the OKH. Pigs! And the Ostministerium is the worst of all. Orders, counterorders. Asses, the whole gaggle of them." Another shot rang out. "I said no shooting!" he shrieked.

During the trip back to Balta poor Vera was unable to drive and I had to take the wheel. She sat huddled beside me, pasty-faced.

"Why, Edmonde?" she asked. "Why Germans they kill like this?"

I felt slightly bilious myself. A hundred and five corpses! Why indeed? "All dictatorships are homicidal, Vera."

"Please?"

"Dictators *kill.* That's why they're dictators."

"No understand."

"Totalitarianism. You know what this is, no? Communism, Nazism, Fascism."

"Yes."

"Well, they're murderous forms of government."

"Communists no murder."

"Certainly they do! Balls! What about all the people Stalin purged? Millions and millions of people were massacred. The NKVD and the Gestapo are exactly the same."

"People killed in purge they reactionary."

"Oh, shit!"

We passed a long convoy rolling north. It was the

25th Motorized, joining the advance on Moscow. General Heye, shrouded in dust, rode in his staff-car in the middle of the column. He didn't see me.

"Purge was necessary," Vera insisted. "All were Trotskyites and traitors!"

"Yes, Vera, sure." I was too weary to argue. Why bother!

On the outskirts of town we were stopped at the roadblock and one of the surly GBA thugs said that Sauckel wanted to see me. Vera drove the Ford on to the garage and I walked to the barbershop. I met Gauleiter Koch in the street. He was carrying a basket, prowling in the doorway of one of the empty buildings.

"Good afternoon," I called. He jumped. Then when he recognized me he smiled bashfully.

"I've been collecting souvenirs," he confessed. He showed me the basket. It contained a mildewed Kodak, an alarm clock, a pair of woman's slippers, a broken vase, a portrait of Rimsky-Korsakov, and a rusty goblet. "Who is this?" He held up the portrait. "Marx?"

"No. That's Rimsky-Korsakov."

"Who?"

"A Russian composer."

"And this, look." He lifted out the goblet and showed it to me. "Is it gold, do you think?" We examined it. It was brass.

"Yes," I said, "it looks like gold."

"There's a samovar in there too. I'll come back and get it later."

"Are you sure it isn't a bedpan?"

"A bedpan?"

"Russian samovars and Russian bedpans are quite similar. In fact, they're interchangeable."

"Really?" Then his tone frosted. "See here! What's

this Bach tells me about your girls? You're going to
vivisect them? Why wasn't I informed?"

I'd forgotten all about that nonsense. Mon Dieu!
What a pack of simpletons! "He shouldn't have mentioned that, Herr Koch. It's a state secret."

"*I* am the state here, girl! I'm the Gauleiter!"

"Yes, sir. I should have taken that into consider-
ation."

"I'll come to see you tomorrow." He winked. "I
want to sample a few of them before they're cut up."
And he took my hand and placed it on his crotch. It
was as hard as a rock! He chuckled and walked off,
winding the alarm clock and holding it to his ear. The
grotesque pigfucker!

Sauckel was waiting for me in the barbershop, waving a telegram gleefully. "From Berlin!" he cried. "You
are to turn your whores over to me immediately! They
are now the official property of the GBA."

"Who is the telegram from, Sauckel?"

"Bormann."

"I'm very sorry, but Bormann has no jurisdiction
over the SS."

"He has, he has, he has!" He was quivering. "He is
Himmler's superior!"

What a day! I was exhausted. I just couldn't face a
debate with this cockroach. Besides, my mind was
made up—I knew what I had to do then. "All right,
Sauckel, you can have them."

"How many of them are there?"

"About forty."

"Bring them to me tonight."

"Tonight?" No, that was too precipitate. I needed
more time. "Very well, I'll have them here in an hour.
Heil Hitler."

"Heil Hitler."

"Oh, by the way, I found Vera."

He paled. "Where is she?"

"Heye has her."

"Heye?" he twitched and licked his lips. "General Heye of the Twenty-fifth Motorized?"

"Yes."

"They just moved out . . . this afternoon . . ."

"I know. He took her with him."

He stood there an instant, stung. Then he began shouting for his car and driver. Five minutes later he was speeding out of town.

I ran back to the garage.

By eight o'clock all the girls and rations were loaded in the truck. I decided to leave the car behind. We didn't have enough gasoline for both vehicles.

Vera drove. To avoid the roadblocks we crossed the pastures behind the garage, then turned south, following a maze of cowpaths toward the Dniester. At midnight we bumped out of the fields onto a road and rolled along it all night under the bright moon.

At dawn we stopped for breakfast in the ruins of a sugar refinery near, near what? I hadn't the faintest idea.

"Where are we, Vera?"

"Dniester just there is." She waved toward the horizon.

The girls alighted, cold and miserable, and sat down in the rubble. Mopsa and Dorcas cooked a pot of soup. The three snipers continued to stare at me.

"How long do you think it will take us to reach Poland?"

Vera shrugged. "Are four hundred kilometers. Three days."

"Do you know the way?"

"We follow river." She pulled off her trousers. "North. Soroki, Mogilev Podolski, Gorodenka . . ."

"What are you doing?"

She removed her jacket and shirt. "Enough I am of being a man," she laughed. And she put on a dress.

Then I saw the high pillar of dust moving toward us from the west. At first I thought it was a windstorm, but then the rumble of motors could be heard drifting across the infinity. They were vehicles!

We put out the fire. I drove the truck out of the ruins into a hollow in a field. Vera herded the girls into the deep grass bordering the road and hid them.

An hour later three of von dem Bach-Zelewski's halftracks appeared. They surrounded the refinery and a company of yelling gunmen searched the building.

They were looking for us, I knew it in my bones. Bach must have found out I had the maniacs from the asylum and he was . . .

At that moment two of the mad girls came out to the field and stood on the road, tossing a ball back and and forth. I was too far away from them to do anything, and the others hadn't seen them. Jesus! They were laughing and shouting and jumping up and down! All anyone in the refinery had to do was glance out a window and . . . Mopsa and Dorcas dashed to them and dragged them back into the grass.

I held my breath, waiting for disaster to fall upon us.

But no. The thugs climbed into their halftracks and roared off to the south in a tempest of dust. We all jumped into the truck and slipped away in the opposite direction.

We drove all day, stopping only to refill the tank with gasoline. I fell asleep, and when I woke we were crossing a river on a pontoon bridge.

"Is this the Dniester, Vera?"

"No. Is another. I do not know it what its name."

"Let me drive for a while."

"No. Is all right. I am no tired."

The sun set and it began to snow. We slept in a demolished house on a lonely crossroads, God knows where, all of us piled together on the floor like dogs in a kennel.

During the night Vera and I, buried in snoring bodies, managed to ease ourselves between each other's legs and we made love tiredly.

The rising sun melted the snow and turned the road to a creek of slush. We drove on, averaging no more than a kilometer or two an hour. At noon we came upon a wide river.

"Dniester!" Vera announced triumphantly.

"So we head straight north now?"

"North, yes."

We followed the winding bank for hours and hours while the sun set to the left of us. At twilight it began to snow again. I decided not to stop that night. The temperature dropped to below zero and the ground froze like concrete. I took the wheel, accelerating as fast as I could to cover as much distance as possible before the morning thaw returned.

The road disappeared in an immense hiatus of white nothingness, but the river was a perfect guideline, leading us northward.

Worms of doubt began to gnaw at my insides.

Northward? Yes, we were driving north, because the sun had set to our left, in the west. But . . . I was an idiot! The river was to our right. Which meant that we were on the *left* bank!

How on earth did we ever get on *this* side of the Dniester?

"Vera!"

"Yes?"

"This can't be the Dniester."

"No. Is not."

"Are we lost or what?"

"Me not lost. Know where we are precisely at."

"What is this river?"

"Is the Dnieper."

The *Dnieper!* Shit! We were thousands of kilometers to the *east* of the Army Group, right in the middle of the Russian front! I turned to Vera. Her teeth gleamed in the darkness like the jaws of a shark.

Then I saw something even more frightening.

Just ahead of us, stretched across the entire bank, was a cordon of horsemen mounted on shaggy little ponies.

She leaned out the door and shouted to them. They came galloping toward us. I pressed the brakes, and as we skidded to a stop I jumped out of the truck.

I ran to the river and slid down the bank. Shit. I was trapped like a bear in a 'ole. Charles Boyer said that in *Algiers*. I'd seen it in Berlin with Lucie. "I cannot leave the Casbah, I'm trapped like a bear in a 'ole." This was a fine time to be thinking of Lucie and Charles Boyer!

A 'ole. Yes! I lifted a heavy stone and heaved it into the water. Hooves pounded on the frozen ground, converging on the splash. I scooped out a 'ole in the snow and crawled into it, entombing myself in an icy igloo.

Horses neighed all around me. Good! They would stamp away my footprints. The pigfucking Cossack vermin! I heard Vera calling to me: "Edmonde! Come back!" *La garce!* "Edmonde! Where are you?" *Sale petite conne!* My rage warmed me. I had my Lüger. If they found me I'd get her first—a bullet right between her barracuda teeth!

The shouting and hoofbeats faded.

Either they were convinced I'd tried to swim across the river and drowned or they were waiting for me to come out in the open. I looked at my watch. I couldn't see it. It must have been about four o'clock.

I counted to a thousand.

Then I crawled out of the hole. It had stopped snowing. The truck was gone; the bank was deserted.

I went through my pockets. I had a pack of cigarettes, matches, the Lüger, extra ammo, *Anthony Adverse*, a bar of chocolate, and a box of raisins.

I began to walk north, staying in sight of the Dnieper. Rivers always led somewhere.

Five o'clock, six o'clock, seven o'clock. I ate the chocolate. Eight o'clock. The sun came up. The air warmed immediately and the ground became gluey. I smoked a cigarette and descended the bank, walking along the edge of the water to minimize my silhouette.

I drew the line of the Dnieper in my mind. Northeast from Odessa to Dnepropetrovsk, then northwest to Kiev. I was somewhere on this northwestern turning, between Dnepropetrovsk and Kremenchug—maybe!

A map! My kingdom for a map!

Nine o'clock, ten o'clock. I ate some of the raisins.

Then I turned and saw the horses behind me! I jumped into a thicket. Had they seen me? They came closer, moving slowly along the top of the bank. Three, four, five, six of them. They passed just above me and I saw them clearly. Vera, Mopsa, Dorcas, and the three awful snipers, all of them wearing fur coats and carrying spears.

I looked down. Lying in the grass before me was a paddle. And farther on, concealed in the high rushes,

was a canoe. I pulled it into the river and climbed into
it. I paddled into the current to the opposite bank. In
midstream the bow began to leak. The water splashed
over my feet. Shit! But Vera and her witches hadn't
seen me yet. They were far ahead of me, just six black
blobs on the skyline. The water rose higher, filling the
canoe, lapping at my legs. The right bank was as far
away as Samarkand! Then it was much closer. I paddled like a galley slave. Then I was there. I jumped
out to the bank. The canoe sank.

I took off my boots and stockings and lit a fire. It
was eleven o'clock. The sun rose higher. I ate some
more raisins. By noon I was on my way again, running
to keep warm.

I was dry and the temperature was rising. I could
last about five hours. When night fell . . . Well, that
was another story. I would freeze to death.

Where was the Führer now? And little Joseph and
Hermann and Himmler? The pigfuckers! What were
they doing at this moment?

The important thing for the time being was to keep
sane. For instance, I could not close my eyes or I
would think I was walking along the Quai des Tuileries
and the river would become the Seine. And I had to
stop looking for Papa. And calling to him.

Papa!
What is it, Edmonde?
Papa!
Stop shouting! What do you want?
Where are you?
Was that a pun? Seine? Sane?
It's one o'clock, Papa. I'm famished.
Why do you insist on speaking English?
I'm hungry, Papa.
Do you want to go into town for lunch after mass?

All right. What shall I wear? It's getting chilly.
The wind's rising. It's going to snow again. Mass?
Is today Sunday?

Virgo singularis, inter omnes mitis, nos culpis solu-
tos, mites fac et castos. Eat some more raisins.

No, no! I refused to go mad! I would not die in
the middle of Russia, raving on the banks of the pigfucking Dnieper!

Edmonde!

"No, no, I won't answer."

Edmonde!

Rest, rest, perturbed spirit! Shut up! Leave me
alone! I won't answer. I . . .

"Edmonde!"

I stopped. It wasn't Papa! That was Vera's voice! I
jumped down the bank and crawled into the grass. The
six horses were coming along the slope in *front* of me!
How did they get over here? There was surely a ford
farther upstream. Good! I was lucid again.

They passed me, almost touching me. Dorcas first,
then Vera, then Mopsa, then the three grisly snipers.
I slipped my Lüger from the holster—I would shoot
them all . . .

But I was thinking clearly again, thank God. The
rest of the cavalry was surely not far off. So no firing.

"Edmonde!"

I forgive you, you bitch, because it's Sunday. Peace
be unto you, and grace.

I let them pass, then climbed up the bank. There
were trees in the distance. I raced toward them.

It was snowing. I hadn't noticed before.

I jumped into a ditch and looked back. They still
hadn't seen me. They were dismounted, lighting a fire.
I ran on into the trees and came face to face with a
giant white beetle.

I wanted to scream but I didn't, because that would have been the end of me. So instead I walked up to it and tapped its nose with my Lüger.

It was a Mark IV tank. Painted on its hull was an ϟϟ.

A sentry challenged me.

It was a battalion of the Leibstandarte attached to the Twenty-fifth Motorized. I was taken before General Heye. Sauckel was with him. They both gaped at me.

"Good evening, gentlemen." I felt sozzled.

"Where in God's name," Heye asked, "did you come from?"

"I've been"—I sat down on a log and lit a cigarette—"wandering around, hither and yon."

Sauckel yelped with rage. "The general denies all knowledge of Vera's whereabouts," he cried. "One of you is lying!"

Heye was just as angry. "Did you tell this imbecile I abducted her?" he sputtered.

"He misunderstood me." I had no difficulty at all playing dumb. I was stupid with weariness. "I told him I knew where she was."

"And *where* is she?" Sauckel shouted.

"Over there by the river."

A patrol was sent out; it came back a half-hour later with Vera, Mopsa, Dorcas, and the snipers—prisoners. They were still wearing their fur coats, and I saw for the first time that tiny red stars were sewed on their sleeves.

"Commissars!" Sauckel was incredulous. "All of them!" He walked over to Vera. "You little slut! You told me you weren't even a member of the party!"

She spit in his face.

He turned to Heye, trembling. "You know the regulations, General. All commissars are to be executed immediately upon capture."

Heye grimaced with distaste and called the commander of the Leibstandarte. Mopsa and Dorcas were sobbing. The three snipers just stared at me, as usual.

Vera pulled off her coat and threw it to me. I caught it and put it on. It fit snugly. In one of the pockets I found a jar of cherry jam.

The six of them were tied to trees and shot.

I composed a short poem for the occasion.

> The stealing gypsies come
> When the night is still
> To take a clothespin from the windowsill.

I called it "Loss." Then I ate the jam.

We never took Moscow. Or Leningrad. The Russians counterattacked and drove us all the way back to the River Donets.

Then, on the eleventh of December, 1941, the United States of America declared war on Germany.

7

"I'M CERTAINLY NOT going to occupy all of Russia," Hitler said. "I'd need three thousand divisions to do that. I refuse to go any farther than the Urals. I'll divide everything west of the Volga into a checker-board of German military districts and let the rest of the country just go to the devil."

We were in the underground tearoom of the chan-cellery bunker. Eva was pale and moody and visibly in heat and Bormann was in a happy daze, as if he'd just smoked a pipe of opium. They had invited me to lunch so that I could tell them about my experiences in Russia, but so far Hitler had done all the talking, as always.

"I'll rebuild Moscow, of course," he said. "Perhaps a bit farther south, around Kaluga on the Oka River. And naturally I'll rename it. Not 'Hitlergrad' or any silly thing like that, no. A good German name."

"Wocsom," I suggested.

He frowned at me. "Wocsom?"

"That's Moscow spelled backward."

Eva burst out laughing. Bormann looked at me as if I had belched.

Hitler shook his head. "No. I was thinking of a sim-ple battleship-type name. Like 'Bismarck.' Or 'Wag-ner.'"

His hand was shaking as he sipped his tea, and his

eyes were puffed and red. He kept licking his lips, as if he'd just eaten a wormy apple. In fact, he was a mess. The cold winter winds of Russia had blown all the way to Berlin that year.

The meal and his monologue went on and on all afternoon. Finally he excused himself, and he and Bormann went upstairs to a meeting.

Eva showed me around the bunker. It was an enormous, labyrinthine sewer system of rooms and corridors and baths and kitchens. She took me into the "Führer Suite" and we locked the door and pulled off our skirts. We made love on a daybed beside a bust of Frederick Barbarossa.

I really wasn't in the mood, but she was leaving for Obersalzberg the next day and I probably wouldn't see her again for months.

"This is the first time," she whispered, "since 1941."

"Who did you do it with in 1941?" I asked.

"A chambermaid in a hotel in Vienna."

The Berlin headquarters of ⚡⚡RUSHA—Rass-und-Siedlings Hauptamt, the department responsible for sending me on my nonsensical whore-seeking mission to Russia—had been closed for weeks. I reported there every ·day, but the door was always locked and the receptionist in the lobby had no idea when the office would reopen. I finally found out that the whole section had been transferred to WVHA on the Zähringerstrasse in Wilmersdorf. I went over there and looked up my old friend Standartenführer Otto Kasper, then in charge of concentration camp transportation. He put me to work in the economic bureau. He also gave me a month's leave.

I telephoned Lisa's mother in Dresden and she told me Lisa was living in Cologne. I still had my Luftwaffe flight pass tucked away in my purse. I flew there on the first of June.

I checked into a hotel on the Severnenstrasse, just next door to St. Johann's. She lived way, way over on the other side of the city, on the Hansaring.

I walked there. It took me hours and every step was a benediction. Cologne was a vast nave of peace. The streets were cathedral aisles, holy incense poured out of all the windows, and saints blessed me in a thousand transepts—Saint Mariae, Saint Kunibert, Saint Gereon, Saint Andreas, Saint Martin, Saint Apostelm, Saint Mauritius, Saint Pantaleon.

I wondered if there was a Saint Rita here somewhere. She was Papa's favorite—the Lady of Lost Causes. He used to light candles in her honor whenever a check was overdue or when his bank account was down to zero. Or when I was ill. She was infallible He swore she saved my life when I had the mumps in 1919.

I finally reached the Hansaring. Lisa's apartment house was just across the street from the Stadtmauer. Her name was on a mailbox in the entranceway. She lived on the ground floor, in a half-moon courtyard facing a park filled with oak trees. It was heavenly!

I rang her bell. The door opened. A dark young man stood before me.

"Is Lisa home?"

"No, she isn't." He stared at the swastika forks on my collar. "Have you come to arrest her?" Irony. A supercilious smile. His black eyes strafed my breasts.

"I'm a friend of hers. My name is Edmonde Kerrl."

"Oh, yes."

What did that mean? Oh yes. He invited me in for a drink. She wouldn't be back until about five. I could wait for her if I liked. Scotch? Gin? Or would I prefer coffee—he was just having some himself. Who was he? He behaved as if he *lived* there.

He introduced himself. Hans Kreutz. He poured two cups of coffee and we sat facing each other, sipping them.

He was about thirty, swarthy, ink-eyed, wearing a light summer suit, a brown shirt and white necktie, and . . . *bedroom slippers!* Ugh!

"You're not in the army?" I asked.

"Afraid not. Government employee. And you?"

"Me?"

"Gestapo? *Kripo?*"

"The WVHA."

"We're Very Harmless Actually."

"I beg your pardon?"

"That's how the Berlin wags translate the initials. WVHA."

"Are you a Berlin wag, Herr Kreutz?"

"No, I'm from Hamburg."

"We're the SS's economics and administrative section."

"Naturally. But what do you *really* do?"

"I don't know." I finished my coffee. "Hideous things probably. But I'm only a clerk."

"Me too." He poured me another cup.

Lisa came back to the flat at four-thirty. When she saw me she shrieked and almost swooned. I'd lost hundreds of kilos in Russia and was still stained with Ukrainian sunburn. Not only that, but I'd been infested with lice in April and had had to shave my hair. I must have looked like a panzergrenadier in a dress!

But she—mon Dieu!—she was still nineteen years old, a little girl, all in pale blue gabardine, with an orange tam pulled aslant over her forehead. She was awesomely lovely! Her eyes were overly painted—

green and mauve!—making her look like an Etruscan vase, but even that was enchanting.

She pushed me into the bedroom and we stood in each other's arms before the open window in front of all those oak trees smelling of summer and the Rhine, and we sobbed and laughed.

"Cocktails!" Kreutz called from the other room.

"Lisa," I whispered, "who is he?"

"Oh"—she wiped away her tears—"he's the shit I'm sleeping with."

I was jolted. Hundreds of girls I'd known had referred to their liaisons in all sorts of ways, but I'd never before heard any of them speak quite like that about a lover.

"And what about your son?"

"A nurse is looking after him, in Siegburg." She groaned with misery. "It was Hans's idea. He doesn't like children."

He took us out to dinner, then to a dismal nightclub near the Heumarkt. It was obvious that Lisa despised him. Then why did she tolerate him? I couldn't understand any of it. What kind of sexual ambiguity was this? After a few drinks he began mauling her sickeningly and she kept shoving him away. When he invited her to dance she refused. When he tried to slip his hand under her blouse she threw a glass of wine in his face. It was awful!

I got up and pulled her to her feet. The orchestra was playing "Lili Marlene." She moved into my arms and we danced off into the smoky darkness, floating on the music.

Holding her tightly, all our curves interlaced, our thighs moving together, everything was suddenly all right. Her lips touched my ear. "Edmonde," she hummed. Her hand moved beneath my collar to the back of my neck. "Wings," she whispered. I was deaf and dumb and blind with bliss. Here was my place. Our bodies danced away from us and we were left hovering in the air, like entwined ectoplasm drifting in a nothingness of beatitude.

I could close my eyes and imagine we were anywhere. And it would be true. All havens were within my scope. No refuge was too far. We swam through the boudoir of my house in Bad Tölz. We walked along the boulevards of Munich and Templehof. We crossed the Dnieper and the Bug and the Isar, the Rhine and the Seine and the Elb. We moved like fog across Vavin to the rue Notre-Dame-des-Champs.

Marie-José! Montparnasse and Papa! Cemeteries! Where did they bury poor Sanders? Are there certain sacred bodies worms refuse to dine upon and the rotting earth will not decay? When I died, where would I roam?

Suddenly I knew!

"Lisa, I had my portrait painted in the nude."

"Show it to me. I want to see it."

"I can't. It's on a door, in a studio in Montparnasse. I'm posed like a ballerina, completely bareassed, beautiful and lithe, wearing only dancing slippers on my feet and straps tied to my ankles."

"Montparnasse? In Paris? Then I'll never see it."

"You might. It will be there forever. You might see it someday, if you look for it. Oh, some scurvy tenth-rate artist might move in and paint something over it, but that won't matter, because it will always be there. And when I die I'll possess it. I'll come into its body and make its eyes light up. It will breathe and its limbs will move and it will be my ghost."

"Air raid!" somebody shouted.

Sirens were wailing. People were stumbling through

the shadows, knocking over tables and smashing glasses.
A maître d'hôtel led us down a flight of stairs into the
club's shelter.

Kreutz was sozzled and fell asleep. Lisa and I sat on
a bench in a dark corner, a blanket over us concealing
our hands.

"Who painted it?" she asked.

"A girl named Marie-José. Who is Kreutz, Lisa?"

"Marie-José." She tasted the name. "How pretty. Did
you ever read *Anthony Adverse?*"

"Yes. No. I haven't finished it yet. I keep putting it
aside; then, when I start to read it again, I have to go
all the way back to the beginning, otherwise I'd lose
the thread of the plot. Now I'm in the middle of Book
Six, Chapter 41—'A Glimpse into the Furnace.' Anthony is in Africa, buying slaves. He has a black mistress named Neleta."

Her gown opened down the side and she unbuttoned
it, offering me her legs. I opened my blouse so she could
have my breasts. We played with each other like cats
torturing mice until we were both giddy with excitement.

"Lisa, who is Kreutz?"

She put her head on my shoulder. "I can't tell you."

"Why not?"

"I can't."

"Where did you pick him up?"

"He picked me up." Her fingers stroked my nipples.
"He came into the apartment one afternoon and said,
'Take off your clothes but keep your stockings on.
Now put it in your mouth.' "

I was shocked. "And you did?"

"Yes."

The all-clear howled. We carried Kreutz outside and
they got into a taxi and drove back to the Hansaring,

leaving me standing alone and baffled on the Pipin-strasse. At the hotel I phoned Otto Kasper in Berlin. He called me back in the morning with the information I'd asked for. Hans Kreutz worked for the Abwehr.

"What the hell is that, Otto?"

"Military intelligence. Admiral Canaris's outfit."

"Wehrmacht or SS?"

"Wehrmacht. They have absolutely nothing to do with the SS. It's a nonparty organization. Problems, Eddy?"

"Yes indeed."

"Can I help?"

"I don't think so, Otto."

"Then perhaps you can help me."

"Gladly. What's happening?"

"I've been offered another job. I don't know whether to accept or not. It will mean leaving Berlin. Tell me what I should do."

"Can it wait until I get back?"

"Sure."

"All right then, I'll see you in July."

Lisa phoned at eleven and we met for lunch in a restaurant behind the Völkerkundemuseum. When I saw her I was glad I'd decided not to wear my uniform. She wore a long yellow summer dress with a red band in her hair. She took my breath away. We sat at a table on the terrace, and I moved my chair closer to her to absorb some of her illumination.

"You look like a goddess," I told her.

"So do you," she laughed. "We're two Rhine goddesses sitting in the sun, nibbling hors d'oeuvres."

She was right, of course, I was lovely too. I felt beauty emerging from me like pure mist from a marsh, filling the air around us with shimmering amber haze.

"Tell me about Marie-José," she said.

"She hated me." I was weeping with joy. The odor of grass and wine and Lisa and July were almost too captivating to bear. "She hated me right from the very beginning. She whipped me and she stuck things in me and she hated me, Lisa, she hated me. There was another girl in the Ukraine named Vera. She hated me too. She tried to capture me alive so that she could smother me in sulfur or drown me in Russian urine. And there was a third girl in Berlin, a Jewess named Lucie—she hated me even more than Vera and Marie-José did. I took her to Bad Tölz and gave her my house and she befouled everything with hate. Hate, Lisa. Did you know that hate stories exist side by side with love stories? Did you know that one can sing hate songs just as one sings love songs? That there are hate affairs, like love affairs? That you can fall in hate like you fall in love?"

"I know, yes." She smiled and held my hand. "She was a Jew, this Lucie? Suppose they had caught you?"

"Himmler almost did." I shrugged. "But he didn't seem to care too much. Those old party hacks are sentimental about the Munich days and all that."

I knew right away that she had made up her mind to confess everything. She hadn't told me before because she didn't trust me. Imagine that! Lisa losing confidence in *me!* Incredible!

We walked along the Bayenstrasse past the port, then down to the Holzmarkt. She still seemed hesitant. It was unnerving

"Tell me, Lisa," I prompted her.

"Hans is with the Abwehr," she admitted finally.

"Are you in trouble with the Abwehr?"

"My husband is." She leaned against the parapet of the quay. "Or he could be. He wrote a very incriminating letter to Field Marshal von Rundstedt last December. Hans intercepted it. He hasn't shown it to anyone yet."

"He's blackmailing you?"

"Yes."

"What does he want?"

"Just me. Or my mouth, actually. He says I have 'aristocratic lips.' I've been swallowing him every day for almost three months now. That satisfied him until yesterday."

"Yesterday?"

"You made quite an impression on him. Now he wants to sleep with both of us. Tonight."

I bought a tube of sleeping tablets in a pharmacy on the Severinstrasse.

On the Ubierring was an SS supply depot. The Sturmbannführer in charge gave me a jerrycan of gasoline in exchange for a bottle of Irish whiskey I'd bought from the bartender at my hotel.

I put the can in a shopping bag and lugged it to a streetcar. I arrived at the Hansaring at nine o'clock. It was still daylight and crowds of children were playing under the oak trees, making an awful racket. Lisa was alone in the apartment. Kreutz wasn't due until after ten. I put the bag in a closet and we sat in the dim kitchen drinking lime juice.

She was nude, wearing only her stockings under a *robe de chambre*. And she was horribly ill at ease. "You don't have to go through with this, Edmonde, not really."

"I don't mind."

"You'll loathe his body. It's ghastly! He's covered with boils and hair and moles ..."

"Please, Lisa."

"And he smells like a lavatory."

"Stop it."

We sat in silence for a long moment. She looked at her watch miserably. "Nine-fifteen."

"Come on." I took her by the hand and led her into the bedroom. I undressed and she removed her robe.

"You see, he makes me keep my stockings on."

"He's right. You're very erotic."

"You understand," she pleaded. "It's not my husband I care about. It's Eduard."

"I understand, Lisa." I kissed her breasts and moved my hands up and down her waist and over her hips until she was oblivious to everything but her need for me.

"Why are you so beautiful?" she cried. "Are you a girl or are you a naiad born in the bottom of a lake?"

"My father said he found me in an ashcan behind the Theater-am-Gärtnerplatz in Munich."

She stared at me wildly. "Look at your eyes. They're unearthly. You're not a human being, admit it. You're Pallas Athena or somebody. What's that on your leg?"

"Platinum."

I pulled off the chain and clasped it around her ankle. Then she sat on the bed and I knelt between her knees and obliterated all her vexations and sorrows while she caressed my hair.

Kreutz came strolling in a half-hour later. We'd just had a shower and were sitting in the living room wrapped in towels. When he saw us he smacked his lips.

"Bravo!" He clapped his hands. "Don't move! Let me admire the tableau! How is it that upper-class young ladies are always so chic, even without their clothes on? What's the secret?"

I got up and dropped my towel. "Tell us about your

experiences with upper-class young ladies, Herr Kreutz." His eyes flew at me like startled bats. "Have you known many?"

"Only one," he admitted, smiling again. "Until recently, my specialty has always been chasing girls who work in department stores. And to tell the truth, I wasn't very good at it."

"A drink?"

"Let me get *you* a drink. After all, I'm the host. I live here."

"Tonight you're the guest of honor."

"In that case, gin and pineapple juice."

Ugh! I poured gin and juice into a tall glass. The tube was tucked into the band of my watch. I pulled it loose, opened it, and emptied all the sleeping pills into the revolting mixture. I stirred it with a spoon and carried it over to him. He took it and drank half of it down in one thirsty gulp.

Lisa said nothing. She just sat on the couch, her arms folded, looking dismal. I glanced out the window. It was dark now. All the children who had been playing under the oak trees were gone and the park was as silent as a forest.

"I don't suppose you care," Kreutz announced, "but the goddamned Americans just sank half the Japanese fleet off Midway."

"I care," I said. "The sooner America wins the war the better. I miss Hollywood films terribly."

He stared at me, agog with amazement. "Are you serious?"

"Naturally!"

"That's a fine patriotic thing to say!"

"And you, Herr Kreutz? Are you patriotic?"

"Certainly I am."

I laughed. A patriotic blackmailer! Oh, what a pigfucker!

"What are you giggling at?"

"I always giggle when I'm sexually aroused." I posed
before him, à la tart. "Finish your drink and let's get
going."

He chuckled and slobbered down the rest of his gin.
"You and her first," he smirked. "Kiss her."

I went over to the couch and lifted Lisa's towel. She
smiled at me forlornly and opened her arms. We kissed
slowly.

Kreutz began wheezing like an elk and pulling off
his clothes. "Her stockings!"

They were in the bedroom. I went to get them and
when I came back he was naked. Lisa was right. His
body was atrocious!

I sat down beside her and she lifted her legs. He
watched, his pole flapping at us, as I pulled on her
stockings. I smiled at him. "What shall I put on Hans?
A tutu?"

He wasn't listening. He was standing before me, aiming straight in my face. He lunged at me. I turned
away, simpering coyly, and it plunged into my hair.

"It's not ready yet." I eased it away from me. "Make
it bigger."

This confused him. "Bigger."

"That's nothing," I chided. "I want it *enormous!*"

He stood there foolishly. We waited.

"Come on, Hans," Lisa sneered. "You can do better
than that. Up, up!"

He took a step toward her, then stopped and looked
down at himself. His erection had languished sadly. He
laughed, disconcerted. Then he wobbled back and
dropped into a chair.

"Let's help him, Lisa," I cooed. We slid together.

"Watch, Hans." Her kisses moved across my stomach and down my hips. She came off the couch to the floor, her breath blowing up my legs. I lounged back, gazing at him triumphantly. He was trout-faced. He tried to rise and pitched forward to his hands and knees. I blew a kiss at him as she entered me, her tongue frolicking in me, flooding me with sweetness. I gasped with exultation, my rejoicing spilling out of my lips like gibberish.

He turned yellow, then green. He slumped to the rug, croaking.

Lisa burrowed deeper into me, smiting me. She glanced up at me, her eyes immense and gleaming. That look was the coup de grâce, more diabolic than a hundred skilled caresses! I boiled over, disemboweled!

Kreutz brayed in agony.

When I come out of my stupor it was ten-thirty and she was still on the floor beside him.

"Edmonde, I think he's dead!"

I got up and took his pulse. "Not yet, but he will be shortly."

"What happened to him?"

"Heart attack, I suppose."

"Christ! What are we going to do?"

"Get rid of him."

"But if he dies, what about Richard's letter?"

I searched his clothing. It wasn't there. Not that I expected to find it. It was far too precious to carry around in his pocket. And for the same reason it wouldn't be in his office either.

"Where does he live, Lisa?"

"On the Machabäerstrasse."

"That's where it is, then. We'll need a shovel or something."

"A what?"

"Don't get dressed. We'll take a bath afterward."

"What are you talking about?"

In the kitchen I found a large trowel. It would do perfectly. I switched off the lights, pulled back the curtains, and opened the window. We lifted him and threw him out into the courtyard. Still naked, we climbed after him.

The moon was cloudy and all the windows of the apartment house were blacked out. We carried him across the lawn to the oak trees. With the trowel and our hands we dug a long, deep, narrow grave in a flowerbed and buried him. He was still alive.

We came back to the apartment and closed the window. I stepped under a shower. Lisa took a bath.

"I'll be back in an hour," I told her.

"Where are you going?"

"To find the letter."

I dressed, gathered up all of Kreutz's clothes and belongings, and put everything in a valise. Then I took my shopping bag out of the closet. I found a taxi on the Hansaring and drove to the Machabäerstrasse.

He lived in the top-floor studio in an old building near the river. I unlocked the door with his key. The letter was surely there somewhere, but I didn't bother to search for it. I pulled the jerrycan out of the shopping bag and poured gasoline over everything. Then I struck a match and the whole room burst into flames.

I ran downstairs to the street. There wasn't a soul in sight. In a café on the Domstrasse I called the firemen. Then I walked back to the Hansaring.

Lisa was still sitting in the bathtub. She was humming to herself, playing with one of her son's rubber toys. I pulled her out of the water and put her to bed. I undressed and crawled in beside her and held her in my arms all night. In the morning she was no better.

I called a doctor. He gave her an injection of something and took her away in an ambulance.

She spent the rest of June in a nursing home and I went back to Berlin.

"The Sixth Army has taken Stalingrad," Otto said. "Where's that?"

"I don't know. Down south somewhere, on the Volga."

We were sitting in his office, drinking cognac. He didn't have any cigarettes so I was smoking one of his cigars. It was delicious.

We were both preoccupied. My problem was Lisa again. After her breakdown, General Heye had returned from the front on emergency leave. They were in Berlin now, living in the house on the Warthe-Platz. I'd tried to visit her several times, but he forbade her to see me or even to talk to me on the phone.

Otto's problm was the WVHA. He'd been offered the command of a camp in Gotha, in Thuringia, and he didn't know whether to accept or not, although it probably meant a promotion.

"It's one of those restricted areas," he brooded. "You know what that means. Everybody there becomes an inmate. Even the guards."

And there was *another* problem looming that concerned us both, that concerned everybody in the SS. Russia! A directive from Himmler had been making the rounds, warning the various departments that a new Einsetzgruppe was being formed for a special mission in the Ukraine. We were all eligible for assignment and of course no one wanted to go. Especially me. Ugh! The very idea of recrossing the Dniester terrified me.

"The Ukraine." He poured another cognac. "With

winter coming. Anything would be better than that. Including a concentration camp."

"Otto, can you get me some of these cigars?"

"Yes, but they're hellishly expensive. They come from Cuba via Stockholm and a box costs a month's salary. Which reminds me, I'm having lunch with the girl from the Swedish embassy who sells them to me. Why don't you join us?"

We drove to Spandau, to a small inn in a wood near the stadium. It was a warm, brown autumn afternoon. The air reeked of cider and dampness. It was the kind of day when nothing seemed important—not the war, nor love, nor a debit in the bank. I'd received a tax notice that morning, reminding me I owed the Reich ten thousand marks. I tore it up.

While we were waiting for the girl we had several more cognacs and got slightly sozzled. She arrived at two o'clock. Her name was Naima Josephson.

She stood before us and the woods sang.

Suddenly everything became as vital as breath. If my heart stopped beating at that instant I would die and never see her again. I prayed to live just a while longer—at least until the end of lunch!—just long enough to renounce everything except her presence.

She was a Norse vision! A divinity! An idol! A Scandinavian sacrificial pine tree standing in the ice on the highest slope of Kebnekaise! An altar! I longed to tear out handfuls of my entrails and burn them before her, to slash my veins and offer her a cup of blood. I wanted to lie before her and let multitudes of Vikings slice me up with battleaxes just so I could worship her with my shrieks.

"How is it," she asked, "that there's no mention of El Alamein in the German papers?"

"El Alamein?" Otto could hardly keep his eyes focused. "What's that? A cigar?"

"It's a battlefield in Africa," she laughed. "You just got the shit kicked out of you there. Rommel has been routed."

"The hell with Rommel. What have you got to sell?"

She laughed again. Ah, that laughter! A lute ode! Mozartian! A harp-string sonatina! How unfamiliar! No one laughed in Germany anymore. I tried . . . but I could only choke and squeak like a broken valve.

She looked at me strangely. I was certain I repelled her. I was foul and repugnant! My skin was blotchy! My teeth were crooked, my tongue was covered with scales! My body threw off a skunk stench of sourness and putrescence! She would excuse herself in a moment and rush away into the thickets and vomit!

How could she not abhor me? How could she even tolerate my *being* there? She surely wouldn't be able to eat, not with me sitting beside her like a leper! She would pretend she was dieting and order only a glass of sherry and an aspirin.

But no! She ordered sardines, spaghetti, cake, and apricots and ate everything!

Then she sold us two boxes of cigars, three cartons of Chesterfields, six tubes of British toothpaste, and a bottle of American shampoo.

At four o'clock Otto had to go back to the office. He paid the bill and left us there.

I folded my hands on my lap and bit my tongue, afraid to speak.

Papa, what do you do when you forget your lines?

What's the matter now, little beast?

I'm sitting in an inn with a girl and I'm unable to say a single word. Help me, please!

Pray to Saint Rita.

You pray for me. My mind is a chaos.

Gladly. O Rita! if my deep prayers cannot appease thee, but thou wilt be avenged on my misdeeds, yet execute thy wrath on me alone, spare my guiltless daughter.

That's Richard the Third!

Loss, little Edmonde, everything is loss. Look at her a moment, then watch her go away.

Why is it so, Papa? How can I make her stay? The sun is going down and Spandau is turning black!

"Hey," she whispered. "What's the matter with you?"

I leaned on her shoulder and sobbed all over her.

She lived in a rooming house in Steglit, on the Willdenowstrasse behind the Bontanischer Garten. That's where I found myself when I sobered up. I was lying on a bed beside an open window. I was naked.

Naima was sitting on the floor reading a book. A monstrous Doberman pinscher was lying on a mat beside her.

"His name is Faust," she said. And she laughed her merry laugh. "Are you feeling better?"

It was seven o'clock. My uniform was hanging neatly over the back of a chair. I was thirsty. She poured me a glass of something dark and tasty.

"Root beer," she announced. "Made in USA."

The dog came over and sniffed me. I pulled his ears. He growled at me.

"Can I borrow this?" She showed me the book. It was *Anthony Adverse*. "Excuse me for going through your purse, but I didn't have any change to tip the taxi driver."

"I haven't finished it yet."

"Loan it to me when you're through."

"All right." I stared at her. *"Loulou,"* I said.

"Please?"

"You look like Louise Brooks. Especially when you smile."

"I know a Bulgarian who says I look like Greta Garbo," she laughed. "It seems all the world is just a silver screen, and we are but stars. Do you want to take a shower?"

Faust followed me into the bathroom. The water was scalding and the soap was American Palmolive! I scoured myself from head to toe, trying to scrub away I don't know what.

She slipped through the shower curtain and stood before me. "In the event of our not meeting again," she said, "I want to take advantage of your visit."

She was exactly my height. That was gratifying, because I'd thought she was much taller. But her eyes were just level with mine and our shoulders were parallel. How revealing nudity is! Clothing is so deceptive!

We gazed at each other.

She was like a mirror, reflecting another Edmonde— a former, laughing, smiling, long-ago Edmonde. The Edmonde Papa used to take with him on endless walks. The Edmonde lost in a deep cave with Eva. The Bad Tölz and Munich Edmonde. Edmonde in the woods and fields, Edmonde and Anna, Edmonde reading *Fantômas,* Sturmabteilung Edmonde.

She lifted her leg, putting her knee against my stomach. She kissed my cheeks and eyes. Our hands hung at our sides for a moment, then touched, and she raised my palm to her face and licked it—garroting me, dissolving me in acid, guillotining all my limbs . . . how wondrous that a mirror could do that!

She laughed. "You are a basket of fruit! If I only had

eight hands like an octopus to touch you everywhere!"
She groped beneath my arm, fondling me avidly. Then
our lips mingled and her fingers moved to my breasts,
counting decades of Aves on my nipples. "Two octo-
puses," she whispered, "all wrapped together and slimy."
Her arms circled me. "Say my name."

"Edmonde."

"That's not my name."

"*Loulou.*"

"Who was *Loulou?*"

"It was a film about Jack the Ripper. With Louise
Brooks and . . . I forget."

"That's not my name either."

"Naima Josephson."

"Yes. Again."

"Naima Josephson."

She moaned. "It sounds like an oboe!" Her body en-
compassed me. "I cannot wait," she murmured. "If you
are not ready, *tant pis!*"

She dropped to her knees, sinking away from me—
down, down, down, into the maelstrom.

"Where are you?" I couldn't see her. Where had she
gone? Then I felt her teeth on my hip.

"Yes, Naima, I'm ready." I knelt beside her. "But
we must do it together."

We crawled out of the waterfloor to the bathroom
floor, tumbling into each other, engulfing our heads
in our thighs.

Faust lay watching us, thumping his tail on the tiles.

She was still my mirror. I was bent double upon myself, hunched impossibly, convoluted and twisted, like
a contortionist, between my own legs, my face in my
own arbor, my kisses paying homage to my own pas-
sion, my mouth tasting myself, my tongue deep in Edmonde.

She laughed. "A pity no one can see us . . . This must be a spectacular sight . . ." Another laugh. "Faust is shocked." More laughter. "In fact, so am I!"

Then we were both laughing, rolling on the floor like hysterical clowns, yowling, tickling, and biting, scissoring our necks with our legs, baying, splashing in puddles, banging against the wall.

But finally our hilarity and our fervor collided, smashing together like nitroglycerin meteoroids and exploding—bursting us asunder, crumbling us.

Faust barked at us.

At eleven o'clock she had to deliver a dozen bottles of black-market Scotch to a client at the Luftwaffe Ministry. I went with her to help her carry the bags.

The building was in darkness, the windows were boarded up, and sandbags were piled everywhere, mountains of them. A night porter let us in through a side entrance and led us along the familiar maze of passages to the operations section in the back.

We passed my old office. I looked through the door of the typists' room and saw Lucie's desk by the window.

> But thoughts, the slaves
> of life, and life, time's fool,
> And time, that takes survey
> of all the world,
> Must have a stop.

as Hotspur said. Then he dropped dead.

The client was waiting for us in the headquarters lounge. All the lights were turned off except for one blue blackout lamp, and he sat beneath it, slumped in an armchair, staring at the floor.

It was Hermann.

"Come in, Naima, come in." He didn't even bother to look at us. He was "out of it." His mouth hung open, his eyes were smeared with exhaustion, his whalelike bulk petrified with swollen blubber.

"How are you, Reichsmarschall?" Naima kissed the top of his head. "This is Edmonde."

"Hello," he rumbled.

He didn't recognize me.

"How's your war coming along?" she asked him. "Here's your scotch." We took the bottles out of the bag and set them on the table beside him.

He took a handful of marks from his pocket and handed them to her without counting them. "We'll have Stalingrad by the end of the week," he promised.

"What? You mean you haven't taken it yet?"

"No, I don't think so."

"Do you want a poke, Reichsmarschall?"

"Yes, Naima, please."

She walked off into the nearby men's room. Left alone together, Hermann and I eyed each other.

"You don't remember me"—but I was using the lovers' *du;* I corrected myself quickly—"You don't remember me, Herr Reichsmarschall."

"Certainly I do," he smiled, all the heavy festoons of flesh hanging from his jaws wobbling. "You're Oberleutnant Kerrl's little girl."

I was amazed. "Yes, that's right."

"Jasta 12/JG 2."

"Yes." Mon Dieu! There was a spark of life in him after all!

"How is your father?"

"He's dead."

"I'm sorry," He looked at the floor again. "He was a fine young man. It will be a tremendous victory. And we need a victory now. Stalin is in a panic. Throwing all his armies down there on the Volga. Dozens of them. It will be a butchery!" His monumental body shifted, almost snapping off the legs of the chair. "But the Führer is highly displeased about the air raids." He rubbed his plump hands together. Rings clicked on all his fingers. "Those Flying Fortresses are master-pieces of destruction. I need more fighters. Of course I remember you. Kerrl, yes. All those splendid young-sters. Voss, Loewenhart, Udet . . ." He chuckled. "And Göring too! They called Immelmann 'The Eagle of Lille.' And Manfred was 'The Red Baron' if you please! But I was always just 'Big Hermann.' "

Naima came back into the room holding a syringe. She handed it to me while she helped him take off his tunic. It was like undressing Mont Blanc!

"It's the RAF every night now," he mumbled. "And the American Eighth Air Force every blessed day."

"Would your wife be interested in some stockings, Reichsmarschall?"

"Stockings, Naima?"

"Brand new." She rolled up his sleeve. "Right straight from New York."

"Very well. Bring them around. What I really need though is . . ." He scowled, trying to remember. "Yes, five hundred more Focke Wulf 190s and the pilots to fly them. And two or three Nachtjäger squadrons to neutralize those damned Lancasters every night. Stock-ings, yes, Emmy will be delighted."

"I'll bring them around tomorrow." She plunged the needle into his arm.

Air-raid sirens began to moan all over Berlin.

He got up brusquely and went off into the opera-tions wing, pulling on his tunic. "Remember me to your papa!" he called to me as he left.

"What an elephant!" Naima laughed. "I gave myself a jab too." She waved the needle at me dreamily. "Oooo, I'm beginning to feel it. Do you want some, Edmonde darling?"

"Yes."

She sawed off the tip of an ampule with a tiny blade and filled the syringe. I lifted my skirt and she pricked me in the thigh. Then she kissed the wound and licked away a drop of blood. We started to make love right there on the spot, but two Luftwaffe officers came hurrying by, so we opened one of the bottles of Scotch instead. We sat drinking it until the all-clear sounded.

The injection crashed into me as we were leaving the building. Boooom! I remember Naima throwing me down on a pile of sandbags and pouncing between my legs like a growling panther. Then we went off on a tour of churches, looking for a statue of Saint Rita. Then we were in the Volkspark in Mariendorf. I was sitting in the grass, smoking a cigar and watching her kneeling before—I think—a sailor, biting his penis. He ran off, blattering with pain, and she chased him, laughing, beating him with a stick. Then we were away over in Zehlendorf, drinking beer in some dive. Then we were somewhere else, dancing with—I think—midgets. I woke up at eight o'clock in the morning, at the Schlesisches Tor stop on the U-bahn.

I felt marvelous, as if I'd slept ten hours. I went home, took a bath, changed my uniform, and had breakfast.

Then I read a newspaper and almost collapsed.

A girl had been killed last night in Tempelhof. Her body was discovered this morning on the Gottlieb-Dunkelstrasse near the canal—stabbed. Chills ran up and down my spine. Shit! That was only five minutes away from the Volkspark Mariendorf! I remembered

Naima and I crossing the canal bridge, then passing the Neuköllner Cemetery, then walking along the Rixdorferstrasse toward the park . . . Shit! What time had it been? Midnight? Two o'clock in the morning?

I read on.

It was the third knife murder in three weeks. There was obviously a homicidal maniac on the loose in Berlin.

Good! I poured a drink, trembling with relief. A homicidal maniac, fine! There for a moment I thought *we* had killed the poor girl during our wild spree. I wouldn't have been surprised. We'd done everything else! Balls!

The entire area around my pudendum was ice cold, as if I'd just given birth to a glacier. I was sticky with sweat. I had to take another bath.

The shock proved to be beneficial. It cracked open the crust of lazy complacency that had been coarctating me all these weeks, and I made two momentous decisions: one, no more syringes for me, and two, I would see Lisa today!

I went to the Warthe-Platz determined to have it out with General Heye, even if it meant a brawl. I kicked open the gate à la Gary Cooper entering a saloon in a Western, stormed to the house, and pounded on the front door.

An old woman who lived next door leaned over the fence and snarled at me. How dare I make so much noise at this hour of the morning when her two sons were fighting for the Fatherland on the Russian front.

I snarled back at her and showed her my ⚡⚡ card. She was immediately humble. No, the Heyes weren't there, they'd left the night before. No, she had no idea where they were.

I walked up the Oderstrasse and sat down on a

bench. I smoked a cigar. Two policemen passed and
gaped at me as if I were a freak in a cage. I got up
and walked around the block, coming back to the bench,
expecting to find Lisa there, waiting for me. Of course
she wasn't.

I went over to the airport and had a drink in the
bar. The bookstall where she'd bought me *Anthony
Adverse* was closed, shuttered like a pillbox. Two
French POWs were sweeping the floor.

Who was it who said—an English writer, one of the
better ones, Thomas Hardy or Conrad or Henry James
—who said—what did he say exactly? That life was
like a Persian carpet, intricate and exquisite, but mean-
ingless, except for its tangle.

Naima invited me to the Swedish embassy whenever
they showed an American film. They had a projection
room in the basement, and there I saw four magnificent
new Hollywood chefs d'oeuvres, imported from Stockholm.

The first was *All That Money Can Buy,* with the
fantastic Walter Huston playing the devil. Then
Kings Row, with another remarkable actor named
Claude Rains and a fabulous musical score by Erich
Wolfgang Korngold. Then *The Sea Wolf,* with a phe-
nomenal girl named Ida Lupino, who looked exactly
like Eva! And finally *Dr. Jekyll and Mr. Hyde,* with
the extraordinary Spencer Tracy, who was absolutely
superb! I emerged from these sessions reeling with bliss,
longing to be transferred to Sweden so I could go to
the movies every single day.

Instead, I was almost sent to Russia.

Himmler summoned me to his house on the Walchensee. He was alone in the living room, in his smoking
jacket—the same one he had been wearing the last time

I was there—drinking a cup of coffee and munching pretzels. He looked at me and shook his head, his thick glasses twinkling.

"What am I going to do with you, Edmonde?"

"Is anything wrong, sir?"

"Don't call me sir. We're old friends." He was using the *du*. Excellent! He was in one of his fatherly, old-comrade moods.

"What is it, Heinrich?"

"She's a spy, you know."

"Who is?"

"Naima Josephson."

The room spun around me for an instant. He jumped up and took me by the arm. "Heavens! Sit down! Do you want some schnapps?"

"Yes."

I sank into a chair. He poured me a glass of something revolting and held it under my nose. I almost puked. "Thank you."

"We can't touch her because she has diplomatic immunity. So we use her. Feed her bits of false information."

"You mean she's a Swedish spy, Heinrich?"

He made a loud barnyard sound—"Heehahhak! Dearest Edmonde! A *Swedish* spy! Heeeehoohh!"

He took off his glasses and wiped his eyes with a handkerchief. I took advantage of this to empty my glass into a nearby flowerpot, like the murderer in *The Dragon Murder Case.*

"No, you little goose, she works for the British. And the Yankees too, I believe. Tell me now, how did she contact you?"

I had to keep poor Otto out of this at all costs "I don't recall . . ." I looked vague and stupid. "Oh, yes . . . it was in a restaurant . . . No, on the U-bahn . . ."

"It doesn't matter. Has she tried to pump anything out of you yet?"

"No! Never! Certainly not!"

"She will. Very well, give her this. We're going to invade Malta."

"Malta?"

"Tell her that."

"But, Heinrich, I couldn't! That would be treason!"

"Just do as I say, Edmonde."

"All right."

"Do you want another schnapps?"

"No, thank you."

Then Frau Himmler came home and we spent the rest of the afternoon talking about the forthcoming victory at Stalingrad. Then we had dinner. Then we listened to records—*The Merry Widow*—ugh! I didn't get out of the place until almost midnight.

Naima a spy! It was all nonsense, of course. Typical Gestapo batshit.

I went directly to her rooming house on the Willdenowstrasse. She wasn't home. I sat in the Botanischer Garten until two o'clock, waiting for her. She finally came stumbling up the street, drunk and mirthful. When she saw me she yelped and almost carried me to her room.

"I've got something to show you," she sang. "Pretty pictures! Wait till you see them. Oooooo! You naughty girl!" She was carrying a large envelope. When we got to her room she opened it. "I just had these developed! They're sensational!"

They were photographs. Photographs of *me*. Naked on the bed, with the dog lying on top of me. Naked on the bathroom floor, between her legs. Naked in a room crowded with midgets. Naked with several grotesque old women in a beer garden.

Don't look, Papa! Don't look!

She grinned at me. "I'll show these to everybody in Berlin," she smirked, "if you're not nice."

"Nice, Naima?"

"You can do certain things for me, darling. And, in exchange, I can do certain things for you."

"Are you a spy, Naima?"

She laughed her merry laugh. "Goodness no! I just peddle things. Whiskey, stockings, cigars, information. I'm a huckster."

"Information? Are you interested in Malta?"

"Malta?"

"We're going to invade Malta."

She blinked with surprise. "Really?"

I tried to remember everything I'd read in the newspapers about those three dead girls. They'd all been stabbed—I recalled that. And there was something else too . . . What was it? The first body had been found in a vacant lot in Schöneberg, the second in the Tiergarten. Yes, that was it. And the third was near the canal in Tempelhof. They had all been killed in the streets. *Outside.*

It wouldn't be wise to change the pattern.

Go away, Papa. There's no need for you to watch this.

"Tell me about Malta, Edmonde," she said.

There were several logs sitting on the floor before the fireplace. I picked up one of them and slammed it across her jaw, being careful not to damage her face too much. Just a neat, hard, clean blow—*crack!* She fell to the floor, stunned.

Faust crawled out from under the bed, growling furiously. Shit! I'd forgotten all about him! He came at me, his eyes wild, his jaws open. I ran into the bathroom. He jumped after me, slid past me. I came back into the room behind him and closed the door on him. He began barking crazily.

Make him shut up, Papa!

The barking ceased.

I slid the photos back into the envelope and put it in my purse. Then I found a knife in the drawer of the table.

I turned off the lights, picked up Naima, and lugged her downstairs to the vestibule. I opened the street door.

I dumped her out on the front steps and stabbed her in the heart.

I walked home via the Brentanostrasse and threw the knife into a sewer.

It's all right, Papa, you can come back now.

The newspapers the next day were predictable: KNIFE KILLER SLAYS FOURTH VICTIM—or some such thing. Himmler's reaction, though, was unexpected.

"This is vexing." His lips smacked together querulously. "Extremely regrettable."

"She deserved it, Heinrich."

"Mmmmmm." He obviously didn't approve of the "Heinrich"—not during office hours. "She was useful."

"Perhaps the British themselves killed her. They found out you were on to her and . . ."

"Don't be silly." He looked at me keenly. "You're such a child, Edmonde. You know, I haven't forgotten that business with the Jew—Lucie What's-her-name. Now *this*. What foolishness will you get involved in next?" He pulled off his glasses and tapped them on the desk. Disaster was about to descend on me; I felt it in my bones. "I think the Ukraine would be the best place for you. Keep you out of mischief for a while."

Ugh! I bowed my head meekly. "Yes, sir." I had to

think fast. God! Papa! Somebody! Help me! "Otto," I said.

"What?"

"Otto will be so disappointed."

"Otto? You mean Standartenführer Kasper? What does he have to do with it?"

"He's been reassigned, you see . . ."

"Yes, he's taking the Gotha post."

"I was going there with him."

"In what capacity?"

"He asked me to marry him."

He sprang up, beaming like the Sun King. "But that's marvelous, Edmonde! Why wasn't I informed?"

"I wanted to surprise you, Heinrich."

"Dearest girl! Look here now! Look here! Eh! I insist on giving the bride away! Eh!"

Adieu, Russia!

I called up Otto a half-hour later and frightened him shitless. "Himmler found out about your black-market-ing with Naima," I gasped. "He's altogether outraged."

"Oh, my God!"

"He even threatened to have you court-martialed."

"What shall I do, Edmonde?"

"I told him we were engaged, that softened him a bit."

"En-engaged?"

"We have to get married, Otto, fast. He loves wed-dings. Especially SS weddings."

"All right. Whatever you say."

We were married in November. It was a gala, party festival, with swastikas hanging on all the walls, Himm-ler giving the bride away, and Frau Himmler bustling about like a mother hen, bossing everyone. Hermann showed up, more or less lucid, and Bormann came, representing the Führer.

In the bottom of a valise I found one of Frau Frankovitch's white evening gowns. It made a perfect bridal dress.

After the ceremony we came out of the chapel and walked between two long columns of SS grenadiers holding crossed swords.

A mad dog, frothing at the mouth, ran across the driveway and attacked us, barking and snarling. It was an enormous Doberman pinscher.

A policeman shot him with a Lüger.

‖‖‖

8

ON THE EDGE OF THE Eisenach highway was a simple
sign— ⚡⚡WVHA—with an arrow pointing into the
forest. A long, narrow lane, as wide as our limousine,
twisted through the trees to a high gate.

Beyond the gate was Camp Gotha.

Otto and I arrived on a rainy morning in November.
When the gate opened, a loudspeaker blared a march.
We rolled along a driveway past a battalion of SS riflemen presenting arms, past a casern, past a tan barn,
past lawns and flowerbeds and fishponds. We stopped
before a pretty green cottage with white shutters.

Frau Kasper and her husband were home.

Luckily there were two bedrooms, so Otto and I could
give up the pretense of sleeping together. I learned on
our wedding night that he had no interest at all in my
body. Our three-week "honeymoon" in Vienna had been
as chaste as a novena.

I didn't mind. On the contrary. The idea of physical
intimacy with him didn't appeal to me in the least.
Ugh! That very first encounter, years and years ago in
—where had it been? Stuttgart? Munich? Ulm?—had
been quite sufficient.

"Take your pick," he said, indicating the two rooms
and thereby formally confirming our separation.

I picked the one in the back of the house, overlooking a peach orchard, a high fence, and the forest.

I lit a cigar and stood at the window, surveying my new horizon. An old woman wearing what appeared to be a black nightshirt was in the orchard, pruning branches. On the other side of the fence two guards passed. One of them had a wooden leg.

All rather dismal.

The house was nice, though. Clean and bare and smelling of pine. There was an awful picture on the wall—*Stag at Bay* or something. I took it down and threw it in the coal scuttle.

I put on my raincape and went out to the front yard. A rectangle of lawn framed in barbed wire. A willow tree. Bushes. It was going to be a melancholy winter.

What do you think, Papa? Awful, isn't it?

Running along the far side of the driveway was a tall hedge. I followed it around the border of the camp until I found an opening in the foliage. I stepped through it and there before me, spread out across a muddy plain, was the pit of Acheron.

A hundred barracks stood in ten neat rows, and before each row was massed an immobile formation of one thousand prisoners.

Startled, I multiplied them quickly: ten times one thousand . . .

Good God! Ten thousand people!

Fascinated, I walked closer.

Half of them were men, in black pajamas, and half women, in black nightshirts, five thousand to one side, five thousand to the other, all of them silent and motionless, standing in the rain like a necropolis of funereal colonnades.

A tall man with a broken nose, a shaven skull, and

white stripes painted on the sleeves of his pajamas limped forward and saluted me with a cudgel.

"I am Zintsch, my lady. At your service."

I fought back the impulse to cower away from him. "Heil Hitler," I muttered.

"Alas, my lady, we are not permitted to acclaim the Führer."

He was revolting! I moved past him, my stomach turning. "Why are they standing there like that, Zintsch?"

"They are waiting for you, my lady. If you would care to inspect them . . ."

Twenty thousand lizard eyes watched as he led me past the ranks, their scrutiny bombarding me with despair.

"Barracks 1 through 50 are masculine," he explained. "Barracks 51 through 99 are feminine. Barracks 100 is for gypsies."

"And who are you, Zintsch?"

"I, my lady"—he showed me his cudgel—"am the Chief Club."

There were other striped-sleeved men and women in the multitude, armed with rods. They bowed as I passed.

"Where are the gypsies?"

"Gypsies front and center!" he yelped.

Eighty women and twenty men shuffled out of the last formation and stood at limp attention before us, their dark olive faces glowering at me.

Here they were, the springtime night fiends, the shadows that came out of the woods at twilight to steal my childhood.

I stared at them. Did they remember me? Surely they did, because I recognized all of them—all but one. Among their aspic heads was a face that didn't belong there. A girl stood in a middle column—blonde, fair, blue-eyed, taller than the others.

"Who is she, Zintsch?"

"That is Uiberreither, my lady. The former commander, Oberführer Pleiger, put her in 100 to teach her a lesson."

"Edmonde!"

Otto and another officer came striding through the mud toward us. "What the hell are you doing?"

"Just having a look around."

"You're not supposed to be in this part of the camp, darling."

"Why not?"

"It's against the rules."

"Stop behaving like a flunky, Otto. *You* make the rules here."

The other officer laughed. He was a handsome young man, no more than twenty, with a patch on his left eye. Otto introduced him, Hauptsturmführer Karl-Jesko Weber.

"She's right, Kasper," he giggled. "You're the boss now. Zintsch!" He clapped his hands. "Let's have some music!"

"Yes, sir, Hauptsturmführer!" Zintsch waved his club. "Music!" he barked.

And the ten thousand prisoners began to hum and whistle Mozart's Overture to *The Marriage of Figaro*.

Every morning at seven o'clock the prisoners marched out of the camp into the forest and spent the day chopping down trees, sawing logs, and uprooting thickets. When I asked Karl-Jesko what they were supposed to be doing he laughed. He was always laughing. I thought at first that he was comically inclined, but I soon realized that he was in a perpetual state of giddy hysteria.

"They're building a road," he said.

"A road where?"

"Nowhere."

I went out and looked at the road several times. It was broad and level and wound on and on and around and around, bisecting itself in dozens of crossings and going, in effect, in no direction.

"But what is its purpose?" I asked Otto.

"It keeps them occupied." He shrugged. He opened another bottle of vodka. He drank at least four liters of the stuff a day and was continuously bleary.

"But couldn't they do something useful?"

"What, for instance?"

"I don't know. They could paint the house perhaps."

"All right."

The next day over a hundred of them showed up at the cottage. They plastered and painted all the walls and ceilings, varnished the floors, and reshingled the roof. Then they marched away, dead-faced and silent.

I discovered the road's secret in January.

I happened to be passing the barracks one evening during the prisoners' roll call. They didn't look as numerous as before. In fact, some of the formations were down to just a few hundred men and women.

I counted them. There were only four thousand present! Four thousand from ten thousand . . .

It was unbelievable! In three months we'd lost six thousand people! I couldn't believe it.

"What happened to them, Otto?"

"They died."

It was almost as bad as Stalingrad. In ninety days the Sixth Army had lost twenty-two divisions!

"What do you do with all the bodies, Karl-Jesko?"

He giggled and giggled and giggled. And he pointed to the pajama- and nightshirt-clad specters filing out of the gate into the woods, humming and whistling Beethoven's Eighth. A wagonload of fresh corpses followed them.

I had one of the Clubs saddle a horse for me and galloped out to the site. I watched them bury the bodies in a row and build the road over them.

It was a political camp. The prisoners were all charged with antiparty felonies. Some fifty percent of them were Social Democrats. Twenty percent had belonged to the Catholic Center, ten percent were Hanoverians, and the rest, Communists. There were a few ex-Nazis too. And some, like Zintsch and the gypsies, were just flotsam.

From February on, once a month, a train would pull into the tiny station in a clearing by the back gate and four or five or six thousand more outcasts would march into the barracks to replace the dead. About half of them would live three weeks. The rest went under the road.

"Fräulein 100"—as everyone called her—always managed to survive.

She intrigued me and I went to the casern office to read her dossier. Her name was Faustina Uiberreither. She was born in Braunschweig in 1922. She was arrested by the Gestapo in '41 in a students' purge at the University of Bonn. She'd been a law sophomore.

When Karl-Jesko found me studying the file he added a few more laughing details to her story.

"Old Pleiger, your esteemed predecessor, kept her off the work gang and, hah-hah, and made her his cook. He also installed her in his frugal and, hah-hah-hah, austere SS cot. Then she did something that displeased him, I don't know what—perhaps her cuisine didn't agree with him—so he threw her in with the scurvy gypsies, and everybody says, hah-hah, they put the *hex* on him, because he dropped dead one morning while doing push-ups in the orchard."

I found her behind Barracks 100, standing in the mud, combing her long filthy hair with a fork. She turned as I walked up to her, and we stood for a moment appraising each other.

"The gypsies are afraid of you." She pointed to the window. Blank, swarthy raven faces were peering out at us. "They say you are their judgment. They want to know what they're accused of."

"The wrongful carrying off of the personal goods of another," I said. "They're thieves."

"Fifteen of them died today," she remarked. "There are only eleven left. Did it ever occur to you that you will be judged too? You will have to account for all these deaths someday."

"Then I'll need a good lawyer. Will you defend me?"

She smiled. It illuminated her, cleansed her, choked me with pity. Her teeth were yellow.

"Come with me"—I took her by the hand—"and I'll fix your hair."

"No." She pulled away from me. "I will stay here."

"Don't be a martyr, Faustina. You will do as I say."

I took her back to the cottage and cut and washed her hair. Then I made her take a bath and brush her teeth. My heart melted when I saw her naked. Her body was just bones.

Her black nightshirt was alive with lice. I burned it and telephoned to the supply sergeant to bring her a new one.

She protested bitterly. "This is too cruel!" She was

on the verge of tears but refused to cry. "Going back to the work gang now will be unbearable!"

"You won't have to go back," I assured her. She didn't believe me, of course. She was convinced that I was torturing her, poor girl. I put her to bed in my room and she slept for twelve hours. I spent the night on the sofa in the living room.

Otto was so sozzled he didn't even know she was there. But Zintsch, when he found out I'd abducted her, came to see me, cringing with indignation.

"I should have been informed, my lady," he simpered. "After all, I am the Chief Club. All changes in the work schedule are my responsibility. You didn't even consult me." His hideous face twisted with polite vexation and he waited for me to apologize.

This was the crisis I was certain he'd been waiting for. It gave him the opportunity to force me to affirm his authority.

I took my riding crop from the closet and slashed it across his shaven head. He scampered away from me, astonished.

"Zintsch," I hissed at him, "get down on your knees and beg my pardon for your affront."

He obeyed quickly. "I'm very sorry, my lady, but . . ."

I slashed him again. "Now get out of here. No, wait. First carry this sofa into the pantry."

He got even with me a few days later when he discovered that the old woman in charge of our garden had pruned all the trees to nothingness. The orchard was now a corpse of poles. He clubbed her to death, and another few meters of road were built on top of her.

I told Otto to put him in the work gang. He refused.

"I need him," he grumbled.

"What for?"

"He does what I'm incapable of doing. He gets the job done. Please don't interfere with him, Edmonde."

The next day a new gardener reported for work. It was one of the gypsies.

Faustina moved into the pantry. She cooked for us and kept house. The days and the weeks and the months passed. Her body gained weight and curves and breasts and her clean hair grew, blonde and fine. The Sixth Army surrendered, and Stalingrad was added to the long list of cities we never captured. Von Mannstein was put in command of the Southern Front. The Afrika Korps was booted out of Tunisia. The Americans and British invaded Sicily and Italy. Otto was promoted to Oberführer and Karl-Jesko to Sturmbannführer.

We went into Gotha to celebrate. We sat in a grubby nightclub, wearing paper hats, throwing handfuls of confetti at one another, and eating roast duck. The place was crowded with Luftwaffe and Wehrmacht officers and their girls. They all left—very gradually, one or two couples at first, then three or four more, then everybody. Soon there was no one there but us.

"Where did they all go?" I asked.

Karl-Jesko chuckled like a mad jackal. "We frightened them off. When the wolves come out of the forest the lambs hide."

"Reminds me of my father," Otto mused. "Coming home from the slaughterhouse stinking of butchered hogs' blood. And the neighbors would sneer at him and call him the Lord High Executioner."

Karl-Jesko made a face. "Your father worked in a slaughterhouse, Oberführer Kasper?"

"My father owned the slaughterhouse, Sturmbannführer Weber. And nobody would shake his hand, but everybody would eat his meat. Pigfuckers, as Edmonde would say."

"Odd." Karl-Jesko stopped laughing for a moment.

"Odd? Why?"

"My father was an undertaker."

"What's so odd about that?"

"But here we are, Otto, both of us, hah-hah-hah, carrying on the family traditions. We must be obeying some secret law of heredity."

"It's true," I agreed. "My father was an actor, and here am I now, the leading lady of a freak show!"

We drank five bottles of *vin rosé* and Otto got sozzled. We carried him to the car, unconscious, and drove him back to the camp. We put him to bed, then sat in the living room drinking coffee.

Karl-Jesko became soggy and amorous and tried to kiss me. But I wasn't having any of that. I pushed him away.

"Please," he begged. "I have an ungodly erection!" He took my hand and put it on the bulge on his lap. "Just hold it for a moment."

"Hold it yourself."

"I do, a hundred times a day, but it needs a woman's touch."

I hadn't felt a man's penis since that long-ago afternoon in the Gestapo basement on the rue . . . the rue . . . What was the name of that street?

Sanders's body floated down the river of my mind. I suddenly had an urge to touch him again, to *feel* him, to tug him gently, to make him throb between my fingers and watch him spurt into the air. "Show it to me," I said.

"Really?"

"Take it out."

"Will you kiss it, Edmonde?"

"Perhaps."

"Have you ever done that before?"

"Oh, yes."

"Taken it in your mouth?"

"Yes."

"Does it disgust you?"

"Disgust me? No more than a banana."

"A banana!" Giggle-giggle-giggle. "A banana!"

"Stop braying, you'll wake up Otto."

He undid his belt and lowered his trousers. "Get ready," he cooed. "Here it is." He pulled something out of his underwear, something pliant and serpentine "Voilà!" He placed it in my hand. It was cold and rough and *hollow*. I looked down at it, astonished. It wasn't a penis. It was a knotted length of rubber hose! "See?" He bawled with laughter. "I lost it in Belgium," he hooted. "Isn't it silly? Have you ever seen anything more absurd? Hah! hah! ho! hah! ho!"

Then he sobbed.

I jumped up and pulled him to the door and threw him out into the yard.

The pigfucking monstrosity! What was the name of that street? The rue Balzac? The avenue Marceau? The rue François 1er? Shit! Was I losing my memory? No, the Gestapo pig in charge was named Ohlendorf. I remembered that. And his successor was that bison-faced leering simpleton—Rauss. No, Reitsch . . . no, *Roesch!* Yes, Roesch!

I went into the kitchen for a glass of water. A ghostly angel of requital was standing in the shadows by the pantry door, her eyes shooting flint sparks at me.

"You're all degenerates!" Faustina whispered.

I bowed and almost lost my balance. I must have been more sozzled than I thought I was. "Let me remind the prosecuting attorney," I declared, "that every-one has their little faults."

"SS riffraff," she said.

She was wearing one of my *chemises de nuit*. I could see her nipples through its sheerness and her new ripeness swelling its hems. I found myself moving to-ward her, my hands aching to caress her. I took her in my arms, pulled her against me, and kissed her lips as they opened in protest.

She spun away from me and ran into the pantry. I followed her, tearing at the gown. We fell across the sofa. I pinioned her against me and buried my face in her breasts.

"Leave me alone," she spat. "Get away from me."

Her elbow jabbed me, her nails gashed at me. We fell to the floor and she escaped again. I sprang after her. She backed into the kitchen. "Don't touch me," she hissed. "I don't want your hands on me."

"All right." I leaned against the door, breathless. "Tomorrow I'm sending you back to Zintsch."

"I knew you would."

"No, you didn't, because I didn't know myself until this minute."

"I knew. I've known all along you'd send me back. That's the only reason you brought me here."

"That's not true."

"It is, it is."

"Good night, Faustina." I went into my room, my head spinning. O misery! I felt putrid! Balls to them all! She came through the darkness behind me.

"Very well," she said. "Very well."

"Very well what?"

"What do you want me to do?"

"Get in bed. Take that off."

She pulled the *chemise de nuit* over her head and

crawled under the covers. I undressed quickly, spilling my clothes all over the floor. I slipped in beside her. Her feet were icy and her hands smelled like potatoes. The poor girl. The rue Galilée! That was the name of the street . . .

I took her in my arms and fell sound asleep, dreaming of snow.

The dog woke me just before dawn. I sat up. Faustina was curled beside me, snoring. The barking came from the orchard. I jumped out of bed and opened the shutter.

It was snowing.

A Doberman was standing on the far side of the fence, barking at the cottage.

Then Karl-Jesko went on leave. And Otto found a boy. Or, rather, Zintsch found him for him. In one of the trainloads of wretches was an eighteen- or nineteen-year-old lout named Haase, a Hitler Youth leader from Koblenz convicted of immorality.

In the morning I found him sitting in the kitchen drinking chocolate, wearing Otto's dressing gown and smoking one of my cigars.

He grinned at me. "Hello there. Who are you?"

He was a gawky, vacant-faced little thug with yak eyes and gold teeth. I called Zintsch and had him removed.

When Otto came home for lunch he was actually sober! Not only that, but he'd spent the entire morning out in the forest, supervising the latest burials in person. He was as happy as a bridegroom!

"Where's young Haase?" he chirped.

I delivered my ultimatum. "He's not going to live here, Otto."

"Why noth?"

"What?"

"I said why noth?"

I couldn't believe my ears. He was *lisping!* "First of all, there isn't enough room. I couldn't stand having the clod hanging around all day. Second, if a WVHA inspector should drop by, he might object to having our household turned into a homosexual ménage à trois."

"A ménagth à quatre, you mean. What about Faustina?"

"Faustina is ostensibly our domestic, Otto. Haase couldn't possibly pass for anything but what he actually is, a goddamned male whore."

"You're right." He waved the whole matter aside jauntily. "We planted fifty-five of them under the road this morning."

Zintsch put Haase to work in the stable, and thereafter he would come to the cottage only at night, after the curfew, and leave in the morning before I got up.

So there we were.

The nights were long. Otto and Haase would mumble and thrash and bump against the walls for hours. And in our bed, Faustina and I would lie side by side like cadavers. Her only comment was: "God will punish them."

I tried everything to thaw her out, but she wouldn't respond. Finally, in desperation, I forced open her legs and raped her with my tongue. Her body resisted me even as it spasmed. Then I pulled her down on top of me and impaled myself on her face. When her lips touched me they were like scythes slicing into the deep, deep, permeable strata of my frustration, releasing all my harassment in a glorious burst, making me geyser beautifully.

Her only comment was: "You're just an organ."

After that we would do it simultaneously, night after night two female machines lying with their mouths fixed in each other, like drills digging artesian wells. And when we climaxed it was as automatic as burglar alarms ringing.

Her only comment would be: "Is it over? Can I sleep now?"

When I tried to talk to her, she would snore. When I tried to kiss her cold nipples, she would cover them with her arms. When I tried to touch her cheek, she would turn her head away.

But one night I woke up warmed and thrilled and found her arms around me and her face on my shoulder. I wept like an idiot, but silently, so as not to disturb her. It made the whole world war worthwhile!

And every morning, just before sunrise, the dog barked outside the fence.

Mannstein recaptured Kharkov, and a thousand Russian tanks and guns were destroyed. Little Joseph made a special blaring radio broadcast and called it "the miracle of the Donets." In Gotha and Eisenach churchbells rang all day, and our prisoners stood at attention and hummed and whistled the third movement of Beethoven's Fifth. Then Guderian was appointed inspector general of all the Panzer armies and everyone began talking about Fall Zitadelle, which was going to end the war in the East in a single battle.

Nineteen forty-three was to be the Year of the German Phoenix.

"Oncth Stalin ith out o' the way," Otto lisped like a fop, "the poor Yankth and English will collapth."

"Otto," I warned, "if you continue to enuciate like that, I swear I'm going to hit you with Zintsch's club!"

"It amuses Will."

"Who?"

"Haase. His name is Willi."

"Well, it doesn't amuse me."

He looked at me coldly. "That's too bad."

"I'm telling you that for your own good, you fool!" I was furious, I don't know why. "You sound like a gruesome old fag!"

"I *am* a gruesome old fag, darling."

He was at that. Why should it exasperate me and what right had I to complain? I was responsible for this outlandish marriage, not him. For better or for worse, ugh, in sickness and in health. "But O! the pity of it, Iago!"

"Do you know what Will calls me?" he sniggered. "Grandpa!"

Well, I thought, perhaps the war *would* be over this year and then I could divorce him and, and, and what? And, in the meantime, he'd stopped drinking. That at least was positive.

Summer came to Thuringia. The branches of the peach trees in the orchard sprouted. Roses camouflaged the barbed wire in the yard, vines grew over the fence, and bogs of dust rose from the camp every time anyone moved.

And day by day our wandering road wound through the forest like a lost caravan, leaving the endless pavement of graves in its wake.

And the clocks ticked and the hours tolled.

5:00. The barking dog wakes me. *5:30.* The loudspeaker wakes the prisoners and they march to work, whistling like the wind blowing through an empty house. *6:00.* Haase leaves the cottage, slamming the back door defiantly. Otto has breakfast alone in the kitchen, then shaves and leaves too. *6:30.* As soon as he's gone, Faustina crawls out of bed and takes a bath. *7:00.* I have my shower and dress. Faustina and I sit silently in the kitchen drinking ersatz coffee and eating crackers. I listen to the morning news on the radio, from Berlin, then Vienna, then Budapest, then Brussels. Faustina reads and rereads the back copies of *Marie-Claire* I brought from Paris. The advertisements fascinate her. *"C'est surtout aux femmes qui ne peuvent supporter aucune autre gaine qu'il faut recommander la gaine SCANDALE." "Mon mari ne pouvait en croire ses yeux! Il dit que je parais 10 ans plus jeune!" "J'ai maigri et mon fiancé me trouve plus élégante!" "Attention à votre INTESTIN—Fructines-Vichy."* I watch the lights change in her eyes, knowing exactly when she's going to laugh or smile or scowl. I love girls' eyes! I love the way they widen and narrow and wink and squint and blaze with green and blue and gray and beige. *7:30.* The gypsy gardener is digging and clipping things all around the house, mowing and watering the grass, burning rubbish, sweeping the walks. His presence is loathsome. I wait until I'm sure he's in the front yard and escape via the back door—or vice versa. *8:00.* I take a horse from the stable and ride to the lake. If I'm in the mood I undress and swim. On the second of June a watersnake bit me on the back of the arm. I couldn't suck the wound and was certain I'd be dead within the hour. I sat down on the bank and waited, terrified and resigned and angry and indifferent. I smoked a cigar. I masturbated. I prayed. I dived into the water and swam around. Nothing happened. I dressed and mounted the horse and galloped as far as the highway and watched a column of new Mark V Panther tanks pass. *10:30.* Back at the stable I turn the horse over to Haase. He smirks at me, his gold teeth like a mouthful of tacks. I walk through the camp. The barracks are empty and smelly; the Clubs are collecting the night's corpses and piling them

in a wagon. Two male suicides, four old women and
two gypsies. *11:00.* Faustina has another cup of coffee
waiting for me. The beds are made, the laundry is
hanging on a clothesline in the orchard, the floors are
scrubbed. I change from my riding clothes into a
uniform and read for an hour. I found a stack of novels
in English in a secondhand bookshop in Eisenach, so
I've put *Anthony Adverse* aside again and am now
reading—oh, scores of things!—*The Wisdom of Father
Brown, Fer-de-Lance, Ivanhoe, Northwest Passage,
Oliver Twist, All This and Heaven Too, The Daughter
of Fu Manchu, The Egyptian Cross Mystery, Rebecca,
Murder on the Orient Express, The Warlord of Mars,
U.S.A.* by John Dos Passos, and *The Web and the
Rock* by Thomas Wolfe. *Noon.* Otto and I have lunch
together. Then he usually takes a nap before going to
the office. Now that he's sober and steadfast, he spends
all morning out on the road and all afternoon at his
desk. Now and then he sneaks over to the stable to
visit his beloved "Will." The SS guards call them Tris-
tan and Isolde. *13:30.* On certain days, if there's a
vehicle available, I drive to Gotha. There are three
cinemas there and a department store. I see a film, then
do some shopping, then have pastry in a tearoom. As
I walk through the streets everybody stares at me. They
know who I am and where I'm from. In the store I'm
served immediately by the manager himself. When I
enter the tearoom all conversation ceases. I'm given the
best table and a special menu to choose from. The
other customers get up and leave. Only in the darkness
of the movie am I anonymous and unobtrusive. I watch
insipid shit like Hilde Krahl in *Anuschka,* or Margit
Symo in *Styx,* or Laura Solari in *Guépéou*—awful pictures made for halfwits! But I wouldn't miss them for
anything. One afternoon Papa sat down beside me. He

slumped back, as he always does, and put his knees
on the seat in front of him. And suddenly all the years
vanished magically and I was a little girl again, with
a new soul. I longed for the film to end so we could go
home together, and I prayed it would go on and on
so we could sit like that forever. Happiness choked my
throat. I couldn't swallow. The screen blurred with
tears. I lay coiled in my seat against him, like a sleepy
python stuffed with a huge lump of bliss. An immense
donjon of certitude closed around me and I slept for
eons in peace—Edmonde the Princess of Tranquillity,
serene in her sepulcher built by her father, the King of
Love. Then the lights came on and I awoke. And he
was gone. *14:00*. But I hardly ever go to Gotha now.
After lunch Faustina and I take out the Ouija board
and try to communicate with any errant spirits who
happen to be hovering about. She receives messages
from someone named Alecto, short cryptic communi-
qués such as "Youwillbe" or "Itwillcome." I get nothing but gibberish—"Uwkmvjazmsiqbe" and the like.
Twice though, two days in a row, the same sentence
came through clearly, chilling me: "Bewareofsteps."
14:30. I take my Lüger and go for a walk in the
woods. I'm determined to find that goddamned dog
and kill him. No matter what trail or pathway I follow
I inevitably come upon our Flying Dutchman road and
its latest cargo of dead, piled up like firewood. And
there are the prisoners, toiling with the earnest diligence
of coolies, digging and chopping and sawing as if their
senseless labor had some meaning, as if they were going
home at the end of the day to their wives and husbands
and children with a paycheck. Instead, where will they
go? Back behind the fence, into their fetid barracks to
eat watery soup containing not even enough calories to
nourish a cockroach, and perhaps to die of malnutrition

and exhaustion before dawn. Why don't they try to escape? Thousands of them are guarded by only five or six sentries, Zintsch, and a few Clubs. Are they waiting for some Spartacus to come and rally them? Why doesn't one of them at least brain Zintsch with a shovel? How can they abide that ghoul? As I watch, a sunburned girl drops dead. Her body is dragged beside the other corpses. *16:00*. I report to the office to help Otto and the clerks with the paperwork. The mortality rate is appalling!

21 June	92
22 June	120
23 June	85
24 June	109
25 June	72
26 June	94
27 June	63

18:30. The haunted-house whistling approaches the camp. Then the humming can be heard. It's Schubert this evening. The "Unfinished" Symphony in B Minor. The funeral procession of prisioners marches in through the gate. Zintsch makes them stand in formation for an hour while he and the Clubs smoke their cigarette rations. Now it's execution time. Three men from Barracks 41 have lost their wooden shoes. A woman from Barracks 65 has lost one wooden shoe. A woman from Barracks 62 has broken an ax. A man from Barracks 8 has broken a saw. A man from Barracks 22 and a woman from Barracks 86 were caught in the woods fornicating. A gypsy from Barracks 100 was caught picking berries. Two men from Barracks 34, a man from Barracks 46, and a woman from Barracks 58 overslept at reveille and failed to answer roll call.

They're all dragged to the center of the parade ground
and batted to death by the Clubs. Zintsch kills the
gypsy because he knows I'm watching. *19:30*. A bath,
schnapps, a cigar, and *The Daughter of Fu Manchu*.
I finish it. There are seven or eight volumes in the
series: *The Mask of Fu Manchu, The Shadow of Fu
Manchu, The Bride of Fu Manchu,* and more—I'd
love to read them all. What now? Should I return to
Anthony Adverse or begin *Northwest Passage? 20:00*.
Faustina has prepared *tomates farcies aux champignons*.
Otto eats like a hog. "Will" and mass murder become
him. Gorgonzola cheese and an apple cake for dessert.
20:30. Zintsch knocks humbly on the door to report
that one of his Clubs has the clap. Since sexual inter-
course with the prisoners is forbidden, this automati-
cally forfeits the fellow's guard privileges and Otto
orders him to be transferred to the work gang. He'll
be defunct within twenty-four hours. Ex-Clubs *never*
survive the first day on the road. *21:30*. There's a play
on the radio, Euripides' *Medea,* with a cast of un-
known Bavarians. The chorus's opening lines are dis-
concerting: "If the trees in Pelion Forest had never
been chopped down to build the *Argo,* then Jason never
would have sailed to Colchis to seek the Golden
Fleece and there would be no story to tell." What a
strange way of interpreting events! It makes everything
we do have some bearing on what will, or will not,
happen to us. To forebode the future, one has to be
a chess master, working out a million moves in advance. Who can think that far ahead? It's impossible!
Papa once owed the Munich Income Revenue Bureau
seventy thousand marks. He went to see some tax functionary and told him he couldn't pay because he hadn't
worked for a year and was broke. And the functionary
replied, "That's your problem, my friend, you should

have taken certain precautions." How could Papa have
known in advance that he would be unemployed for a
year? And even if he had known, what "precautions"
could he have taken? According to the newspapers,
Munich was bombed twice this week. I hope the
Revenue Office was pulverized to shit! *23:00*. I go to
bed. Then Faustina comes into my room and undresses
in the moonlight. My mouth waters as I watch her
unveil her hips and her legs, then her shoulders and
breasts. She slides between the sheets, turning her back,
avoiding me. I push my stomach against her derriere
and kiss her spine and neck. She shakes her body, like
a horse twitching a fly from its croup. It's her affirma-
tion of rejection. No matter. She's here, filling my arms
and my mouth, whether she likes it or not. We hear
Haase arrive and go prowling into Otto's room, trip-
ping against a kitchen chair and rattling all the doorknobs. They're at it immediately, filling the house with
bedspring noises. *Thump-thump, mumble-mumble.*
Faustina snorts and shakes her head. I turn her over
gently and taste her nipples. She's as rigid as a girder,
but her flesh will respond in a moment, rebelling
against the bondage of her interdiction. Yes, here we
are . . . the first involuntary tremor! My fingers are ten
Roman legions crossing the Euphrates to invade Parthia. I am Caesar at the gates of Alesia and Scipio
Africanus entering Carthage. All my foes are prostrate
before me and my thighs are on the face of Parthenos.
And now her lips are honoring me reluctantly. After
a mass execution her tongue is always just a bit more
cooperative than usual. If I'm lucky, she might even
moan tonight. *5:00*. The barking dog wakes me . . .

Karl-Jesko came back from leave with the latest news
from the Eastern Front. Fall Zitadelle turned out to be

a fiasco. It was a clumsy frontal attack on massed Russian artillery and trenches at Kursk. All our splendid new Panther tanks were mangled.

The war wouldn't end that year.

Then I began to notice the thefts. *Little* things vanished. Eggs, apples, grapes, a pack of cigarettes, candy, biscuits. It was the gypsy gardener, of course. I watched his every move but couldn't catch him in the act. I summoned one of the female Clubs—I think she was a female, but she had a face like an elk—and had her guard the house when I wasn't there. Still things continued to disappear. A comb, a spool of thread, matches, two melons, a pear.

"What difference does it make?" Otto complained. "Stop making an issue of it."

"Just turn him over to Zintsch," Karl-Jesko suggested.

"No. I want to catch him first." But I couldn't. The pigfucker was too cunning.

Then I forgot all about the matter when a telephone call came from Berlin. It was from the Reichsicherheits Hauptamt (RSHA), and one of Himmler's top aides, a man named Eichmann, was on the line. He informed Otto that henceforth Gotha would be placed under the direct command of something called "Amt VI."

Neither of us had any idea what this branch was, so we asked Karl-Jesko. When he heard the news he turned splotchy. "We're in for it," he warned. "It's one of RSHA's more lurid projects."

"What is its function?" Otto asked.

"Dealing with minorities."

"Dealing with them in what way?" I asked.

"The Amt VI way," he giggled. "We'll have to widen the road."

And a few days later our first trainload of Jews arrived—twelve thousand of them! Men, women, children, Poles, Hungarians, Germans, French, Russians, Italians—an incredible rabble of scarecrows, most of them hardly able to walk. They filled all the barracks and were too feeble to join the work gang, or even to assemble for roll call.

Zintsch was flustered. "What am I to *do* with them?" he bleated.

The supply sergeant too was flurried. "I don't have enough uniforms for so many people," he announced. "They'll have to wear the clothes they came in and that's against the regulations."

Six thousand of them died the first night. We were all accustomed to multiple death, but this sudden massiveness of corpses shook us. The "able-bodied" prisoners spent three days burying them. Our road leaped ahead two kilometers in one bound.

The following week another train pulled into the station with eleven thousand more.

"God!" Otto wailed. "I just cannot accommodate all these creatures."

"You'd better," Karl-Jesko crooned, "or they'll find somebody who can. Remember Kursk."

Kursk, yes. It hung over us like a shroud. After our defeat there, the Wehrmacht was in full retreat all over Russia, and the menace of being sent to the East was more dire than ever.

That night Otto got sozzled for the first time in months. He and Haase had a wild party and danced and sang and frolicked until three o'clock. The next morning their love nest was a swamp of vomit and schnapps. Ugh! Faustina refused to touch the mess, so I had Zintsch and his Clubs clean it up.

There were now over twenty-five thousand prisoners

jammed into the barracks, including the Gentile inmates. To make room for the next shipment, at least two-thirds of them had to be "evicted" and their bodies eliminated.

Amt VI solved the first problem. They sent us five enormous buses, each capable of containing two hundred passengers. They were long, broad vehicles without windows and on their roofs were bolted large tanks filled—as one of the RSHA technicians who brought them explained—with carbon monoxide.

They were parked in the railroad yard, and when the next train arrived, a thousand Jews were immediately put aboard the machines, gassed, and then driven off into the forest, where their corpses were unloaded and buried. Then back to the station for a thousand more, and so on, throughout the day. Thus, in five or six hours, ten thousand of them could be annihilated without any effort whatsoever.

Karl-Jesko solved the second problem. In the woods was a nameless creek, always dry during the summer months and only a few centimeters deep in winter. It occurred to him that it would make an excellent roadbed, so he simply excavated its muddy bottom and buried the bodies along its course. This avoided the back-breaking necessity of chopping down and uprooting trees and clearing away undergrowth. Furthermore, picks and shovels could dig an ample trench in the soft earth in a matter of minutes. Working continuously, two or three, or even four or five, layers of corpses could be inhumed at the rate of one hundred every half-hour.

Zintsch and the Clubs were put in charge of the buses, and the work gang, fortified with extra food rations and a bonus of beer, was responsible for the unloading and digging.

Train after train arrived in the station, sometimes two a month, but the camp population was always kept down to a reasonable six or seven thousand.

Otto had a month's leave due, starting on the first of January. But on New Year's Eve he was so sozzled he collapsed and had to spend three weeks in a clinic in Gotha. I went to Berlin alone.

It was dismal. The whole city was a bombed junk-heap. Entire streets were gone, all the shops and the-aters and cinemas and restaurants were closed, and ninety percent of the people were living in cellars.

I had lunch with Heinrich, dinner and cocktails with Hermann, and spent an afternoon with little Joseph and Frau Goebbels inaugurating a War Veterans' Center.

They were all firmly convinced that victory was just around the corner.

Heinrich: It's simply a question of persevering. The Führer knows what he's doing.

Hermann: Wait until you see the new fighters we're building!

Joseph: The American-British-Russian alliance cannot last another year. Capitalists and imperialists on the one hand, Communists-Marxists on the other, pah! They'll be at one another's throats before spring. We're expecting peace feelers from Washington and London any day now.

Frau Goebbels: I'll be so glad when this terrible war is over so I can dress properly again and take my children to the seaside.

Their optimism was sickening.

I couldn't find Lisa, and Eva was in Munich. After a few boring days of just wandering around I went back to Gotha.

I arrived at three o'clock in the afternoon. A taxi drove me down the highway as far as the lane and I walked the rest of the way to the camp. I almost didn't get there.

The trees were bare, all the green was gone from the forest, the wind was scented with ice. A puddle on the ground was frozen. A dog barked.

I stopped and listened.

I knew the sound. It was the Doberman. He was somewhere on the bridle path, over by the lake.

I hurried on, shaken. I wasn't armed. If he caught me out in the open like that he would tear me to pieces.

He barked again, much closer.

Run, Edmonde!

I ran. How fast could he move? It was about two kilometers to the gate. I came around the last turning. The rest of the way would be straight ahead,

Hold him off, Papa. Give me just three minutes.

All right, keep moving!

I dropped my valise, pulled off my overcoat and threw it aside, and removed my shoes.

Another bark, just behind me.

I raced along the lane with wings on my heels. The trees soared past me. The phone poles cantered by at my side.

I flew across the creek bridge, then through a clearing, then into a tunnel of naked branches.

The barking followed me, louder and louder. I could hear paws scraping swiftly against the hard earth.

Faster, Edmonde!

I didn't look back.

Five hundred meters more. I hoped I wouldn't have a heart attack. There was the fence! My lungs were bursting. I could hear the monster growling.

Then I was before the gate and it swung open, its

hinges squealing. The sentry gaped at me. "What's the matter, Frau Kasper?"

"Nothing." I tried to smile. "Just keeping fit."

I sent him back to pick up my shoes, the valise, and my coat. As I came into the driveway two buses passed. Their doors were open and they were empty. The killing was over for the day. I wondered how Otto was getting along. I'd have to do something about that pigfucking dog! Of course it wasn't the same Doberman . . . Naima Josephson's beast . . . no. My head was spinning. Another empty bus passed. And yet, the postmaster in Bad Tölz, Herr Lahse, had a police dog. It had once followed him all the way to Munich.

The cottage looked like a witch's hut, a shack in a glade in the Woodland of Grief. I went into the living room and sat down on the sofa, panting.

Something was wrong. *What?* The vibrations were different. The door of the closet was open. So was the cupboard. There was an odor in the air . . . a gypsy stink . . .

I looked down. A burlap sack was sitting on the rug before me. I reached over and opened it, emptying it onto the floor. Out of it spilled a bar of soap, several cigars, a bottle of schnapps, a jar of olives, a box of crackers. Booty!

I jumped up. *He was here!* Inside the house! I had him! I took my Lüger from the desk drawer and went into my room.

Faustina was on her hands and knees by the bed. Haase was standing before her, pulling her hair, his penis in her mouth. The gypsy was behind her, on her back, pushing himself into her derriere.

They all looked at me unconcernedly, casually, as if I were a minor intrusion, a mere passerby of no real importance to their merrymaking. Oddly enough, I wasn't outraged. I understood immediately what they were up to. This was their pitiful vengeance. Haase was getting even with Otto, Faustina was getting even with me, the gypsy was getting even with all of us—he came toward me.

I knew what he was going to do next. I read it in his falcon eyes. He would be under the creek road tomorrow and he intended to take me with him.

I shot him in the face.

Faustina and Haase scrambled past me and ran out into the kitchen.

I went back into the living room and smoked a cigar.

Karl-Jesko laughed and laughed. " 'Love is a Bohemian bird,' " he sang, " 'that nobody can tame.' Shall I put them on a bus?"

"No. On the work gang. Let them dig themselves to death."

"No doubt they will, and quickly too. The creek bed is frozen solid."

"Good."

"Otto will miss Will."

"We'll tell him he just languished away during his absence."

And that's exactly what happened, almost. Haase died three days later, surprising everyone that he could last that long. I rode out to the creek on horseback every morning and afternoon to watch him perish. He finally succumbed, his carcass occupying no more space in the ditch than a child's.

Faustina, though, was a survivor. Zintsch assigned her, first, to the crew unloading bodies from the buses, and when that had no effect he put her to work smashing the frozen, steely topsoil of the creek with a sledgehammer. She lost weight and most of her teeth—when one of the Clubs struck her across the jaw with a truncheon—but remained as sturdy as an ox.

Otto came back from the clinic, pale and soggy and wan. He spent most of his time in bed, taking his temperature and swallowing pills. I found another boy for him, a chubby pretty little Bulgarian of about sixteen.

I also took care of my own needs. From the various shipments I would pick a girl—or sometimes two girls and once three—selecting only the best specimens, naturally, and keeping them with me for a week or a month. Charlotte, Elvira, Dagmar, Christabel, Hanna, Alexandra, Govanna, Valerina—and dozens of others.

When I tired of them I made certain they were not destroyed by Zintsch and his friends. I found jobs for them in the kitchen or the stable or the office or the supply warehouse. I even turned one of the barracks into a dispensary so several of them could become nurses. (It eventually flourished as a brothel for the SS guards.)

The only one who made any impression on me was Mina. She was a Jewess from Amsterdam. Her husband had been a diamond merchant, one of the richest men in the Netherlands. She had no idea where he was by then or what became of her two daughters.

She was as sad as Niobe and in bed more sensitive and clement than anyone I'd ever known. We would lie in each other's arms whispering our tenderness all night long, each of us always knowing just when and where to touch and kiss, to give and receive, to yield and deny.

She was lovely, a blessing, my providence and my unction.

I lost her.

The Doberman came out of the woods only once

that winter, although I had been waiting for him every night. The barking woke me at five o'clock in the morning on Saint Patrick's Day. I jumped out of bed, took my Lüger from the commode, and opened the shutter. I saw the black shadow moving in the snow and fired at it.

The dog streaked off into the trees. The shadow remained on the ground.

I went out to the yard.

It was Mina. She was lying by the fence, her hand extended through the wire holding a bowl of porridge. The bullet had pierced the back of her neck, almost severing her head.

I refused to put her in the creek. I found a secluded glen, deep in the woods, and buried her there. I dug the grave myself.

Only Papa and I came to her funeral.

He hid in a grove behind me, and when I sang,

> De profundis clamavi ad te,
> Domine, Domine, exaudi vocem
> meam. Fiant aures auae
> intendéntes in vocem
> deprecationis meae,

he answered,

> Si iniquitates observaveris,
> Domine, Domine, quis sustinébit?

It was because of Mina that I reprieved Faustina. My rage drained away, melting with the snow. I took her off the work gang and made her a Club. Zintsch foamed at the mouth with resentment but dared not protest.

Poor Faustina. She turned into one of the most

malevolent furies in the compound. The other prisoners, because of her irascibility and her broken teeth, called her Frau Fang.

Once again I immediately understood what motivated her. Spring was in the air; the wind blew the aroma of hope through the fence. Beyond the forest, beyond Gotha, beyond Thuringia, could be heard the faint crumbling of a dying nation. Everyone knew that we were losing the war. And Faustina's sudden viciousness was inspired simply by the desire to *endure* at all costs until the day our defeat came marching into the camp to liberate her.

Then it was April, then May and June.

The soil of the creek thawed and the digging was easier. The trains arrived regularly, every other week. The long lines of Jews boarded the buses and were driven away.

Otto emerged from the cottage and began going to the office every day, tottering but sober. Amt VI promoted him to Brigadeführer. But nobody was fooled. The commander of the camp was really Karl-Jesko. He was everywhere at once, darting like a happy, demented ringmaster, in the station yard when the trains pulled in, on the roofs of the buses fiddling with the gas tanks, at the creek supervising the digging, in the office sending out reports—forever giggling and cracking jokes, always hilarious and hysterical.

He found a score of musicians among the prisoners and requisitioned instruments for them somewhere. So now the humming and whistling was replaced by a full symphonic orchestra playing Wagner and Verdi, Strauss and Donizetti.

He also found himself a mascot. In one of the shipments was a tall, skinny Negro, a Senegalese POW captured in Italy. Karl-Jesko took him under his wing,

garbed him in a loincloth and feather headdress, gave
him a shield and spear, and appointed him his personal bodyguard. The sight of the two of them scuttling
about the camp, the one-eyed German clown and the
black naked plumed spearman, made even the Jews
laugh, occasionally.

And he always knew all the news long before anyone else. It was from him we learned that an American
army had debarked in Normandy and was marching on
Paris.

"It can't be true!" Otto protested. "All the Americans are in Hawaii fighting the Japanese!"

"They have over twenty divisions in France," Karl-
Jesko insisted. "All motorized."

"And what about the Russians?" I asked.

"They're on this side of the Dniester rolling toward
Rumania," he chuckled. "If they keep coming, the next
time Himmler threatens to send us to the Eastern Front,
hah-hah, he'll probably be referring to Leipzig!"

"You're just being fanciful!" Otto protested. "You're
a damned irresponsible gossipmonger!"

In July another sensational rumor made the rounds.
A group of Wehrmacht officers had attempted to
assassinate Hitler and expel the Nazi regime in a coup
d'état.

For once Karl-Jesko was taken by surprise. Otto
was dumbfounded. "Enemy propaganda!" he gasped.
"They're trying to undermine our morale."

I didn't believe it myself. The officers' corps couldn't
have changed that radically since '33. The pigfuckers
were still incapable of energetic action.

But I was wrong. Little Joseph came on the radio
and confirmed the story. He announced the arrest and
summary execution of scores of generals and colonels.

The dam was really cracking!

Otto and Karl-Jesko, and Otto's Bulgarian and Karl-Jesko's Senegalese slave, all got sozzled together in the orchard and spent the night passed out in the grass.

I sat alone in the living room, the Lüger on my lap, waiting for the Doberman to come back.

The Americans entered Paris in August. The prisoners *knew*. One morning I found the name EISENHOWER printed on the wall of the cottage in red, white, and blue chalk. (General Eisenhower was the commander-in-chief of the Allied armies in the West.)

Then the British took Brussels. And the Russians crossed the River Siretul and zipped through Bucharest toward the Danube.

"Thank heaven we have nothing to fear from our enemies," Karl-Jesko quipped. "We're just innocent roadbuilders."

Then I received a letter from Lisa, forwarded to the camp from my old WVHA office in Berlin. Her husband had been implicated in the officers' plot and arrested. She asked me to find out where he was interned so she could visit him. I could get in touch with her at her mother's address in Dresden.

I phoned the Amt VI main bureau in Berlin and talked to Eichmann himself. He informed me that General Heye had been shot by a firing squad in Colmar on the second of August.

Jesus!

I tried to call Lisa in Dresden, but the line was out. I wrote to her instead.

Dear Marie-José,
I've made inquiries and learned . . .

Marie-José? What on earth was I thinking of? Shit! I tore up the page and began again.

Dear Lisa,

I've made inquiries and learned that your husband was released from prison on the second of August, completely exonerated. He's on the Saar front now, fighting the American Third Army. You'll probably hear from him shortly, if you haven't already. As for me, I . . .

I filled two pages with lies and chitchat and false hope.

That night I went into the office and, using the chief clerk's mimeograph machine, typed out a set of identity papers and a travel permit for a civilian named Fräulein Hildegarde Steuben. I stenciled them and covered them with official stamps and initials. Back in the cottage I packed them in a small overnight bag together with a skirt, sweater, raincoat, stockings, underwear, *Anthony Adverse,* a pair of shoes, and 150,000 marks.

The next day I drove to Gotha. I mailed Lisa's letter and checked the bag in the railroad station depository. I also bought a secondhand bicycle and checked that too.

As my *Dictionary of American Slang* would say, "Better to be safe than sorry."

9

THE NEGRO FROZE TO DEATH in November. The Bulgarian died of pneumonia. Food was scarce and four thousand prisoners died.

Otto survived, pickled in schnapps all winter. But O horror! he was lisping again. He sibilated and hissed like a viper all day long, until I thought I'd go mad. In fact, on several occasions I seriously considered murdering him. It was ghastly! He was turning into a psychopathic cocotte, powdering his cheeks, painting his eyes, rouging his lips. Once I found him playing with himself in front of a mirror, wearing my stockings and slip. And every night he'd put on a pair of ragged filthy black pajamas and pretend he was a prisoner. I would have to play the role of a Club and beat him with a belt, forcing him to clean the kitchen or scrub the bathroom floor or polish my boots or some such thing. If I was too tired to indulge in this nonsense, he would rage with pique and wet his bed.

I phoned Amt VI again and talked to Eichmann, telling him that this couldn't go on. He'd have to find a new commander. He assured me everything would be all right. All officers, he said, engaged in "regulating the Jewish population parameter" passed through these phases of instability. It was due, usually, to overwork and acute conscientiousness. He recommended sleeping pills and exercise.

Shit!

As for Karl-Jesko, as usual, he thrived on disaster like a ghoul. True to form he immediately found a practical method of disposing of the dead prisoners. He had the work gang haul hundreds of logs in from the forest and stack them transversely in the middle of the parade ground. Then he ignited them in a titanic pyre and burned the bodies in the flames. The stink was appalling, but the heat of the fire warmed the entire camp.

"Facilis descensus Averno!" he raved.

Luckily, no trains arrived. Fortresses bombed the railroad daily, thus sparing us the ordeal of digging up the creek.

In December an SS Panzer Army counterattacked the Americans in the Ardennes. We were almost wiped out. The few Panther and Tiger tanks we had left were lost and entire divisions dissolved to nothingness.

And the pigfucking Russians were now on the Vistula.

Ugh!

On New Year's Eve the Doberman got through the fence. In the morning I found his pawprints in the snow just outside my window. I spent the whole day following his tracks all over the camp—from the cottage to the stable, from the stable to the station yard, from the yard back to the cottage, then to the barracks.

I finally convinced myself that the prisoners must have captured and eaten him. (Two weeks ago Zintsch had caught several of them cooking the leg of a corpse.)

Then an absolutely abominable catastrophe struck us. The temperature suddenly rose to eighteen degrees, the snow melted overnight, and it began to rain.

It rained for five days.

The creek became a roaring torrent and all the dead were washed out of their mass grave into the lake.

It was unbelievable!

Thousands and thousands of bodies surfaced, floating in the water like algae as far as the eye could see, in an immense, clogged Sargasso Sea of green faces and decomposing limbs and feet and bloated stomachs.

Karl-Jesko stood on the shore, giggling and howling, "Look, there's Will! Ho! There's a Club! Yeee! There's a gypsy!"

Otto came down from the camp to see the spectacle. He swooned like a maiden.

Faustina and Zintsch took one look and fled in terror.

I myself tried to react to the grisly sight but could not. I was just numb. For some crazed reason or other I kept remembering the year I spent in prison, the summer of the elections. I recalled the results clearly. The Social Democrats had gained 133 seats in the Reichstag, the Catholic Center, 75, the Communists, 89, and the NSDAP, 230.

And I remembered too the stooped, uncombed man waiting for me out on the roadside when I was released: "My name is Adolf Hitler."

Eichmann telephoned Otto that night, ordering him to stop the executions, to get rid of the buses, and to "conceal the results"—his very words—"of the Amt VI program." We had a month to comply with his instructions.

Otto was staggered. "What does he mean?" he blubbered. "What does he mean? What is all this? What am I supposed to do?"

Karl-Jesko was no help in this emergency. He had

turned into a chortling, hah-hah-hahing cretin, totally aberrant.

And to make matters worse, the temperature dropped again and the lake froze, refrigerating the frightful mass in the water, fixing them there solidly until the next thaw, their arms and heads and legs sticking out of the ice from shore to shore. "Concealing the results" was quite out of the question.

Then I received another letter from Lisa, begging me to come to Berlin and see her. She was living in the Harnack House.

I decided to go, delighted to have an excuse to leave.

Otto was panic-stricken. "You can't go running off now!" He'd lost his lisp, thank God! "You have to help me organize things!"

"Organize what?"

"Everything!"

"But what?"

"We have to do something about those bodies!"

"There's nothing we can do, Otto, until the ice melts. I'll only be gone a few days. You can manage without me until Saturday or Sunday."

I took one of the buses and left at midnight.

The roads were cold and black and empty. Thuringia was an abandoned icehouse in a no man's land as desolate as Siberia. I drove all night without passing a single vehicle. But in all the villages ashcans were piled neatly on the curbsides, waiting for the morning garbagemen. That was reassuring. Perhaps that was the solution for our disposal problem at the camp. We could wrap up all the corpses as garbage and just put them out on the streets of Gotha for collection.

It wasn't until I reached the Elbe, at dawn, that I saw the first refugees—endless columns of them, men, women, children, horses, carts, wagons, bicycles—fleeing from the North and the East, all swarming west toward the Americans.

A Volkssturm rifleman on a roadblock told me that the Russians had passed Danzig, Poznań, and Breslau and were advancing to the Oder. Shit! Doom was no longer forthcoming. It was upon us, breathing down the backs of our necks.

I drove into Berlin at eight o'clock in the morning and was immediately arrested by the Gestapo. I was accused of deserting my post in the presence of the enemy. Though my papers were in order, I probably would have been lynched from the nearest lamppost if it hadn't been for the bus.

I took the officer in charge of the detachment aside and told him I was on a special mission.

"What kind of mission?" he asked suspiciously. He was a fat lout in a leather topcoat, wearing a Lüger strapped to his wide hips like the sheriff of Tombstone. "Everybody's on some kind of special mission these days. What's your story?"

"I'm to drive certain people south," I whispered confidentially. "Important people from the chancellery."

"The chancellery?" He was hooked. "Let me see your orders."

"My orders are verbal."

"We'll see about that. Come on."

We climbed into the bus together and drove on through the rubble. I was really in the soup. I hadn't counted on his coming with me. What in the name of Christ would I do when we got to the chancellery?

But I needn't have worried. The first person I saw as we drove up to the gate was Bormann, urinating against a pillbox. He strolled over to the bus, buttoning his trousers. "Heil, Comrade Kerrl!" he called. "What do you want?"

"I've come to join you in the barricades, comrade."

He laughed. When the Gestapo nitwit saw I was on speaking terms with no less a personage than the party leader, he excused himself and scurried away into the ruins.

Bormann led me across the garden and down the deep, deep steps into the Führer's bunker. "When will the war be over?" I asked him.

"Yesterday," he said.

"Bormann, do you remember the day you came to visit me in Landshut prison?"

"I remember, Kerrl." He smiled. "Are you thinking what I'm thinking by any chance?"

"Maybe. What are you thinking?"

"That we'd all probably be a lot better off today if we'd lost that goddamned election."

We went through the steel door into the labyrinth.

The dim underground passages were as crowded as the U-bahn. Clerks and secretaries and messengers went flitting by, shouting and dropping papers. Little Joseph came trotting out of an office, bellowing for a telephone. Wehrmacht and Luftwaffe officers passed grimly, carrying briefcases and maps. Heinrich was there, marching around with a bevy of SS generals. When he saw me he came over and put his hands on my shoulders. He was weeping.

"He's decided to remain in Berlin," he declared.

I was taken aback. "Who has?"

"The Führer. He refuses to desert the capital."

Bormann cursed. "Where did you hear that?"

"He told me so himself."

"When?"

"Just now."

Bormann pushed past us and went into an inner corridor.

"We must be brave." Heinrich pulled off his glasses and wiped his eyes. "We must not falter now, Edmonde."

"No, sir."

"We must prevail."

"Yes, sir."

"There's still hope. Reinhardt is counterattacking Zhukov from Stettin. And Sepp Dietrich, God bless him, will attack across the Neisse on Konev's front." He sighed. "They'll surely stabilize the situation."

"Of course they will, sir." What was he talking about? I couldn't inhale. The air was like mud.

"Edmonde!'

Hermann loomed in front of me, wild-eyed, enormous, dripping with perspiration. "Is it true?" He squeezed my arms with his chubby fists. "You've brought a bus to take him to Munich?"

How the hell did he find out about that so quickly! "Yes, I can take a hundred and fifty or two hundred passengers with me." This was becoming ludicrous! Hitler and his general staff escaping from Berlin in an Amt VI gas chamber! Lunatic!

"Thank heavens!" Hermann kissed my cheek, smearing me with sweat. "You're an angel of mercy!"

"He won't go," Heinrich snapped. "He's staying here."

"Here?' Hermann lunged toward him, all his blubber trembling. "In this sewer? That's ridiculous!"

"This sewer, Herr Reichsmarschall, is our Thermopylae."

"Eh?" Hermann blinked, his jowls twitching. "Correct me if I'm wrong, Herr Himmler, but as I recall, uh . . ." He was drugged, I knew the symptoms. "Thermopylae? Wasn't that where the defeated Persians were

all massacred and the victorious Spartans extermi-
nated?"

"It was a sacrificial battle, Herr Göring. So is our
struggle here."

"And may I ask, Heinrich, if you intend to take part
in the struggle and the sacrifice?"

"My orders are to proceed north to Bremen."

"I see."

A loudspeaker called my name. "Frau Kasper! Will
Frau Kasper please report to the Führer's quarters.
Thank you."

Hermann gripped my arm again. "Try to talk some
sense into him, Edmonde. He has to get out of this
trap before it's too late."

I walked deeper into the maze, passing a hive of
niches crowded with maniacs shrieking into telephones.
In a back gallery I found a girl sound asleep at a
switchboard. In one of the offices music was playing
and several couples were dancing. I recognized the
tune. It was from a Fred Astaire film.

> Must you dance
> Every dance
> With the same fortunate man?
> You have danced with him since the
>   music began.
> Won't you change partners
> And dance with me?

Mon Dieu! Ginger Rogers and Fred Astaire whirling
nimbly across white terraces and up and down white
stairs and in and out of huge white doorways and past
white fountains . . . How lithe and exquisite they were!
I loved them! And their songs were so wistful and non-
chalant.

And then

You may never have to change partners again!

In another room I saw Frau Goebbels and all her children sitting on a bench like a row of effigies. I stopped to say hello.

She gazed at me dully. "It's the only way," she whispered. "There's nothing else we can do. We have no choice now."

Eva slipped behind me and took me by the hand. She led me into the Führer's cubbyhole.

She closed the door behind us and we hugged each other tightly.

"I had no idea you were in Berlin!" we cried together.

"I arrived last night," she said.

"I just got here myself."

"I know. Everybody's talking about you. They want to know what you're doing here." Her fingers caressed my face. "Did you come for me, Edmonde?"

"Certainly."

"Sweet little Edmonde!" She put her dry lips against mine and we tried to kiss. It was impossible.

"You have to get out of here," I told her. "The fucking Russians are coming."

"Let them come." She sat on the bed and pulled me down beside her.

"But they'll be here any minute, Eva!"

"Who cares!" She put her head on my shoulder. "You came for me. How marvelous!"

"Yes, I'll take you back to Gotha with me."

"You're the only friend I ever had. Do you realize that?"

"I know, Eva. We have to leave now."

"I can't go."

"Why not?"

"Because we're going to commit suicide."

I looked at her. She was smiling, like a sleeper blissfully dreaming. "Eva, you can't be serious."

"Yes. We're going to lock all the doors and just die here."

Dreaming, yes. That was it. They were all asleep and this was a subterranean dream.

"*Who's* going to die?"

"He and I. Together. And everybody else. You too, if you like. We're going to poison the dog at lunch."

"What dog?" I asked stupidly.

"*His* dog. Little Blondie." She reached out and touched the smooth cool concrete wall. "It's like that cave in the quarry. Remember? We couldn't find our way out and thought we were going to die there. But our time hadn't come yet. There were years and years left to us then. Not now, though. There's no way out of this cave, Edmonde."

She was right. Her time had come. She would never wake from her dream.

I thought of my overnight bag in the railroad station in Gotha. I would need it soon, tomorrow. And the bike too. This was the moment to run.

Could I get away from this ghastly place? I looked at the ceiling. How *deep* were we? What if I couldn't escape? God! Where was the oxygen coming from? Suppose something happened to the machinery? Where was the exit? If I tried to leave, would anybody stop me? Thermopylae? Sacrifice? Shit!

Papa? Are you down here? Come and get me, Papa, please!

"I've got something to tell you." She was in my arms again. "Edmonde?"

"Yes, Eva, what is it?"

"Guess."

"I can't . . . I'm too . . . My mind is . . ." *Papa! Goddamn it! Come here!*

"Can't you guess?"

"No . . ."

"He asked me to marry him."

A dream! A hideous stifling, underground Nazi dream! *Oh, Papa, I'm smothering!*

"He did? Oh, that's good news."

"We'll die as man and wife."

"Please stop talking about dying, Anna . . ." *Anna? Where did she come from?* "I mean Eva. Oh, I'm all mixed up! I don't know what I'm saying! When will you be married, darling?"

"They're trying to find a pastor now."

The door opened and Hitler walked into the room. "I don't trust Sepp Dietrich," he said. "I want Steiner. Have you seen Blondie, Eva? Edmonde! What a pleasant surprise."

I jumped up and he took my hands and held them, beaming. "Good morning, my Führer."

"Morning? Is it? I've lost all track of time. Let me look at you!" He held me at arm's length and squinted at me, his face wrinkling. "You remind me of Paris. Those wonderful buildings. The Opéra. The place de la Concorde. You've come to my wedding, have you?"

"Of course, my Führer."

Eva moved between us, smiling blissfully, dense with moronic exaltation. "My two beloved people," she sobbed.

He patted her shoulder. "The clergyman is here, Eva. But we can't find Blondie."

The marriage took place in a bare cement room with a red light on the ceiling. We all looked like sapphire phantoms. I stood just behind the bride and groom. Hermann was beside me, swaying and grunting. His last injection was wearing off and he had to lean against the wall to keep from falling. His stomach thundered. The pastor droned on and on. Hitler folded his hands and stared at the floor. Eva turned to me once, her eyes shining. Two scarlet gargoyles stood on the opposite side of the room—Bormann and Heinrich. And all around us was the Goebbels dynasty, the children carrying bouquets, little Joseph holding a bottle of champagne, Frau Goebbels whimpering into a hanky.

Hermann wheezed into my ear, "I have to go to the bathroom," and backed off, knocking over a stool. Nobody paid any attention to him. Out in the corridor a woman brayed, "Who disconnected my telephone?"

The ceremony was over at last. Joseph popped the cork of the bottle and we all toasted the newlyweds. Then Hitler, standing under the red glow, looking like a tired and murky old Sioux chieftain, made a short speech.

"My comrades," he said, "you have all been with me, each and every one of you, since the very beginning of my struggle, sharing in my setbacks and my victories, my deceptions and my triumphs. I ask for no greater proof of the sincerity of your loyalty"—he was looking straight at *me!*—"than your presence here at my side today, as my long combat draws to a close. I thank you from the bottom of my heart for your faithfulness."

Then he shook our hands and he and Eva went back back into their quarters, two sleepwalkers moving through a vermilion haze. As she passed me I whispered, "Good-bye, Eva," but she didn't hear me.

"Come along, Kerrl." Little Joseph pulled me out into the passageway. "We need some more champagne."

He pushed me into a dark recess and put his arms around me. "I've been waiting for this for a long time, you little slut!" he growled, and he tried to kiss me. I turned my face away. "What's the matter? There's nothing to stop us now, is there?" He stepped back, undoing his trousers. Then he rubbed his swollenness against me. "Come on, come on now!" He jabbed at me, his hands tugging at my coat.

"There she is!" someody shouted. "Blondie! Blondie! Blondie!"

He turned. I jumped past him and ran down the corridor.

"Blondie! Here, Blondie! Blondie!"

All around me field marshals, admirals, ministers of state, Gruppenführers, Obergruppenführers, and chiefs of staff were scurrying through the dimness, whistling and snapping their fingers.

I opened a door. It was a closet. A girl screeched. She was standing with her skirt pulled up over her hips. An officer in a cape was kneeling before her, his face between her legs. He turned, agog. It was Heinrich!

I slammed the door shut and ran across another passage into another corridor. *Where's the fucking exit, Papa! Beware of steps! Remember what the Ouija board said? Bewareofsteps! If I don't find those fucking steps I'll die down here, Papa!* Another gallery, more rooms.

Then the steel door slid open just in front of me and three soldiers came into the bunker. I ran between them and ascended the stairs—up, up, up, up!

Daylight glowed above me. I came out into the garden.

The Harnack House was as smashed and gutted as everything else in Berlin. The façade was gone and its dangling floors exposed. There wasn't a soul in sight. I parked the bus in a mountain of rubble and went into what was left of the main foyer.

A man was lying in a hammock suspended between two pillars. I thought he was asleep. But he wasn't. He had no nose or jaw, and there was a gap in his chest filled with worms as large as pencils.

A space had been cleared in a corner, and there stood a message board covered with hundreds of scraps of paper. I found Lisa's note easily; it was pinned to the frame.

Dear Edmonde,
What is keeping you? I've been waiting for you all week, day after day. Perhaps you won't come after all. My son was killed in an air raid in Düsseldorf. Richard is dead too, he was shot at Colmar. You lied to me about that, didn't you? It doesn't matter. When I was in Dresden I was raped by three boys. They took my money and my papers and my jewelry. I've been bleeding ever since. Oh, Edmonde, why didn't you come? If you ever read this, you'll find me down in the basement.

                                        Lisa

The stairway was blocked with rocks and planks. It took me an hour to tunnel my way through the mess.

The basement was heaped with garbage and alive with rats. I could hear them, gossiping and capering all about me.

I wasn't afraid. Papa was just behind me and they would never attack him.

Lisa was hanging by her neck from a rope tied to a

hook on a rafter. On the floor beneath her was a thick smear of dried blood covered with bugs.

Poor girl.

I refused to weep or even to think. I just left her as she was. She was safe from the rats there. And besides ... she looked comfortable.

I told told you—didn't I?—about how we used to hide in Papa's garage and smoke our Wings. And I believe I told you too that she was my Pamina. I mentioned, I think, that . . . mon Dieu! . . . I would often hold her tightly, squeezing the breath out of her, and sing:

> Zum Leiden bin ich auserkoren;
> denn meine Tochter fehlet mir . . .

What more can I say?

The streets were jammed with women building barricades, little boys drilling, and old men pulling guns through the rubble. I drove all day and by nightfall was farther south than the Dubrowstrasse in Zehlendorf.

And there, God bless my luck, I met the same Gestapo detachment commanded by the same fat pigfucking lout who had stopped me that morning.

"Where are your very important passengers?" he sneered.

"They decided to stay and fight," I told him.

"Good for them. Since you're no longer on a special mission then, you can drive us to Tegelort."

Tegelort! Christ! That was in the opposite direction, a million kilometers away. "All right," I said, "climb in."

He jumped in beside me. The others—there were about fifteen or twenty of them—got into the back.

I drove past the Schlachtensee into the Grunewald. He leaned against me and slid his hand across my lap. Oh, ugh! "What's your name, girlie?"

"Charlotte Brontë."

"Me, I'm Schwabe. Let's us make music together, huh, Charlotte?"

"Are you a musician, Schwabe?"

He laughed and tickled my knee. There were two buttons on the dashboard. One locked the rear door, the other released the gas from the tank on the roof. I pushed both of them.

There was a din of thumps and shouts behind us.

"What's that?" he asked.

"Oh, I forgot to warn you," I laughed. "Gaston, my pet python, is in the back."

"Pull up!" he screamed.

I took out my Lüger and shot him in the ear. Then I dumped him out of the bus and turned south again.

I made much better time when I got away from the Berlin area. Once again I drove all night, using the same empty highways, repassing the same dead villages with the garbage cans lining the sidewalks.

Just over the Elbe I was stopped at a Wehrmacht roadblock. I told the captain in command that I was transporting casualties from the battle of Berlin to a military cemetery in Thuringia. When the soldiers opened the rear door and saw the pile of bodies they bayed in horror and waved me on.

I arrived in Gotha at sunrise. The first person I saw, marching determinedly along a deserted street, was "Frau Fang," alias Faustina!

She was in civilian clothes. In fact, she was in *my*

civilian clothes—wrapped in my fur coat, wearing a
pair of my Parisian shoes, carrying one of my purses!

"Faustina!"

She stopped and turned. When she recognized me
she bolted off into an alley.

I didn't try to follow her. What would have been
the point of that? I wished her Godspeed and hoped
the Gestapo woudn't catch her. Exit Faustina.

But how on earth had she managed to get away from
Zintsch?

I then did something extremely foolish. I changed
my plans. Instead of taking my bag and the bike from
the station and getting the hell out of there as quickly
as possible, I decided to go to the camp and see what
had happened during my absence.

There were no sentries on duty and the gate was wide
open.

I drove past the casern. It was empty.

I got out of the bus and walked toward the cottage.
At the end of the driveway Zintsch's head was sticking
out of a barrel of frozen water. He was purple. His
bare skull glittered with icing. He was alive. His eyes
and lips were moving. He looked up at me witlessly
and squealed.

"Zintsch." I bent over him. "Where is my husband?"

His jaws closed and opened. I could see his tongue
wag as he tried to speak. I rocked the barrel, attempting to dislodge him. It fell over on its side and rolled
down the driveway past the stable, his head spinning
around and around and around.

I went into the cottage, smelling the rank blood as
I came through the door.

Karl-Jesko was sprawled on the sofa, stiff and slaty
with rigor mortis. His hands were tied behind his back

and his rubber penis was knotted tightly about his throat. He was grinning, of course. He probably died yapping with laughter.

I went into the bedroom.

Otto's body was hanging by its tunic belt on the clothes rack in the corner. It had no head.

My mouth filled with bitter juice and my heaving stomach pushed me into the bathroom. I coughed out my bile into the sink, turned on the tap, splashed water on my face. Then I saw his head in the mirror. It was in the toilet, his eyes peering over the seat.

I went back into the living room. The Doberman walked out of the kitchen, growling softly. I ran outside, slamming the door on him.

An orchestra played the Overture to *The Marriage of Figaro*.

I turned.

Thousands of prisoners were massed all over the lawn and driveway. The musicians were standing in formation on the sidewalk, blowing their horns and scraping their violins.

I reopened the door and stepped back. The dog came bounding out of the house, streaking past me. I ran into the living room and on into the kitchen and out the rear door.

I flew across the yard and the orchard and jumped up on the fence.

They came after me like an army of hobbling lepers, pouring out of the kitchen and along both sides of the cottage. The Doberman led them. He leaped at me and snapped at my heels. I sprang down on the opposite side of the wire and raced into the forest.

They clamored behind me, hooting and wailing and jeering, flinging rocks at me, calling my name, toppling the fence, stampeding through the thickets, scrabbling over one another for the prize of being the first to catch me.

But I could outrun them. They were too feeble to keep up with me. My main concern was that pigfucking dog bastard! I had to hide my scent or he would have me in five seconds!

Luckily I reached the creek before he overtook me. It was frozen but only a few centimeters deep along its edges. I jumped on the ice, cracking it, plunging my feet into the water to obliterate my odor. I sprinted downstream, smashing the surface as I ran, keeping in the shallows, my legs moving tirelessly in a steady, unrelenting trot—*crack! crack! crack! crack!*

The barking was far enough behind me finally to risk coming out of the water to the firm ground of a pathway. I followed it, galloping faster.

And there was the lake!

I ran out on the ice, skidding among the protruding legs and heads and arms and faces of the gelid corpses.

I stopped running and my velocity carried me forward like an ice skater. I slid effortlessly and swiftly for a dozen meters. I ran on again, stopped again, slid again.

I looked back. The Doberman and the horde were coming out of the woods and down the shore. They saw me. A unanimous roar echoed, like the howl of a packed stadium.

A pool opened in front of me. I skirted it. The ice began to crackle beneath me. I willed myself into the air and planed over it, touching it only with the tips of my toes. It continued to splinter and snap. It sounded exactly like Sanders's bones breaking.

I slipped, spun, fell—I sledded on my derriere into the head and shoulders of a frozen woman holding a frozen infant in her arms.

We stared at each other. Her eyes were wide and round and maroon and on her face was a grimace of distaste. The baby was coal blue and spotted.

I looked past them. All the bodies here were upright, submerged to their chests in the ice—a dozen men, four or five women . . . and the Senegalese, naked and inky, still wearing his headdress of feathers.

They all gazed at me slyly, contemptuously, an audience of supercilious basilisks.

I addressed them! "Ladies and gentlemen, for my first number I would like to sing *'Wien, nur du allein, Wird stets de Stadt meiner Traüme,'* accompanied on the harpsichord by my father . . ."

Get up, Edmonde, on your feet—stop clowning!

A rolling vortex of fog spread across the lake. Good! They couldn't see me. And I couldn't see them. I pulled myself up. In fact, I couldn't see anything. I moved on, lurching and sliding. I passed the Negro and he smiled at me through the haze.

The dog kept barking and voices mooed all around me. Then there was an enormous brittle *click-click-click* as the ice broke asunder like a pane of glass splitting. Then a chorus of echoing shrieks and bleats.

The water rose to my kees, then dropped to my ankles. I found myself ascending the steep slope of a bank.

The Gotha railroad station was open, but there was no one there—not a single passenger or employee. I shot away the lock of the depository door with my Lüger. I removed my boots and socks and pulled off my uniform. I found my overnight bag and put on the clean underwear, the stockings and shoes, the skirt and sweater and the raincoat. I pocketed my false papers, the 150,000 marks, and *Anthony Adverse.* Then I lifted the bike off the hook and pushed it outside. I climbed on the saddle and pedaled out of town, keeping to the back streets.

Exit Edmonde Kerrl!

I was now Fräulein Hildegarde Steuben, fugitive.

10

BIKING THROUGHOUT THE DAY across the gloomy countryside was a resurrection. All the windows of heaven opened and the bleak misty landscapes were Elysian.

I saw only one person, an old woman drawing water at a wayside well. She ran away as I approached, dropping her bucket.

I spent the night in an inn in a village beside a pond. I took my precious bike into the room with me because the pigfucking landlord looked like a bandit. At four o'clock in the morning he tried to climb into bed with me and I smashed his head open with a chamberpot.

I left at dawn and again pedaled all day, navigating by the sun, following a cobweb of back roads and cowpaths toward the west, or northwest or southwest—but never east.

I roved like this for a week, avoiding the cities and keeping off the autobahns, buying food at remote farms, sleeping wherever I happened to be at sunset—one night in a barn, the next in a chapel, the next in a boathouse. I was always cold and hungry, but my freedom was so exhilarating that hardship became a joy, and the woods and the rivers, the morning and afternoon, meadows and roads, dawn and nightfall, were so sufficient unto themselves that they sustained me in luxury.

It was, alas, all too brief. The bell was tolling and the season changed.

In a gymnasium on the outskirts of Marburg I bribed a caretaker to let me take a shower. He turned on the heater and I spent an hour under the hot water, scrubbing myself raw. It cost me a thousand marks.

As I was dressing, he came stumbling tragically into the locker room, sobbing his heart out. The war was over; he'd just heard the announcement on the radio.

Three days later I saw my first Americans in Frankfurt-am-Main.

Frankfurt was a turmoil. I simply became part of the shambles and nobody paid any attention to me.

I rented a room in a warehouse and lived there for five months. I got a job, first, at the post office, then, in a kindergarten. Finally I went to work for the American PX. There I could have stolen all the cigarettes, clothing, and eatables I could get my hands on and made a fortune on the black market. But I didn't. I was honest and steadfast and saved my pay. When I had enough scrip (occupation money), I moved to a larger room in a Catholic hostel out by the airport.

That's where the Doberman found me.

They say that in the deep, deep calm that follows a terrible storm, the sharks go mad and attack everything in the ocean. I read that in a romantic novel about the South Seas. I forget the name of it, but it was made into a film in the thirties starring Dolores Del Rio.

On my way to work one morning I heard that familiar bark, and the dog came out of the bushes and jumped at my throat. I think it was the Doberman. Perhaps it was a wolfhound or a shepherd. Anyway, he tore my clothing to shreds and ripped open my face and arms and shoulders.

I ran into a bakery and hid there, terrified, until the firemen came and drove him off. There were two nuns in the shop. Just before I passed out, I distinctly heard one of them say to the other, "God is probably punishing her because she sleeps with American soldiers."

I was bleeding all over. That must have attracted the sharks. I was taken to a hospital and, lo and behold, one of the doctors was a former prisoner at Gotha. He recognized me.

The military police came for me the next day and I was whisked off to Nuremberg. It seems the Allies had been searching for me for months, so my arrest caused an international sensation.

The French sharks insisted on my immediate extradition to Paris, where I was wanted dead or alive for every atrocity that took place during the occupation. They accused me of being a Gestapo Torquemada and claimed that I had tortured and murdered, not only Marie-José, Mad, and Sanders, but dozens of other Resistance heroes and RAF pilots as well.

The Russian sharks wanted me to stand trial in Moscow. All the members of the Central Committee, led by Stalin himself, signed a bombastic partition containing an incredibly long list of war crimes I'd committed in the Ukraine. Among other things, I was supposed to have personally executed every partisan and commissar captured by Army Group South during the 1941–1942 campaigns—including a certain Vera Kuznetsov, by then known in Communist folklore as the Freedom-Fighter Maiden of the Steppes. (Sergei Prokofiev was composing an oratorio glorifying her exploits and her biography was now being filmed in Kharkov.) And, O irony of ironies! they had somehow found out about that absurd lie I'd told von dem Bach-Zelewski, and I was formally charged with practicing human vivisection!

Shit!

Even the Abwehr sharks swam out of the murk. They were being heralded as the only nonparty organization that existed during the reign of Hitler and thus represented everything that was democratic and honorable in the otherwise putrid German body politic. Their indictment stated that I was responsible for the mysterious disappearance of one of their valiant anti-Nazi agents, Hans Kreutz. Kreutz! That sneaky little rat! His diary was discovered in a safe-deposit box in a bank and several entries mentioned my name. Naturally, there was no reference at all to his intercepting Heye's compromising letter or his blackmailing poor Lisa! So he was now Herr Joan of Arc, and *I* was the fanatic totalitarian who burned him at the stake. Ugh!

But accusation number one was the Gotha camp. Everything else diminished in comparison. The horrors found floating in the lake and unearthed from beneath the road and the creekbed turned the stomach of the entire world. And every festering corpse was dropped in my lap.

Even before the case was brought to court the newspapers condemned me gleefully. Overnight I became:

THE GRUESOME GAS-BUS CONDUCTOR!

—The Chicago *Sun*

GAULEITER GHOUL-GIRL!

—The New York *Daily News*

THE GRIM GUARDIAN OF GOTHA

—*Time* Magazine

GESTAPO GRETCHEN!

—*The Stars and Stripes*

THE LESBIAN LADY MACBETH OF THE MACABRE
                      —The London *Daily Mirror*
THE QUEEN OF THE NIGHT

                                        —*PM*

SS HIGH PRIESTESS OF NAUSEOUSNESS
                      —*The Saturday Evening Post*
LA DEMOISELLE DES DAMNES!

                                   —*Le Figaro*

The long and the short of it was that I was tried and convicted simply for awfulness.

The chief witness for the prosecution was one Faustina Uiberreither, by then a lawyer living in East Berlin. Her testimony reduced the judges to tears. Ah! When she told them how I had given her the choice of either becoming a Club or dying in a gas bus, sobbing spectators shouted, "Shame! Shame!"

The night before I went into the courtroom for the last time I finished *Anthony Adverse.*

The following day I was sentenced to be hanged.

Well then, my story is finished.

It's eleven-forty-five. They'll come for me at midnight.

Sitting here, waiting for them, I found myself singing just now, that old song Mademoiselle de Marigny taught us at l'École des Jeunes Filles:

> Promenons nous dans les bois
> Pendant que le loup n'y est pas
> Si le loup y était
> Il nous mangerait . . .

All I ever asked of life was just to go for long, long,

long walks with my father, the two of us strolling along, side by side, both of us alive.

Not dying would have been so pleasant.

We would have returned home together to our house in Bad Tölz after our walk. We would have had dinner, then we would have gone to Munich, perhaps, to see a film. Then you would have gone to the theater and I, I suppose I would have seen *Die Zauberflöte* again if it were playing. Perhaps I would even have solved the mystery of the Queen of the Night eventually.

You would have grown old and I would have grown up, and surely we would have dwelled in the House of the Lord forever.

What a pity we had to meet the wolf in the woods and be devoured.

Oh, Papa, the priest came this afternoon and we prayed, and he told me to be brave, because he thought I was afraid.

Afraid?

The poor fool doesn't know we have a rendezvous tonight, you and I.

I'll meet you at the theater after the play. When you come out of the alleyway I'll be there, sitting on that bench across the street, remember?

You'll call my name and I'll run to you—God! I can hardly wait!—run to you and we'll be together again at last—together, together, side by side—and we'll walk along the avenues and through all the endless streets of our hearts' desire—we'll walk forever, and walk and walk and walk . . .

Here they come.

Please, Papa, be there, please!

They're all in khaki like the Brown Shirts.

*   *   *

It's bitter cold in the courtyard and as bright as day under the floodlights.

The wind is blowing, the north wind, bringing winter and snow and Christmas. But no more of that for me.

Here are the steps. *Bewareofsteps!* And that fat sergeant must be the hangman. But wait. Before they pull that awful sack over my head I'm allowed to say something. What shall it be? There's something terribly hackneyed about doomed indomitable prisoners muttering famous last words on the gallows.

I'll just say:

"Auf Wiedersehen, you pigfuckers!"